# THE PURSUIT

## Marissa Shrock

CIMELIA PRESS

Published by Cimelia Press, Greentown, Indiana
Printed in the United States of America

Print ISBN-10: 0-9969879-1-6
Print ISBN-13: 978-0-9969879-1-2
Library of Congress Control Number: 2016913708

*For my nephews Greysen, Rylen, and Landen.*
*You bring joy and fun to my life.*

"Whoever pursues righteousness and love
finds life, prosperity and honor."

Proverbs 21:21

# CHAPTER 1

## *Vivica*

No matter how often I dreamed of a happy ending, turmoil wasn't finished with my life—and I couldn't escape its tumultuous grip. Taking a breath of suffocating August air and ignoring the lump clogging my throat, I gazed at the shimmering lake on the fifty-acre compound where I lived with my mother, the president of the United Regions of North America.

My son Isaac turned one today, and I wasn't with him to celebrate. But he was no longer mine, so it shouldn't matter. Yet it did.

Pulling a twisty from my wrist, I gathered my blond hair into a ponytail. My mother's stylist had changed it back to my original golden color after all of the disguises the Emancipation Warriors had given me during my time fighting with them in the revolution. I tore off my bathing suit cover-up and charged off the porch into the lake.

The change in temperature robbed me of my breath, but I waded forward until the water covered my shoulders. I should've found a way to send a gift. What kind of mother didn't send a present to her child on his first birthday?

If I still had my courier, my son's adoptive mother Alma could send me pictures. Photos of a beautiful brown-eyed boy enjoying his first birthday cake.

But I'd surrendered to my mother's demands and returned to live with her, and that meant giving up the device, along with my freedom and the people who'd come to mean so much to me. Now, all I had was the government-monitored doc that all citizens carried, and pictures from Alma weren't safe. They could be used to track us.

Eyeing the distant shoreline, I swam toward it, hoping the exercise would clear my funk. Though the activity eased the tension in my muscles, the dull ache in my heart remained. I stopped and floated, gazing at the white streaks crisscrossing the hazy sky. For weeks, it had rained daily, but today the sun had decided to appear.

I swam back toward the deck that led into my suite, eased out of the water, wrapped myself in a towel, and lounged in the chaise. I'd thought my mother would let me leave the presidential compound when I turned eighteen. But a month had passed, and here I was, still shackled to wealth, power, and political intrigue.

On the expansive patio that surrounded the presidential mansion, the uniformed household staff bustled around setting up tables and placing flower arrangements for tonight's state dinner. I caught a whiff of garlic on the breeze.

I closed my eyes as the afternoon sun warmed me and birds chittered. There was time for a nap before I had to shower, wasn't there?

"Vivica, sweetie, you need to start getting ready."

I opened my eyes. Melvin, my mother's assistant, stood at my feet holding a garment bag.

"I know." I got up and took the bag. "I hope the alterations are right."

"Me too." He scrutinized me. "You've lost far too much weight. We can't have the Peacekeepers or the media thinking Genevieve is starving her daughter."

No. We wouldn't want that. I unzipped the bag and examined the gown as I walked into my bedroom. My mother's designer, Zelda, had taken in the waist and added padding to the bust. The form-fitting baby blue gown would give the illusion of curves and enhance my aquamarine eyes, but it would do nothing to disguise my twiggy arms.

"Thanks, Melvin. I promise I'll hit the shower now." I hung the dress in my armoire.

Melvin hesitated next to the door that led from my suite. A frown creased his forehead, and he ran his fingers through his thinning gray hair.

"Is there something else?"

He adjusted his purple silk tie. "You know how important Secretary General Zahedi's visit is to your mother."

That was an understatement. Ever since she'd brokered a peace deal and ended the revolution the Emancipation Warriors had started, the Council of World Peacekeepers, led by Secretary General Zahedi, had been keeping a close watch on our country for signs of conflict. If the peace agreement didn't hold, then the Peacekeepers planned to take over URNA.

"Melvin, I've been a model prisoner these past eight months."

He shook his head. "Don't let your mother hear you say that."

"We both know it's true."

He sighed. The man would never say a disloyal word about my mother. Ever.

I held up my right hand. "I promise. I'll be a perfect first daughter at the dinner tonight. I do have social skills." I removed the twisty and shook my wet hair. "I think."

Melvin stepped back to avoid the water spray. "I know. It's just that…"

"What?"

"Secretary General Zahedi has a specific request." Melvin studied his perfectly polished loafers.

*Uh oh.* "Let me guess. It somehow involves me."

"He'd like to meet with you privately in the library before the dinner. There's a matter he'd like to discuss."

I sat on the edge of my bed. "Did he say what?" Since I'd never met the man, I found it hard to imagine what he'd want from me.

"No. Your mother asked, but he refused to say. She was infuriated."

"But she feels pressure to comply."

"Exactly."

"Then I don't have a choice, do I?"

# CHAPTER 2

## *Vivica*

The presidential library was a book lover's dream, and even though I'd rather be on a computer practicing my hacking skills than reading, something about the room had always excited me. I'd found plenty of entertainment here. Floor-to-ceiling bookshelves lined three of the four walls. The fourth wall consisted of a stone fireplace with a window on each side that provided a view of the lake.

It was here that Secretary General Navid Zahedi sat in a wingback chair smoking a pipe while two men from his security team flanked the door. I hesitated outside. When Secretary General Zahedi saw me, he motioned for me to enter. He was dressed for dinner, and a pair of white gloves rested in his lap. His ebony hair was slicked a little too perfectly.

"Miss Wilkins, please have a seat." He pointed at the chair opposite his. "You look gorgeous this evening." His dark brown eyes gleamed. "You are as beautiful as your mother. Perhaps even more so." He leered at me with the confidence of a man who was accustomed to getting what he wanted.

"Thank you." Clutching a wad of my skirt and wishing I could disappear within its folds, I sat and pushed away the memories of the boys who'd stared at me with the same desire—boys I'd once given myself to without a thought of the consequences.

"Your mother's hospitality is top notch." His English, tinged with a hint of an accent, was flawless. "I am looking forward to this evening's dinner." He flashed the smile he'd used to charm the Council of World Peacekeepers into giving him his powerful position in spite of his age. At thirty-eight, he was the youngest person on the Council.

"Excellent. What did you need?"

He blew out smoke and chuckled. "You like to get to the point."

"Yes."

He examined his pipe. Carved bird talons clutched the bowl. "I don't suppose you smoke?"

"No. I care about my lungs."

He laughed. "Pity. There's something appealing about a woman who enjoys such indulgences." He met my eyes and held my gaze.

My stomach clenched. "I'm not that kind of woman."

"I see. Very well." He took another draw on the pipe. "Has your father attempted to contact you during the last several months?"

I blinked. "No."

"Really? I find it interesting he has not."

I hadn't seen my father since he'd disappeared when liberation forces destroyed Fortune City.

"Why would he, Secretary General?" I said. "We're talking about a man who faked his death and abandoned his four-year-old daughter years ago. Why wouldn't he repeat that pattern?" I tried to keep the bitterness from my voice but didn't succeed.

A slow smile spread over his face. "Miss Wilkins, I like your directness. And please, call me Navid."

"Fine."

"You see, the Peacekeepers have a problem."

"How so?" I raised my eyebrows.

He looked me directly in the eyes. "You are aware that the rebels' presence on this continent will inevitably cause difficulties."

I studied my hands. "My mother has things under control."

"She does, and I am pleased. But I must be prepared in case problems should arise."

"What's that have to do with me? I don't enjoy politics."

"Yes, after observing you during your time in Fortune City, I realize your strength is technology. A gift from your father. Also, the fact that you are multilingual is both impressive and useful."

I crossed my arms and tried to suppress the chill that started in my heart and spread throughout my body. He'd spied on me in Fortune City. The cameras had been everywhere—except the bathrooms. What all had Navid seen?

He chuckled softly as if he could read my thoughts. "You possess your mother's charisma and beauty. A combination that could do wonders for the Council. And me." He drummed his fingers on the chair's arm. "I have many enemies who would like to see me replaced. Therefore, I must anticipate and deal with any possible complications. Enhancing technology will provide the edge I need."

"You want to recruit me."

"Yes."

"And since neither of us have any idea where my father is, you think I can take his place."

"Precisely. Though if I find him, I would be inclined to have him join you."

"How could charisma and beauty possibly help while I'm shut away behind a computer?"

"Your bluntness is charming." He laughed and gazed at me.

His lack of a direct answer confirmed my suspicions that he wanted more than a working relationship. But I forced myself to stay calm and folded my hands in my lap. "Have you spoken with my mother about this?"

Navid lifted an eyebrow. "You are no longer a minor. Your mother's permission is not necessary."

"I'm not interested."

"You will find your role quite fulfilling."

I stood and tried to keep the disgust from my expression. "Thank you, but I'm still not interested." The Council's version of world peace and harmony required citizens to sacrifice personal liberty—for safety and security.

He narrowed his dark eyes and gazed at me as if he could elicit a different response simply by hypnotic force.

But I didn't blink.

"We will revisit this matter another time. Perhaps it will be best if I wait until you decide to come to me." He rose and towered over me. "I will see you at dinner, Miss Wilkins." With shoulders squared, he strode from the room with his bodyguards.

A few minutes after his exit, I hurried to the banquet hall and passed a massive, white staircase embellished with gold. Somehow I'd have to get through this white tie event with a churning stomach. Navid's parting words reverberated in my mind. I locked myself in the ladies' powder room, wet a towel with cool water, and dabbed it against my neck. Everything would be fine. My mother would never allow Navid to recruit me. I leaned against the sink and closed my eyes.

"God, please help me," I whispered. I was learning to listen to God and to let him guide me, but it was a difficult process. Especially because I liked things to go my way.

I stepped into the corridor and caught sight of Navid at the end of the hall. Though his back was to me, I recognized his perfect posture. Annoyance bled from his tone while he spoke on his MD3, the advanced model of the docs that government officials carried.

I slipped back into the ladies' room, peered through the crack in the door, and strained to listen.

"I am working on a solution. It will be beneficial in many ways."

Who was he talking to? Navid curled his gloved fingers into a fist. "I will not be usurped. Understand I will do what it takes to defeat my brother and maintain my position!" He disconnected the call and swore as he stashed the MD3 into his pocket.

His brother was trying to usurp him?

When he disappeared around a corner, I emerged from the powder room. If desperation was driving Navid, then he'd do anything to get his way.

I reached the banquet hall just as the staff escorted guests to their seats. Scanning the crowd, I caught sight of Drake Freeman. Our eyes met, and his handsome face broke into a grin as he hurried toward me. Like the rest of the men, he wore a tailcoat and matching trousers with a single satin stripe.

My heart issued the tiniest blip before falling back into rhythm. Dismissing my reaction as nothing more than excitement over reconnecting with a friend, I held out my hands, and he grasped them before raising my right hand to his lips.

I held my breath.

Amusement danced in his expression as if he enjoyed making me uncomfortable. "My dear, it's wonderful to see you again." He'd gelled his blond hair into spikes that advertised his prickly personality.

"We need to talk," I whispered and pulled my hands from his grip. "It's important." Drake would know what to do about Navid. When I'd worked with the Emancipation Warriors, Drake had been my supervisor and had helped arrange the peace deal with my mother—though he hadn't been in favor of my returning to her custody. He was a guest at the state dinner because his stepfather, Oliver Matheson, was governor of the Coastal Plain Region.

Drake tilted his head, and his blue eyes sparkled. "Always focused on business. But then, I wouldn't expect you to say how much you missed me." He straightened his white bow tie.

I fought a grin. "Shut up." The last thing he needed to know was that I *had* missed having him around.

"I'm much too interesting to be quiet."

"So you think." I glanced at the dissipating crowd and caught Navid's eye. He flicked his gaze to Drake, and his expression darkened.

I turned away and rested my hand on Drake's arm. "We'll talk later," I whispered.

We headed through the double doors, and the heavy scent of the various flowers adorning the tables reminded me of a funeral. I found my place next to Melvin and some members of URNA's Council of Representatives. I exchanged pleasantries with the men and women. Also seated at the long table were governors from the seven regions and their significant others. My mother presided next to Secretary General Zahedi, and I was thankful to be far from the man.

Operating in first daughter mode, I answered the representatives' questions and engaged in meaningless small talk. When tuxedo-clad waiters served dinner, I picked at my asparagus and filet mignon, but I could only manage to swallow a few bites. The memory of Navid's request lingered, taunting me.

I met Drake's eyes, and he winked. He didn't enjoy these events any more than I did, but it was an excellent opportunity for him to gather information that could help the continuing efforts of the Emancipation Warriors.

I needed his take on my situation. We hadn't spoken since our friends' wedding in January, because my exile had prevented it. I'd often found myself wondering if he was okay. The work he did for the Warriors was sometimes dangerous.

I turned my gold fork over on my plate to signal the waiter I was finished. How much longer would this dinner last?

When the wait staff had cleared away the remaining dishes, my mother stood, looking regal as ever. With her blond hair coiffed in her signature updo, she radiated elegance. Her draping gown was red, the national color. "I hope all of you enjoyed the dinner my staff prepared for you this evening."

The guests applauded.

My mother smiled. "Thank you. I'm delighted to share with you the wonderful news that Secretary General Zahedi has for us this evening. I'll allow him to explain." She took her seat, and Navid rose.

"Ladies and Gentleman, as you are aware, the Council of World Peacekeepers has been closely monitoring the political situation in your country. During the past six months, we have been pleased that conflicts have been minimal. Therefore, the Council will be withdrawing the majority of our officers from your country a few at a time throughout the next three months. I am pleased with the work President Wilkins has done to make this possible." He held up a wine glass. "I propose a toast to peace and harmony in the United Regions of North America." My mother rose to join him, and they drank to the sentiment.

I clinked my untouched glass of champagne against Melvin's.

This was political theater. Considering my conversation with Navid, I'd be surprised if the Council followed through and removed their officers.

***

When the dinner had ended and the guests lingered, I made my way to the deck overlooking the lake. The breeze that had chased away the afternoon humidity rippled the moonlit water. It was a perfect evening.

"My dear, you look stunning. You were the most beautiful woman in the room tonight."

I faced Drake and prayed the darkness concealed my burning cheeks. What was with the flattery? We hugged quickly and stood facing each other, the past months of no communication an awkward barrier between us.

"Thank you." I turned and leaned against the deck's railing. The memory of my first mission here at the presidential mansion with Drake resurfaced. I grinned when I thought of how he'd coaxed me into slapping him…and how much I'd enjoyed it.

So much had happened since that night.

He joined me, glancing over his shoulder, and I followed his gaze. The nearest cluster of people was out of earshot. "Where's your doc?"

"In my suite." I hated the thing because of its tracking and listening capabilities.

"Good." He lowered his voice. "That was quite the speech the secretary general gave. Do you believe him?"

"No." Falling into our old pattern of focusing on work relieved the tension between us.

"Good. I don't either. The Peacekeepers are up to something."

"I think so too." I told him about Navid's proposal but left out the insinuations. Drake didn't need details that would make him think less of me.

The muscle in his jaw tightened, and he put an arm around me. "We still have agents all over the world gathering intel on the Peacekeepers. Factions from other countries are working with us as well. The Warriors aren't done with our mission of restoring freedom to this country. Especially since URNA's Council of Representatives didn't vote down PPASDA." He dropped his arm. "We still have huge obstacles, though."

"I know." I fidgeted with some sequins on my dress and thought about the law my mother had glibly promised to abolish. PPASDA, the term law, was the Posterity Protection and Self-Determination Act. It required underage girls and adult women with more than two children to terminate their pregnancies. "Peacekeepers are powerful. I'm not sure the Warriors have enough resources to stop them." I searched his face.

"I agree." He ran his fingers through his hair.

My shoulders slumped. "That's not what I wanted to hear."

"It may be reality."

"So we give up?"

"Nope." He grinned. "I'm not planning to go down without a fight." His smile faded. "But our beliefs may get us killed."

"I accepted that risk when I joined the Warriors."

"I did too." He straightened and shoved his hands in his pockets. "For so long, I never doubted we'd be able to restore freedom and everything would be great. But what if we can't? What if it isn't meant to be because God has a different plan?" He hesitated. "Maybe what we need to look forward to is Heaven and accept that our lives on Earth might not be what we'd hoped."

I opened my mouth to protest and then snapped it shut. Looking forward to Heaven was something I should be doing. I just wasn't there yet because there was still too much I wanted from life.

"Anyway, the Warriors may've stopped the war with the URNA government, but we're not done fighting."

I raised my eyebrows. "How so?"

He leaned closer, and my pulse raced. Why was he *so* close?

"Like I said," he whispered, "there's still hope. The Warriors have shifted focus." He brushed a stray hair from my face. "We're planning to move as many of our people as possible into the Coastal

Plain Region, secede, and declare our independence from URNA."

I stepped back to get some space between us and stared at him. "Shouldn't there be some kind of vote?"

"The Peacekeepers would have to allow it."

"And they won't." I groaned. "You think the Peacekeepers are going to stand by and let a new nation form? That URNA's military won't fight back with the Peacekeepers' help?"

"I think they'll stand by if we have nukes."

I covered my gaping mouth. URNA had disarmed years ago when the Council of World Peacekeepers had combined Canada, Mexico, and the United States. "You'd really kill innocent people?"

Drake grimaced. "Having the weapons will serve as a deterrent. We hope to never use them."

"But you might?"

He looked away.

"How are you going to get nukes?" I shook my head.

"Don't worry about it. We'll take care of it." He twisted his monogrammed cufflinks.

Since the Peacekeepers controlled nuclear weapons, they were the only source. "How are you going to ensure that the Peacekeepers don't use them on the new country?"

"Mutually assured destruction—they fire at us, we fire at them." It made sense, but even Drake didn't seem as confident as he normally was.

"A lot of things could go wrong," I said.

He shook his head. "What's happened to you? Has your mother been influencing you? You used to be willing to fight."

I bristled. "Really? You're the one saying things might not work out. I prefer to fight when we have a shot at achieving our goal."

"Fair enough. I can't give you details, but I'm working on plans to increase our chances of success."

It was strange that he didn't keep arguing with me. Unless he knew I was right. I cleared my throat. "Well, when my mother lets me leave, I want to help."

He placed his hand on mine. "I'll find a place for you."

I pulled my hand away.

He faced me. "How are you *really* doing?"

"Okay. I miss Agatha and everybody else in the Warriors." I clutched his arm. "How is she? How's Chad?" When I'd first joined the Warriors, Agatha had become my closest friend. She and Chad had gotten married in January.

"They're both fine. Working for the Warriors in the Great Plains Region. Agatha sends her love. She demanded that I give her a full report on your wellbeing."

I laughed. "That sounds like her."

"I've been praying for you."

"You have?" Tears stung my eyes. "Thanks. I've felt so isolated. Online church services aren't the same. And I've been reading my Bible, but…"

"It helps to have other Christians around," he said.

"Yeah."

"I've missed you, my dear."

"I've missed you too. I wish I knew what my next step is. I thought when I was eighteen, I'd be free to move on, but my mother hasn't let me go. My life is pointless."

He took my hands. "No it's not." He hesitated and gazed into my eyes. "There's something I need to talk to you about."

"Of course." I forced nonchalance into my tone, but the intensity in his expression sent a ripple through my stomach.

"I've been doing a lot of thinking and praying during the last several months." He drew a deep breath. "My dear, I'm in love with you, and I intend to make you my wife."

15

# CHAPTER 3

## *Vivica*

I laughed. "You're kidding, right?" My mind tried to process a conversation that had taken place months earlier. Hadn't he told me he thought of me as a little sister?

But the look on his face indicated this was no joke. "It must come as a shock to hear me say this, but—"

"You *think*?"

He grinned, leaned against the railing, and crossed his arms.

I stomped my foot. The cocky—never mind. "You were just talking about *death*. Why are you doing this? Why now?"

"Telling you how I feel? Being honest? It's about time one of us does something about the elephant in the room. As the man, I felt it was my duty."

I blinked. "What ele—?"

"Vivica Suzanne Wilkins, don't you dare deny it. There's been a pack of elephants in the room since the day I met you, and I'm tired of them coming between us. I'm serious about making you my wife."

"You didn't even *ask* me. You assumed I want to marry you." I put my hands on my burning face. "I'm not ready to get married."

"I'm happy to wait, which is why I didn't ask and just let you

16

know my intentions. It's probably better since you're still quite young."

I ignored the comment about my age. "What if I don't want to get married at all?" My hands dropped. "To anyone. Ever."

His face darkened. "You were more than willing to marry Ben."

"Not right away. Besides, I thought Ben and I had a future, but it was ripped away. I never want to feel that way again." I began walking the length of the deck.

He followed. "I felt the same when I found out Faith betrayed all of us, but I swore I wouldn't let her ruin the rest of my life."

The tears I'd been fighting all day spilled over. "I don't want to get married." Why did Drake have to do this? I needed a friend, not a complication. "I'm sorry."

Drake gently grabbed my arm and turned me to face him. "No. I'm sorry, my dear. Clearly my timing is abhorrent."

"No kidding." I faced him. "I have a lot on my mind right now."

"I won't pressure you." He released my arm. "Nothing has to change between us."

"Thank you."

But it already had.

# CHAPTER 4

## *Vivica*

After a night of fitful sleep, I paced the length of my bedroom. Someone needed to invent a way to delete unwanted memories. I'd give anything to purge the memory of the day I'd learned Ben was going to marry someone else. Yet, God had allowed it to happen, and I believed it was his will. God had a different plan for me—one that didn't include Ben as my husband.

During the past few months, I'd thought of Ben less and less. The hurt had begun to heal, but Drake's declaration ripped open the wound.

I couldn't risk loving again.

Would I ever be able to think of Drake that way? He was handsome. Charming. Confident. I'd always found him attractive, but…that wasn't a solid foundation for a relationship, especially when we were experts at annoying each other.

It didn't matter. I wasn't willing to pursue it.

A knock interrupted my thoughts. "Come in."

My maid Carol entered. Her warm hazel eyes were rimmed in red, and the lines on her face appeared more pronounced.

"What's wrong?" I rushed to her.

Fresh tears spilled over, and she swiped them away with the back of her work-worn hand. "My son-in-law called. My daughter and her babies are sick."

"I'm sorry." I gave her a quick hug. "Of course you can have time off. That's no problem. Do you need extra money for travel?" Her daughter and family lived in the Great Plains Region.

Carol shook her head. "No. Your mother pays well. It's just…" She began to sob, and I guided her to my sitting room, where we sat on the couch.

"Tell me."

"The doctors don't know what's wrong with 'em. They're bad off. It began yesterday with a mild fever that kept climbing. They started throwing up. Couldn't keep anything down. Not even water. Now they're coughing up blood and getting weaker and weaker." She buried her head in her hands. "They're gonna die. I've got to try to get to 'em. I have to tell them I love them one more time."

"Oh, Carol. I'm so sorry." My mind whirred. They were all so young. There had to be something we could do. "We could send my mother's doctor. Dr. Alstead is up-to-date on the latest treatments and—"

"Your mother already offered. Dr. Alstead called up my girl's doctor and gave suggestions, but he said it was too late. There's nothing they can do. Laureen's only thirty. Her babies are five and three."

I closed my eyes and absorbed the impact of her statement that put my own problems in perspective. I rested my hand on her shoulder. "Could I pray for you before you go?" It was all I had to offer.

Carol raised her head. "It's why I came to you."

Tears stung my eyes, and my nose tingled. At least I'd made an impression. I'd begun to wonder if I'd been outspoken enough about my faith. I grasped her hands. "God, thank you that you're sovereign and faithful. Heal Laureen, Kallie, and Brenden. Give the doctors wisdom. Comfort Carol and her son-in-law. Give her safety as she travels. Amen."

She squeezed my hands. "Thank you."

"How else can I help?"

"Keep praying." She stood and headed for the door. Pausing with her hand on the knob, she turned. "And pray that whatever they got don't start spreading like wildfire. That could be real bad."

I swallowed when I thought of Agatha and her husband Chad, who were working in the region. "I will."

"God bless you, Vivica. I'll never forget how good you've been to me." She closed the door behind her.

I wrapped my arms around my waist and stared at the door.

She wasn't expecting to come back.

# Chapter 5

## *Vivica*

"I attempted to persuade your daughter to come work for the Peacekeepers, but she was not interested," Navid said to my mother the next morning at breakfast as sunlight streamed through French doors. He took a slow sip of tea.

My mother rested her fork on her plate, and her fingers trembled ever so slightly. "I see. It *is* her decision." She glanced at me, and I gave her a tiny smile. Would Navid notice her reaction?

"Yes, but I thought you might be able to help persuade her." He leaned forward and gazed at my mother, as if to mesmerize her into compliance.

"Any conversation involving my daughter's future will be a matter that's discussed privately. I see no reason for you to be privy to such a debate." She raised her chin. "Now, what are your travel plans, Secretary General?"

He emitted a throaty laugh and rested his teacup in the saucer. "Eager to get rid of me, I see."

"I merely asked so as to ensure my staff could best accommodate you regarding your plans."

"Of course." His polite, yet patronizing, tone conveyed his

disbelief. "I believe my security team is taking care of that."

"Very well." My mother flashed a half-smile.

"There is another matter that one of my staff members brought to my attention this morning." He swiped his MD3 and projected a newsfeed onto the wall behind me. I glanced over my shoulder as he stopped on one article from the national news service. "Have you been informed of this?"

My mother's lips moved slightly as she read the article. When she finished, she eyed Navid. "The governor of the Great Plains Region was here for the dinner and didn't mention this problem." She turned to Melvin. "Go investigate this."

Melvin tossed his napkin on the table and scurried from the room.

"Obviously an epidemic is a serious crisis," Navid said.

I gripped the arm of my chair. I'd gather details now and explore later. Were they talking about the same illness that Carol's family had? If so, my mother was playing dumb.

Unless Carol had lied about my mother offering Dr. Alstead's services. But that didn't seem likely.

"I assure you, Secretary General, my country's Health Management division is well equipped to handle serious epidemics. Although, from the information presented in the article, I see no reason to panic. There only seem to be a few cases, and the researchers haven't ruled out environmental causes."

Navid nodded slowly. "Nevertheless, I am willing to offer assistance, should such measures become necessary."

My mother took a long sip of orange juice. "That's very kind of you, Secretary General."

He smiled. "How many times must I insist you call me Navid?"

"*Navid*, it's my hope that we won't have a crisis that causes the Peacekeepers to waste energy and resources on my country—especially when so many other places in the world are in need." She hadn't loosened her grip on her juice glass.

Navid folded his napkin and placed it on the table. "I thank you for your hospitality, Genevieve. I must prepare for my journey home."

My mother and I rose and shook his hand.

When he'd exited the room with his security team, I met my mother's eyes.

"We'll talk later," she whispered.

\*\*\*

The presidential mansion had three sections—each to symbolize one of the former countries that made up the United Regions of North America. Because my mother and I were from the part of the Great Lakes Region that had once been in the United States, we lived in the area of the mansion that represented that former country.

Located outside of the nation's capital, Union City, the mansion sat in the middle of a vast parcel of land. A security fence bordered the property, and it was along this line between my prison and the outside world that I walked in the evening. The sun was sinking behind hazy clouds, and cicadas buzzed.

I needed to have a clear plan when I talked to my mother about my future. I'd taken online courses, because I hadn't been allowed to leave the grounds of the presidential estate to attend school. I'd earned my high school diploma a couple of months ago.

Though I'd spent the last eight months praying, I wasn't sure what God wanted me to do. But I was *certain* it didn't involve working for Navid and the Peacekeepers. Helping the Emancipation Warriors form a new nation appealed to me, but that probably wasn't realistic—if my mother had her way.

And what about Drake's declaration? It hadn't been a proposal, but he *had* made his intentions clear.

I stopped next to an oak tree and sat down, allowing the roughened trunk to support my back. Drawing my knees to my chest, I began to pray.

"God, help me hear you clearly. Show me what to do."

I sat with my head resting on my knees, thinking and praying, until twilight surrounded me.

It was time to talk to my mother.

\*\*\*

I found my mother in her suite, projecting a report from her MD3 onto the grayish-blue wall of her sitting room. I knocked on the doorframe.

"Come in."

Commander, my mother's black Lab, raised his head, stood, and clicked across the wooden floor to greet me.

"We need to talk." I patted the dog's head, and his tail swiped my legs.

"Yes." She waved to a chair next to the couch.

I sat and curled my legs underneath me. "Working for Navid isn't an option." With a groan, Commander collapsed next to me.

My mother scowled. "I'd never ask you to. I don't trust him, and I'm certain he's not done with this country. No matter what he says, his agenda is to take over. National sovereignty means nothing to him. One-world government has been on the Peacekeepers' agenda for years."

"I know." I let out a breath. For once, we agreed. "But I want to talk about my future."

"And?"

"I want to go to college. I could start next semester." If I went away, I might be able to help the Warriors in my spare time.

"I anticipated you might, and several months ago, I had Melvin

24

start researching some appropriate institutions. However, none of them have been able to assure me of your safety from my enemies."

I hated being so predictable. "I should have a say. When I agreed to come back and live with you, I didn't know you'd keep me trapped forever."

"I wish you wouldn't think of it that way." She pointed to the document projected on the wall. "I've been doing some more reading and following up on the information I have about Carol's family. I have a bad feeling about this sickness in the Great Plains Region."

I grabbed a throw pillow and clutched it to my chest. "I haven't been able to get them off my mind all day. I keep praying—"

My mother grimaced. "I've been sending them positive thoughts as well."

For a few seconds, silence grew between us. Then I refocused. "You changed the subject. Can we get back to—?"

"Did you notice how Navid brought the outbreak to my attention? And then offered to help?" She studied me.

"What does that have to do with my going to college?"

"I want you to work for me instead."

I blinked. "Doing what?"

"Hacking. Spying. Investigating. Whatever it was you did for the reb—I mean, the Emancipation Warriors." She smoothed her hair. "I should've thought of it before now. It's no wonder you're restless. You're like me. You have to have a purpose. A goal."

I bit my lip. I'd never thought of the possibility myself. In fact, I wasn't even sure how much my mother knew about what I'd done for the Warriors or my range of abilities. Before I'd run away, I'd kept my activities to myself. Changing my friends' grades and hacking security systems weren't exactly activities a girl shared with her mother.

"What changed your mind?" I asked.

She leaned forward. "Yesterday afternoon before the dinner, I had a lovely conversation with your friend, Drake Freeman."

I couldn't believe she liked Drake so much when she knew he was a Warrior. Her opinion would definitely change if she were aware that he was plotting secession.

"He shared some suspicions about this sickness in the Great Plains Regions that I found concerning. He suggested that I utilize your talents and have you investigate the epidemic's origins." She examined her French manicure. "And you must be good if Navid wants to recruit you."

My eyes begged to be rolled, but I'd be respectful if it killed me. "You think the Peacekeepers caused the outbreak, and you want me to figure out how?"

"Yes, I believe anything's possible where Navid is involved. You have your father's gift of working with technology, so you'll be an important asset."

My father's *gift*. Funny how she'd used the same words as Navid.

"I haven't agreed yet." I hesitated. "But if I do, will you let me live on my own?"

"No. But I'll see that you're well compensated. And when I determine the threat to our safety has passed, I'll allow you to leave. You may go to college then." She rested her hands on her knees and straightened.

It had been worth a shot, but her promise was definitely vague. Still, it was better than where I'd been this morning. Plus, finding out what the Peacekeepers were doing could also help the Warriors. This could be the answer to my prayers.

Part of my problem the last few months had been a lack of direction. If my new purpose was keeping an eye on Navid and the Peacekeepers, then it was a mission I was willing to accept.

Besides, I still had to convince my mother that she needed God.

It could be why God was giving me this opportunity to stay and work.

"I need the best possible technology," I said.

"I'll see that you get it." She smiled. "In fact, I'll even persuade Drake to visit and assist you. I'm certain he'll be far more forthcoming with you than he was with me."

Great. That wouldn't be awkward. Still, I held out my hand. "We have a deal."

# Chapter 6

## *Vivica*

Two days later, my mother had an office set up for me down the hall from her own. Filled with the latest computers, it would make my job much easier. It also had a view of the lake. I awoke early on my first day and strode into my workspace where Drake stood sipping coffee.

"Good morning, my dear," he said.

"Top of the morning, Sugar Bear."

He spat coffee. "*Sugar Bear?*"

"It's only fair. You always call me *my dear* in spite of my protests. I thought Sugar Bear was fitting."

"How so? I'm neither sweet nor grouchy."

I tilted my head. "I've seen you in both states."

"But my default is charming and aloof."

"So you think."

He grinned. "I'd keep working on the nickname." He leaned into my space. "You'll want to get it right," he whispered.

"I'll make it top priority." I rolled my eyes and stepped back.

He took a sip of coffee. "You don't seem to care why I'm here."

I settled at my desk. "It's either to make good on your promise to woo me or to share intel." I waved toward my computer. "Since I have a lot of work to do, I'm hoping it's information about the outbreak."

"Actually it is, since I was so rudely rebuffed during our last encounter."

He didn't sound offended, but I wasn't sure. "Drake, it's not about you."

"My dear, that's dangerously close to, 'It's not you. It's me.' I thought you were more clever than that." His eyes twinkled.

"Fine. It's *not* me. It's Sugar Bear."

He chuckled. "There's the sign of life I was looking for."

"Could we get to work?"

"Gladly." I turned from his intense gaze, hacked into the compound's security system, and disabled the camera in the room— we didn't need my mother spying on us.

Drake closed the door and then rolled his chair next to mine. "Your mother was intrigued to hear about some research files we found in the ruins of Fortune City."

I raised my eyebrows. "The blast didn't destroy everything?"

"Nope. Oh, I almost forgot." He reached into the backpack he'd slung across a chair and pulled out a courier that looked just like a doc. "I thought you might like this."

I examined it, and when I realized it was the exact device I'd used during my time with the Warriors, I squealed and threw my arms around him. "Thank you."

"You're easy to please."

I scrolled through the messages and found new pictures of Isaac his mother had sent. My heart leaped when I found a picture of him with birthday cake smeared over his face, his brown eyes sparkling with joy. I turned the device so Drake could see.

"Now I understand." His face softened. "He's a cutie—and he has your smile."

It was true, but I didn't want to dwell on that. "He's getting so big." I found more pictures and gazed at them before I realized I was wasting Drake's time. I looked up and rested the courier in my lap. "Sorry."

He put a hand on my arm. "It's fine."

The gentle expression in his eyes caused my thoughts to scatter. "I'm ready to focus now." If I said it aloud, maybe I'd believe it.

"Our people found a computer hard drive and recovered pieces of an investigation your father was doing on a man by the name of Dr. Colin Gates."

"I've met him," I said.

"Really?"

"Yeah. I'm pretty sure he's the guy I know as Dr. Ear Hair."

Drake laughed. "He must have a pretty serious problem to earn that nickname."

I wrinkled my nose. "It's bad."

"What else do you know?"

"He's an epidemiologist specializing in nanobot research. I met him when I was working undercover in the government." I drew a breath and leaned forward. "Drake, I made the offhand comment to Dr. Gates about him being the man we'd call if we need to keep people healthy. And he said something like, 'Who said anything about keeping people healthy?'" I shuddered. "Maybe it's nothing. I mean, he *was* a little tipsy at the time, but—"

"Your father didn't trust him."

"Right. Because my father thought Dr. Gates might have been using nanobots to manipulate his mind."

"Open the Wilkins Research file," Drake said. "Your father was on to something, but part of the research got destroyed."

Of course it had.

I perused the file—portions of electronic journals my father had written. Piecing them together wouldn't be an easy task, but I projected the documents onto the wall and began reading. I found bits of information about smart viruses, but I had difficulty pinpointing how they worked. After a few minutes, I got up and poured a cup of coffee. "It'd be nice if we could find my father and get his opinion."

Drake took his courier from his pocket. "Let me see what I can do."

"Hold on. I'm not sure my father's trustworthy."

"I'll talk to my contact. Just trust me." He left the room, and I went back to reading the file. My father seemed to take a special interest in the pregnancy-prevention vaccines the government administered to underage girls. The shots also stopped STDs, so the boys received a modified version.

Drake returned. "My contact will get a message to your father."

I narrowed my eyes. "Who's the contact?"

"My dear, if I wanted you to know, I'd tell you. Any progress?"

"If I wanted you to know, I'd tell you."

Drake's deep laughter filled the room.

I grinned. "Seriously though, my father did mention once that the pregnancy-prevention vaccines we all have to take are more about limiting life expectancy than anything else."

"Did you believe him?"

"Yes." I bit my lip. "I tried asking for more details, but he always changed the subject or made excuses. I figured it was because we were under surveillance."

"You truly think the technology exists to make it possible for the Peacekeepers to limit life expectancy?"

I considered all the advanced technology I'd seen during my time as a prisoner in Fortune City, especially the nanobots that they'd hoped to use to track us in the city. "Yeah." I nodded slowly.

"Especially with what I'm reading about smart viruses."

Drake ran his fingers through his hair. "Then it wouldn't be a stretch for Dr. Gates and the Peacekeepers to engineer an epidemic."

I leaned back and wrapped my arms around my waist. "Right. Which is what my mother suspects." And why she was choosing to trust Drake. And me. "If this epidemic is engineered, then we have to figure out how they're dispersing it."

"And who they're spreading it to."

***

After brainstorming, Drake and I decided the food supply was the most obvious place to start searching for suspicious activity. I looked for a number in my courier, and when I found it, I typed in the required security code and placed the call.

Drake's brow furrowed. "Who are you—?"

I held up a finger. "Judd? Hey, how's it going? This is Sarah Miller." I winked at Drake, and he gave me a thumps-up.

Sarah was the alias I'd used when I'd hidden at Judd's farm during my illegal pregnancy. Though Judd was aware I'd gone on to be an agent, I wasn't sure he knew my true identity—especially since I'd been in disguise when I'd lived at his farm. So, I didn't use video mode for this call.

"All right," Judd said. "Getting remarried here in a couple of weeks. Special woman. Twins are doing fine too, and Tammy loves 'em like her own. Growing up too fast. Starting kindergarten this year." His children, Emma and Jesse, had won my heart when I'd lived in the cottage next to their farmhouse.

"I wish I could see them again, but it's not safe."

"Yeah. Someday when things settle down. Now, you didn't call to chitchat."

I pictured him adjusting his ever-present cowboy hat. "No. I have a few questions about Agricultural Management."

He chuckled. "I got a few questions about them myself."

I smiled. "You have to give eighty-five percent of your crops to Ag Management, and they're distributed throughout the country, right?"

"Yes ma'am."

"Does Ag Management regulate *how* you grow the crops?"

"You better believe it. We can only use chemicals the government supplies, and we have to apply them on a mandated program. One and only exception for getting off schedule is inclement weather. Been a lot of that lately."

I sat down and crossed my legs. "Any changes to the chemicals?"

"Nope. Same smell, same schedule, same results."

"Thanks, Judd. I appreciate it."

"No problem. You take care now."

I disconnected the call and chewed on my lip. Maybe the government contaminated the food after it was gathered and before distribution. "Not what I was hoping for."

"It was a good theory," Drake said.

"I'm glad Judd and the kids are okay." I stretched my arms and yawned. "It's nice to be able to catch up with friends again."

Drake smirked. "Speaking of which, I can't believe you haven't asked."

I furrowed my brow. "Asked what?"

"About Ben."

"I figured if something was wrong, you'd tell me." I swiveled away and stared at my computer screen. "Are he…and his wife okay?"

"Yes."

"Good," I said.

"You don't want details?"

"Why are you doing this to me?" I hissed. "Don't you get it? I don't want to think about him. It hurts too much."

He winced. "I'm sorry."

"No you're not. You did this on purpose to see how I'd react."

The edge of his mouth quirked.

"Did you find what you were looking for?" My cheeks burned.

"I'm afraid so," he said.

"And what's the diagnosis, Dr. Freeman?"

"You're still not over him."

I leaned into Drake's space. "Listen very carefully. I *am* over Ben." I took a deep breath. Why had I leaned so close? The scent of his aftershave sidetracked my thoughts momentarily, and his eyes twinkled as if he could read my thoughts. "We're talking about a guy who refused to fight for me. I'm *not* pining for him. He's married!"

Drake leaned back and crossed his arms.

"Did it ever occur to you that I don't want to hear how happy his life is while I'm stuck here?" I asked.

"It should've." Sincerity flitted though his expression. "I'm sorry."

"It's okay." I started to turn back the computer, but I raised up my hands and dropped them back into my lap. "Now I'm curious. Where are Ben and his wife living?"

"Coastal Plain Region. Ben's working as a private pilot. Does some work for the Warriors once in a while."

"Good for him. Anything else I should know before I get back to work?"

Drake swiped his courier and projected a document onto the wall. "Nope."

***

Later that night, I used my courier to call Agatha, and she shrieked when she answered the call. "Viv, I can't believe we finally get to talk!"

"I know. It's been forever." I changed the call to video mode.

She'd let her red curls grow to chin length. "What's going on?" she asked.

I filled her in on my new job and our theory that the Peacekeepers might be spreading the epidemic by contaminating the nation's food supply.

"I'm glad your mother suspects something's not right about this outbreak, because Chad and I do too. We've both been in and out of clinics and hospitals talking to as many doctors and nurses as we can." She grimaced. "It's nasty stuff."

I didn't like the thought of my friends being that close to danger. "Are people surviving?"

"There's a twenty-five percent survival rate once people contract the disease."

I said a silent prayer for Carol and her family. "Does it have a name?"

"Great Plains Virus."

"Doctors are sure it's a virus?"

"Yep. I confirmed it with an epidemiologist. The virus causes a headache. Nausea. Chills. Hemorrhaging. Then in most cases— death. Those who survive don't hemorrhage." She hesitated and looked as if she wanted to say more.

"What else?"

"Chad and I discovered a pattern. Frankly, it freaks me out, so I hate saying this out loud, because I don't know how it could be true. The virus seems to target people without biochips. In fact, we've been doing some figuring, and about ninety percent of the patients who get sick don't have biochips. The other ten percent have weakened immune systems, but they usually pull through—so do the patients who take the chip in the hospital."

I prayed Carol's family had received chips in time.

Could GPV be the smart virus my father had been researching? I tensed and rubbed the scar on my upper arm where a biochip had once resided against my will during my time as a prisoner in Fortune City.

After my mother had become president, the Global Health Organization had begun to implant biochips in citizens' arms in order to monitor their health data. Most people had voluntarily complied—since there was monetary incentive to do so—but everyone associated with the Emancipation Warriors had refused. Because of my negative experience with biochips, my mother hadn't pursued the fact that I remained chip-free.

Surely she wasn't aware that the chips had that much power.

"You and Chad should leave the Great Plains Region," I said. "Go somewhere safe."

Concern creased Agatha's forehead. "There's no place safe."

"Then we've got to figure out how to stop it. We can't let a virus wipe out the Warriors. If I can pinpoint how they're spreading it, then it won't matter if people have a chip or not."

"It's not always up to you to save the world."

"Then why do I keep trying?"

"Because you're so capable." She smiled. "Anyway. Enough of the doomsday stuff. How's Drake?"

I told her about his declaration.

She clasped her hands. "Excellent. It's time one of you owned up to your feelings."

"What do you mean, 'one of us'? I don't have feelings for Drake other than friendship…and attraction."

"Seriously? How long are you going to keep this up? Everyone knows you're in love with him."

"I am *not*. He's an attractive friend. That's all."

"Viv, you wouldn't know what love looked like if it walked up and slapped you in the face."

"I loved Ben."

"You did. But your feelings for Drake are different."

"You sound so matter-of-fact. Like you know exactly what I'm thinking. But you don't."

She shrugged. "Just because you don't see it doesn't make it less true. You've always been too obsessed with Ben to notice."

"That was in the past. I'm content to be single now. I've even been reading about it in my Bible. Think of everything I could do without a husband to slow me down."

"God's calling you to be single?" She crossed her arms.

"You don't know how much it hurt trying to get over Ben. I don't want to feel that way again. Love isn't worth the risk."

"Yes it is. And you never answered my question."

I chewed my lower lip. "I don't know *for sure.*"

"See? What if God's plan is for you to get married?"

"Then he better make it clear, because I'm not interested."

"You'll change your mind when Drake gets to you and you finally realize you're in love with him." She smirked.

"He won't. He's too annoying."

"How so?"

I recapped our conversation about Ben.

"Well, I can't blame Drake for trying to get a read on you, especially after he admitted his feelings," Agatha said. "You were involved with Ben for a long time. How'd you take the news about Ben's baby?"

I blinked. "His *what?*"

Agatha's face reddened. "Drake didn't tell you Ben's wife is pregnant?"

"Um. No. He did not."

"Maybe he didn't know." She wound a red curl around her finger.

"For his sake, you'd better hope so. Lying to me is not going to help his cause." I flashed a phony smile. "But I'm happy for Ben."

"You don't have to fake it with me," Agatha said.

"I meant it when I said I was over him."

"That doesn't make his happy news sting any less. So—I'm sorry."

Even though I didn't want to admit it, I was too.

*** 

The next day, I beat Drake to my office and sat waiting with my arms crossed.

He strolled in. "My company this morning will have to tide you over for a while, my dear. I'm leaving in a couple of hours on a new mission."

"Did you know Ben's wife was pregnant?"

"Good morning to you too." He cleared his throat and studied his feet. "Yes. I did."

"You lied yesterday."

"What exactly did you want me to do?" He crossed his arms too. "You'd just finished telling me that it hurt you to hear how happy he is. I wasn't going to throw that in your face. I'm sorry."

"It's not your job to protect me." I shot out of my chair and faced him.

He flinched. "Not if you won't let me because you think you can do everything on your own. But you don't know what you want, so I'm not sure how to respond."

"How about leaving me alone?"

He shrugged, but hurt flickered in his eyes. "My dear, if that's what you want, then that's what I'll do."

My stomach plummeted. "Good. Thanks for your help. Have a safe trip." I turned away, so he wouldn't see the tears pricking my eyes.

"One final thought."

I blinked and turned. "What's that?"

He grabbed my waist and pulled me close. I didn't resist when his lips met mine. My brain begged for me to escape, but I didn't have the strength to fight when he deepened the kiss.

And I didn't want to.

Drake broke away, left the room, and I collapsed in my chair.

No one had ever kissed me that way before.

# CHAPTER 7

## *Drake*

My stepdad, Oliver, had a favorite catchphrase. "Work is good."

He'd spouted it every day—at least it'd felt like every day—while my brother, Liam, and I were growing up. But he'd modeled it for us, so at least he wasn't a hypocrite. When I was a teenager, I especially hated hearing it, but now I appreciated the old adage.

Work *was* good because it gave me something else to focus on besides the beautiful and infuriating Vivica Suzanne Wilkins. And since secession loomed on the horizon, there was plenty to think about with Operation Coastal Republic.

While heavy rain drove against the windshield, my self-driving car took me away from the presidential compound to an airstrip. There, I'd hop a flight to the Caribbean Region to meet with a defense contractor about purchasing a fleet of personal aircrafts our new military could use when drones or larger planes weren't effective.

Preparing to defend our new country was key, and the Warriors had me working night and day. This little detour to help Vivica had hijacked my valuable time. But Liam had said I should go, especially since the president had asked. I'd done my good deed. Now it was time to get back to work. Vivica was capable of figuring out this epidemic on her own, especially since she didn't want me around.

So she said. I fought a grin. That kiss had told a very different story.

I still had a chance.

The car pulled into the airport, and I took control and steered it to the hangar where I'd leave it for the next Warrior who needed it. A jet waited on the tarmac, so I grabbed my bag and jogged toward it.

When I boarded and saw my pilot, I stifled a groan.

Ben Lagarde. He was a good guy, but I hated the reminder that Vivica had feelings for him. Maybe always would.

"Hey, Freeman. Nice to see you." Lagarde extended his hand, and I squeezed it. Hard.

He wasn't bad looking if the boyish, barely-out-of-puberty look was your thing. Brown hair and eyes. New goatee that helped him look a tad older. Not as tall as me, but taller than most women, including Vivica. "Same. How's your wife?"

He grinned. "Not slowing down at all. If she weren't pregnant, she'd be out helping with Operation Coastal Republic."

"We could find something for her to do."

His grin faded. "Do me a favor and don't mention that, okay? I don't want to lose her."

"No problem." I understood wanting to keep the woman you loved safe.

He moved toward the cockpit, then paused and turned back. "How's Vivica?"

"Great. Trying to figure out how GPV's spreading."

"Heard that stuff's awful." He furrowed his brow. "Is it safe for her to be working on that? We both know how determined she can be when she's tracking down a lead."

"Do you think either one of us could talk her out of it?"

Lagarde chuckled softly. "Nope." He entered the cockpit and closed the door. I took a seat and started to put on the disguise that matched my alias, Jeff Carter.

***

I was posing as a government official from an URNA military base in the Coastal Plain Region. Oliver was now in on our plan to secede—my mother had finally gotten him to come around to the Warriors' side—so it was easy to get fake government credentials that looked authentic and set up a meeting with a sales rep from Winworth Manufacturing.

The Winworth rep had sent a car to the airport, so I put on a pair of shades and relaxed in the convertible while the car drove along the coastline to the manufacturing plant. Palm trees lined the curvy road. It'd sure be nice to take a vacation at my stepdad's beach house for a few days.

I glanced at my watch. There was time for a quick stop before my meeting. I swiped the navigation screen and searched for places to eat. A local joint was just ahead, so I picked it, and the car's self-driving system adjusted.

The restaurant was a weather-beaten shack, but several cars were parked in the lot, even though it was mid-afternoon. Had to be a good sign.

I found an empty table with an umbrella overlooking the Gulf of Mexico. The perfect amount of breeze blew my way, and I sat on the side of the table that was out of the sun. Too much heat made the skin under my mask itch like crazy.

After the waiter took my order—in Spanish—I drummed my fingers on the table and watched the rest of the customers while I sipped a bottle of water. A mother leaned over and cut some meat for her tow-headed son who was probably four or five while the waiter folded a piece of paper into a sombrero and plopped it on the kid's head. A guy who wasn't much older than me nursed a margarita. An elderly couple chewed their food and ignored each other.

An attractive woman sauntered in. Her dark hair reached her waist, and the breeze kept the hair back from her face. When she caught me looking, a smile teased at her lips.

I nodded and turned my gaze to my courier that had a program to make it look like Jeff's government-issued doc. I'd told my sister-in-law, Ophelia, not to make my alias so good looking, but she hadn't listened. She'd said with my natural charm, it gave me an advantage to have a handsome disguise. Made it easier to get information.

A gust of wind blew over the deck, and the kid's paper sombrero flew by. Diving, I caught it before it skittered out of reach and into the gulf. I took it over to the table.

"Here you go, buddy."

He gazed at me with wide eyes.

With a smile, the mother took the hat. "Thanks."

"No problem."

As soon as I was back at my table, the dark-haired woman walked up. "May I join you? You look like you enjoy being the hero, and I totally despise eating alone."

Well, here was living proof that no good deed goes unpunished. "Yes."

She put her purse on the table, sat down, and extended her hand. "Vanessa."

"Jeff." I squeezed her hand.

"Are you traveling on business?" she asked, and when I cocked an eyebrow, she laughed. "You're not exactly dressed for the beach in that preppy polo shirt and khakis."

I leaned back and crossed my arms. "To my dismay."

The waiter brought my food and took Vanessa's order.

"Go ahead," she said. "Don't wait on me."

I hadn't planned on it. "Thanks." I dove into the fajitas.

"I was here on a trip with my girlfriends, and we had an awesome time. Shopping, spa days, lots of drinks—and men. Anyway, their flight left before mine this morning. Then my flight was cancelled, and I'm stuck here for another day." She tucked her hair behind her ear. "It's totally tragic, but I'll live."

My next alias was going to be homely. I'd insist on it. "Yes, you're facing quite a setback."

"What do you do for a living, Jeff?"

I finished chewing. "Work for the government."

The waiter arrived with a piña colada and set it in front of Vanessa. She took a sip. "Oh, that's so fabulous. I *needed* this after my stressful morning." She leaned back. "Where are you staying?"

"Headed home tonight."

She stuck out her lower lip. "That's too bad."

"Yes." I fought a grin. "It's tragic."

***

After paying for Vanessa's drink and escaping the restaurant, I arrived at Winworth's plant and waited in a lobby that had a sectional sofa and pictures of the different airplanes they manufactured. A few minutes later, a gorgeous woman entered. She had shoulder-length, blond hair and brown eyes, and—man—a *killer* figure. I tried not to stare, but her red blouse was cut low. My eyes involuntarily drifted.

My roguishly handsome alias seemed to have no effect on her though, and she extended her hand. "I'm Alona. I'll be your sales representative today."

I grasped her hand and tried not to flinch at the rubbery texture. Sexy Alona was an android. Good grief.

She smiled. "Now that I have confirmed your identity, Mr.

Carter, may I offer you a beverage?"

"Water would be fantastic. Although I'm curious." I rested a hand on her shoulder. "How'd you confirm my ID?"

"I'm equipped with a retinal scanner." She patted the necklace nestled above her cleavage.

Dirty trick. "That's quite clever."

She went to the minibar, where she retrieved a water bottle from the refrigerator.

"Thank you." I took a drink.

"You're welcome." She motioned toward a set of double doors. "Shall we?"

"Please, ladies first."

Alona led me through the doors and into a large showroom. She sashayed across the concrete floor toward a sleek, gray aircraft, positioned between two fighter jets that dwarfed it. When she stopped, she held out a hand to showcase the plane. "This is the V-32 Lobo Solitario. Shall I give you the full presentation with all of the specifications?" She made the information sound seductive. Who had programmed her, anyway?

"Yes." I fixed my gaze on the aircraft.

"The V-32 Lobo Solitario is designed for one pilot and has autopilot capabilities. It also allows the pilot to travel into difficult-to-reach areas, because rotors allow the aircraft to take off, land, and hover like a helicopter. But once it's in flight, it can convert to a high-speed, high-altitude aircraft…"

Had Vivica made any progress figuring out how GPV was spreading? Lagarde's question about her pursuing a lead bugged me, because he'd anticipated something about Vivica that I'd overlooked—she'd put herself in danger if it meant finding the answer.

I set my jaw. I might never be able to convince her to be my wife, but I couldn't deal with the thought of anything happening to her. I dragged my attention back to Alona.

"…the innovative self-healing, fire-resistant materials are some of the many safety features…"

I should call Vivica and make sure she was okay—and wasn't doing anything stupid. But that might be awkward if she was furious at me for kissing her.

"Mr. Carter?"

I blinked. "Yes, Alona?"

"Would you like to purchase the V-32 Lobo Solitario?" She batted her eyes.

"Yes ma'am. I'm authorized to purchase fifteen." I pulled a credit card out of my wallet.

"Excellent." She held the card up to her eyes to scan it. "It will be a moment while I process your payment."

I turned away and glanced at my courier, hoping to find a message from Vivica.

Nothing. I guess that kiss hadn't been such a smooth move after all.

# CHAPTER 8

## *Vivica*

My fingers froze on the keyboard. As hard as I'd tried all day, I couldn't shake the memory of Drake's kiss. Why had I responded? I should've pulled away and smacked him.

I massaged the bridge of my nose while Agatha's accusation haunted me.

A physical attraction didn't equal love, and I knew that as well as anyone. Drake was attractive. I'd never deny that. It made sense that I'd enjoy his kiss. But now I needed to forget it.

Taking a few deep breaths, I sat up and went back to researching how Ag Management moved food through the supply chain. A couple of hours later, my stomach rumbled, so I headed toward the dining room and heard angry voices coming from my mother's office.

"I don't care how sorry he is for the past, he's not coming onto this property!" my mother shouted. "He can't waltz in here and pretend like he never faked his death and abandoned our four-year-old daughter!"

I halted. My father was here? Had he gotten Drake's message, or had something else drawn him? I crept closer to her office, flattened myself against the wall, and peered inside.

"What if he has information that could help?" Melvin said.

"I can't believe you'd betray me like this." She swayed slightly and gripped the edge of her desk to steady herself.

Wow. I'd *never* heard Melvin disagree with my mother about anything.

"Now hold on, Genevieve. I haven't done anything but make a suggestion. This has nothing to do with betrayal and everything to do with loyalty. I want what's best for you."

"And allowing my ex-husband in here is the solution? I ought to have my security team escort him to prison!"

"Technically, he's still your husband."

My mother swore. "Not for long."

"Listen," Melvin said. "Navid will use this epidemic to try to take back control of the country if you don't get a handle on things. If Harrison knows something about what's causing it, and he says he does—"

"You have no proof he can be any help to us. What could possibly motivate him to show up? For all you know, he could be spying for the Peacekeepers."

I burst into her office. "Drake and I contacted Dad. Well, Drake tried, and I guess it worked."

"Why would you let him do that?" My mother's eyes flashed. "And you know better than to eavesdrop."

"I'm sorry." I bit my tongue to keep from adding that they shouldn't have been talking so loudly. "Drake and I believed Dad had information that could help us determine if the Peacekeepers engineered a smart virus to cause this epidemic, and the more I've learned, the more I think they did. I had no idea he'd show up."

My mother and Melvin exchanged glances. "How did your father seem when you worked with him in Fortune City?" my mother asked.

"Unstable. I could never get a read on where his loyalties were. But he claimed our captors were torturing him with nanobots that were causing him mental problems."

"See? Mental problems." My mother put her hands on her hips and turned to Melvin. "We can't let him in."

Melvin's lips flattened. "It would behoove us to talk with him. You've always made bold choices, Genevieve. I don't want to see you back down now out of fear."

Whoa. My respect for Melvin multiplied.

I took a step back and prepared for fire to shoot from my mother's eyes. Instead, she went to her desk, supported her head with one hand, and rubbed her neck with the other. "I have a horrible headache." She raised her head, met my eyes, and flicked her fingers toward the door. "I'll call you if we need you."

*** 

As I was finishing my tomato and cucumber gazpacho in the dining room, Melvin appeared and motioned for me to follow. "They're in the Canadian wing. The boardroom. Your mother refuses to let him in to this section."

I didn't blame her. "Are they fighting?"

Melvin grinned. "Your mother expressed her displeasure and demanded a divorce. Your father took it in stride—like he always has."

That wasn't surprising. My time with him in Fortune City made me realize his style of retaliation was more passive-aggressive. He'd grown his hair long after he'd faked his death because my mother hated long hair on men.

The quickest way to the Canadian section was to walk outside. Dark clouds obscured the sun, and a rain-scented breeze assaulted my nose. More rain. Again. A blast of chilly wind swept away humidity, and streaks of rain adorned the western horizon. We quickened our pace to beat the approaching downpour.

The Canadian section of the house hadn't been used for more than a decade, though the staff maintained it. Deadness permeated the atmosphere. I stopped. "You'll have to lead the way."

Melvin guided me down the hall toward the boardroom where we passed two guards who waited at the end of the hallway. We drew closer, and I expected to hear angry voices, but silence oozed from the walls. Opening the door to the boardroom, Melvin gasped.

"Genevieve!"

# CHAPTER 9

## *Vivica*

Melvin let go of the door, and I had to put my hand out to keep it from slamming into my face. My mother lay on the floor, unconscious, while my father knelt next to her.

I froze and grasped the doorframe.

"She collapsed," he said. "We were talking, and she got pale and fell."

Melvin's face reddened. "And you didn't call for help? Guards!" He used his MD3 to call my mother's personal physician.

"It happened a few seconds ago. I didn't do anything, I swear." My father held up both hands, and his green eyes pleaded with me to believe him.

I wasn't sure. But my mother had complained of a headache, and she had been dealing with a lot of stress.

Regaining my composure, I knelt next to my mother as the guards rushed in.

"Take him away," Melvin barked. "Lock him up until we figure out what happened."

I felt her neck for a pulse. It was faint. Her breathing was shallow.

"Vivibear, I need to talk to you," my father said while the guards handcuffed him. "Take care of your mother first, but please, this is important."

I looked at the guards. "Don't take him off the property yet. Understand?"

They nodded in unison before leading my father from the room. I grasped my mother's clammy hand and began to pray. "God, please heal my mother. Soften her heart. Help her to know you."

Melvin took her other hand and stared at me. "You really have changed, haven't you? Taking all that exclusivist stuff seriously?"

"Because it's the truth," I said softly.

"Your prayers don't bother me." His forehead creased. "Your mother needs all the help she can get."

Ten minutes later, Dr. Alstead ran in with her medical team and a stretcher. She pushed Melvin and me aside and examined my mother. "Get Madame President to the bunker immediately." She tucked her poufy brown hair behind her ears.

I frowned. "The bunker?"

"There's a state-of-the-art hospital facility below ground," Melvin whispered.

That was news to me. I knew about the bunker, but a hospital facility?

\*\*\*

While Dr. Alstead worked with the team of nurses she'd brought with her, there was nothing I could do but wait, so I found Jaxon, the head of my mother's security team, in his office.

He raised his perfectly-plucked brows when I entered. "I suppose you want to see your father?"

"How'd you guess?"

Jaxon escorted me to an elevator that led to the bunker beneath the mansion. We proceeded through a narrow hallway and several doors. At each one, Jaxon swiped his biochip, which allowed us access.

How much longer would I be able to get away with not having a chip?

My father sat shackled behind a window, and Jaxon pointed at a speaker system that I could use to communicate with him. "I refuse to allow you in the same room with him until we determine why Madame President is ill."

"I understand."

"I'll give you privacy, but I'm not going far."

"Fine."

I stood in front of the glass, and my father placed his hand on it. "Vivibear, you have to believe me. I didn't hurt your mother. Yes, she was angry that I showed up, but I swear, I only came to help you. Have they figured out what's wrong?"

"No. But Dr. Alstead says it's more than the shock of seeing you. Something else major is going on. She's running tests."

"We have a lot to discuss," he said.

I put my hands on my hips. "Like how you sided with the Peacekeepers in Fortune City."

"I told you. They were messing with my head and trying to control me."

What did that even mean? "How?"

"Possibly nanobots. Maybe drugs."

"I heard you were addicted to drugs," I said, recalling what my enemy, Martina Ward, had told me in Fortune City.

He hung his head. "Not by choice. I never took drugs intentionally."

I closed my eyes and fought the tears that formed. This was all too much. "I want to believe you and trust you."

"You can. That's why I came when I heard you needed me."

"Are you working for the Peacekeepers?"

"No."

"Then who are you working for?" I asked.

"I'm a man who believes the world should be a free place and who's fighting to undo all the damage I did when I worked in Fortune City."

I crossed my arms. He knew that's what I'd want to hear, given the time I'd spent working with the Emancipation Warriors, but somehow my instincts said to believe him. "Where have you been hiding the last eight months?"

"I can't tell you."

Surprise, surprise. I switched tactics. "Are the Peacekeepers deliberately targeting citizens without biochips?"

"Yes." He cleared his throat. "Well, that's my theory. When I did some spying in Fortune City, Dr. Gates was close to creating a smart virus."

"How does it work?" I leaned closer.

"He created a virus which recognizes a patient's biochip. If there isn't a chip, the virus attacks the body."

"What a perfect way to target people who don't comply."

"Exactly," he said. "The Emancipation Warriors are a real problem for the Peacekeepers. A group that's rebelling makes implementing world peace and harmony difficult."

No kidding. My stomach tightened when I thought of the Warriors' mission to take over one region and form a new country. How could a single country stand against a global government? Especially if the prospective citizens of that new country died from an epidemic that was made to target them.

I grimaced. Agatha had mentioned survivors. "How can they guarantee a normal person's immune system won't fight this new virus, even without a biochip?"

"Exactly. That's what I haven't figured out yet…or how they're spreading it." His shoulders slumped.

"I've been researching the possibility that they might be using the food supply."

He twisted the tiny gold stud in his ear. "That's a good theory. Keep pursuing it."

"Is there anything else I should know?"

"Yes, which is why I'm terrified for your mother."

My eyes widened.

He clutched a handful of his shoulder-length hair in his fist. "Dr. Gates did more than create a smart virus. His work with nanobots was revolutionary, and he was researching how they could be used in medicine."

"How?" I was having trouble keeping track of all of this information.

"Gates was performing trials on patients using nanobots. They could be used for a lot of good because they could target and repair damage from strokes, heart attacks, cancer—you name it."

My heart thudded as my mind comprehended. "But the reverse could be true, and the nanobots could also be used to make a person's illness worse."

"Correct. And someone may've used nanobots to target your mother."

# CHAPTER 10

## *Vivica*

Goosebumps peppered my arms. "How do we stop them?"

"I've been researching and trying to create good nanobots that'll override the bad nanobots and stop them from attacking the body."

"How's that going?"

My father exhaled. "No breakthroughs. My brain isn't what it used to be—plus I've been pulled away to work on some other projects."

That wasn't something I wanted to hear. Besides, who was he working for? I closed my eyes and tried to focus, but my thoughts jumbled, and I landed on the most crucial one at the moment. "If Mother dies, you may be held responsible."

"Not necessarily."

"How can you say that? She collapsed when you started talking to her. Melvin already blames you. What if he finds out about the nanobots and thinks you used them?"

"Nanobots don't work that fast. It can take as long as a week for them to adequately cause damage. Maybe she had a heart attack, and it's unrelated."

It was a flimsy hope I was unwilling to grasp, but then I realized there was a more logical explanation. Navid had done something while he was here.

"The way to know for sure is to get a blood sample and test it for nanobots," he said.

"If I get the sample, who'll test it?"

"I will. When I escape."

"How are you going to pull that off?" I asked.

"With your help."

He was certainly confident I'd assist him. I pulled a stray thread from my lacy shirt sleeve. But my father was my only option, and we both knew it. Could I be sure he was trustworthy?

"Listen," he said. "You don't have to decide to help me right this minute. But promise me something."

"What?"

"If your mother dies, get out of here as fast as you can. Let the Warriors hide you."

I didn't want to think that way. My mother couldn't die. I still hadn't convinced her she needed Jesus.

My father pressed his hand to the glass. "Promise me you'll leave. Don't stick around for a funeral."

"She's not going to die." She was too tough. I bit my lip. How could I even be sure I trusted my father? What if this was all a lie to manipulate me?

We sat in silence until Jaxon entered the room. "Vivica, Dr. Alstead needs to see you right away."

"Is my mother okay?"

His face was stoic.

Tears nipped my eyes, and I met my father's gaze.

"I love you, Vivibear. Remember what I told you."

I turned away and let Jaxon lead me through the bunker to the hospital I hadn't known was beneath us until a few hours ago.

***

Through the window, I could see my mother on a hospital bed. Hooked up to monitors, she took shallow breaths, and her complexion was gray. Melvin hovered next to her bed. I hesitated by the sliding door when Dr. Alstead strode down the hall.

"What did you find out?" I prayed it was something that could be treated.

Dr. Alstead sighed and shook her head. "Your mother had a ruptured aneurysm in her brain, and she's in a coma. We're going to perform surgery as soon as the surgeon and his team arrive."

My heart flopped. "What's the prognosis?"

She touched my arm. "It's encouraging that she's hanging on, and many patients survive surgery. But, you need to prepare yourself in case she doesn't make it."

This couldn't be happening. Hadn't God sent me back to my mother so she could know him? I'd bitten back comments and forced myself to respect and honor my mother because that was what God expected. I'd squelched disagreement so that maybe she'd listen to me. Or see a difference in my life.

But it hadn't been enough.

I'd failed, and now my mother might spend eternity apart from God. Too numb to cry, I nodded to acknowledge Dr. Alstead's statement and stepped closer to the door. It slid aside.

Melvin looked up, and his eyes were red. "She's my best friend."

I ran into his arms, and we sobbed together.

When we broke apart, I scrutinized the monitors. I didn't have to be a medical professional to see her vitals were weak. Arranging a chair next to the bed, I sat and grasped my mother's clammy hand. "Fight. You can beat this. We love you."

I would've given anything to feel a response. Something to know she could hear. Maybe she could. I'd heard stories of people being trapped in their own bodies. Everyone thought the patients were incapable of processing information, but years later, they awakened and revealed they'd heard everything.

I squeezed her hand. "Mother, please listen." I caught Melvin's eye. He shook his head as if he knew what I was about to say. "God sent his son, Jesus Christ, to die for you and me and Melvin—everyone. Our sin separates us from God, but he loves us and made a way for us to be with him. Without Jesus dying as payment for our sins, we'd go to Hell." Tears began to flow. "All the good you've done isn't enough to get you into Heaven. It isn't enough without Christ."

I buried my face on the edge of her bed and sobbed.

The steady beeps of the machines punctuated my sobs. Melvin came over, knelt beside me, and drew me close.

\*\*\*

I awoke in the recliner next to my mother's bed. I wiggled to take the pressure off my sore tailbone and rubbed my stiff neck. The surgeon had been cautiously optimistic about the surgery two days before, but my mother remained in a coma. Melvin had moved to the couch in the corner, and he snored.

Removing my government doc from my pocket, I scanned the national news headlines that praised the new president. Because my mother was incapacitated, Vice President Melivia Sanders had taken the oath of office and was now leading our country. Though she was a Nationalist like my mother, I wondered if she was a closet Globalist who supported the Council of World Peacekeepers' encroachment on national sovereignty.

I put my doc away and said more prayers for my mother.

The glass door slid aside, and Dr. Alstead walked in. "Good morning." She examined my mother.

It took a few minutes for me to ask the question that had been pinging my brain since the surgeon had given a report. "Will she ever be normal?"

Dr. Alstead tucked a piece of hair behind her ears. "If your mother survives, she's likely to experience disabilities. The damage was significant."

"Can she be rehabilitated?"

"Perhaps. I'm simply telling you how it appears at this moment. Of course, you seem very religious, so you can pray for a miracle. Right now, science says things are bleak."

I didn't appreciate the edge that crept into her voice. Or that she'd be so blunt in front of my mother. What if she could hear? Yet I had another question and wanted to see how Dr. Alstead would react. "Why didn't my mother's biochip alert you about the aneurysm? It should've given you warning so you could've treated it before it ruptured. Isn't that one of the purposes of having a chip inserted?"

Dr. Alstead bristled. "Biochip technology isn't perfect. Sometimes the health data is conflicting. Sometimes people have bad genes." She narrowed her eyes. "I can't be responsible for something your mother's body did to itself."

"I never said you were." I crossed my arms.

In the corner, Melvin stirred and awakened.

Dr. Alstead raised her chin. "Perhaps you should return to your quarters and get some rest. I'd hate to see you wear yourself out."

"I'm fine."

I held her gaze until she looked away. "Fine. I'll check back in an hour." She stalked from the room, and I knew what I needed to do.

Thanking God that Drake had returned my courier, I pulled it from my other pocket, sent a quick message telling him my suspicions, and began to research how to draw blood.

# CHAPTER 11

## *Drake*

"So, I messed up," I said to Liam as we bounced along a gravel road in an old pick-up the government couldn't track. "I shouldn't have pushed Vivica so hard, but I just wanted her to know where my head is."

Liam sighed. "Dude, you need to talk to Ophelia about this. I'm not an expert on women. Plus, she knows Vivica better than I do."

"Sorry."

After I'd left the Winworth factory, I'd joined my brother on a mission to scout security protocols at the International Nuclear Containment Facility where the Peacekeepers stored the highly enriched uranium our scientists needed. We'd gone off grid and hadn't even taken our couriers. Now we were on our way back to a safe house on the edge of an abandoned plantation in the Coastal Plain Region.

"You sure know how to pick 'em, though," Liam said.

"What's that supposed to mean?"

"Faith. And now Vivica."

I curled my fingers into a fist. If Liam hadn't been driving, I'd have slugged him. "Where do you get off lumping the two of them together?" Faith had betrayed the Warriors by becoming a mole for the government, so suggesting Vivica was anything like that woman was disgusting.

Liam shrugged. "Sorry. They're both driven and loyal to their cause."

"In Vivica's case, that's not a bad thing."

"Maybe you need someone who's content to stay home and let you do the fighting."

"Yeah, like your wife does."

"Compared to what Vivica's done in the past, Ophelia's job is safe."

"None of us are safe."

Liam pulled into the driveway. Spanish moss-draped trees surrounded the stone cottage. Before he'd even parked completely, I hopped out and marched into the house. Mosquitos emerged from the nearby swamp and hunted me.

I must be sweeter than I'd thought.

Enough bonding. It was time for some space. I retrieved our couriers from a lockbox in the basement and tossed Liam's at him. Then, I grabbed some pretzels from the pantry, cranked up the air conditioning, and shut myself in a musty bedroom. Lounging on a twin bed, I checked my messages and pumped my fist when I saw one from Vivica.

Until I read it.

My mother had an aneurysm. Critical condition. Suspect assassination attempt.

I massaged the bridge of my nose and said a silent prayer. Then, I skimmed news articles about the president's current condition and the new president. If I could help it, I'd never leave my courier behind again.

Not wanting to wait another minute, I called Vivica. "My dear,

I'm so sorry. I would've called sooner, but I've been working on an assignment and just heard. I didn't have my courier."

"It's okay." Her voice wobbled, and my heart broke for her.

"Are you in a place where you can speak freely?" I stood and shoved my hand in my pocket.

"Give me a few minutes."

I gazed out the window at the swamp. A fat alligator covered in green gunk lurked near the wooden bridge that led across the water, and when he swung his head in my direction and blinked, I turned away.

Not a huge fan of those guys.

A door latched. "Okay," she said. "I'm in a supply closet, but I still can't say too much."

"You think it's an assassination attempt. Do you believe the Peacekeepers are responsible?"

"Yes. Navid did something when he was here."

"Do you have any proof?" I asked.

"Not yet."

"Do you believe your life is in danger?"

She hesitated long enough for me to wonder if she was deciding whether or not to lie to me. Lying convincingly had never been one of her strong points, which in a normal world, would be a good thing. But in our upside-down life, it was a huge liability.

"Probably not," she said.

"Do you know of any way to prove this is an assassination attempt?"

"Maybe."

"Are you working on it?"

"Yes."

I ran my fingers through my hair and wished I could wrap my arms around her. "Will you call when you can talk freely?"

"Yes."

"Good. I'll come as soon as I can."

"Thank you." The relief in her voice was obvious. "I'm glad I can count on you."

I caught a glimpse of my lovesick face in the mirror and was thankful no one but the gator was a witness. "I'm praying for you, and… I love you."

I disconnected before she could answer—or not.

# CHAPTER 12

## *Vivica*

"Melvin," I said that evening after Drake's call, "have you spoken to President Sanders?"

He frowned. "No. I suppose I should. Your mother was handling some problems that may need to be brought to her attention." He rose. "I'll go take care of that right now. Call if there's a change."

I smiled. My distraction had worked perfectly.

He hurried from the room, and I pulled the curtain. I rummaged through drawers, and when I found the automated blood extractor and two vials, I mentally recited the instructions I'd read.

I screwed one vial onto the extractor and placed the machine against the crook of my mother's arm. When I pressed the power button, the extractor lit up. The message on the screen read *Locating Vein*. Then, the vial began to fill with blood. When it was full, the screen instructed me to remove the vial. I repeated the process.

My heart thudded when I heard footsteps. Pocketing the vials, I tossed the extractor's needle in the incinerator, replaced the machine, and scurried back to my chair.

The curtain swooshed open. "Everything okay in here?" Dr. Alstead asked.

"No change from what I can see." I patted my mother's arm.

Dr. Alstead pursed her lips. "Keep the curtain open. It's important that we see your mother."

I smiled. "Of course. Her safety is more important than her privacy." My fingers curled around the chair leg. That should be the Peacekeepers' motto.

"Excellent. I'll check back in a bit."

"Doctor?"

"Yes?"

"Would it be okay to bring my mother's dog down for a visit later? She loves him, and it might help.

Dr. Alstead shrugged. "It can't hurt and might be beneficial." She gave a half-smile and walked out.

I shook my head and worked on hacking the bunker's security system with my courier. Since the device looked like a doc, I was willing to take the risk of using it here.

A few minutes later, Melvin returned. "President Sanders is all set." He pressed his lips together. "She'll do an excellent job, but she's not your mother."

"Any word on what's going to happen to my father?"

Melvin's eyes flashed. "The security team will be moving him soon. I told them to get that man out of this compound as soon as possible. He gave your mother the shock that caused this."

"Melvin, I don't think that's wh—"

"She's not been herself since she learned he was alive." He raised his chin.

"Really?"

"You hadn't noticed?"

"She was good at hiding things from me."

"*Is*, sweetie. Your mother is good at hiding things from you."

"Sorry." I ducked my head and then stood. "I'm going to get

something to eat." I wasn't hungry, but I needed nourishment.

Melvin nodded as he removed his MD3 from his pocket.

I slipped down the hall to the cell where my father was imprisoned.

When I entered, he scrambled to his feet. "They're moving me soon."

"I know." It took a few swipes on my courier, but I was able to open the door. He rushed out of his cell and hugged me.

"I'm so sorry this is happening, Vivibear."

I slipped one of the vials in his pocket. "Then let's stop the people who did this." Taking his arm, I led him down the hallway. "If I get you out, can you take it from here?"

"As long as you cover my tracks until I get off the compound."

"No problem."

We rushed through two sets of doors while I prayed my adjustments to the security cameras were enough.

We burst outside into the moonless night. A fine drizzle misted my face.

"Remember what I told you," he said. "If your mother dies, don't stick around. There's no one left here to protect you."

"But—"

"I don't want her to die either. In spite of our history, I'd never wish her ill. If I were in your shoes, I'd want to say good-bye too. But you have to trust me. The Peacekeepers are going to do whatever they must to take over the world and create a global government. And they're not going to stop until everyone who opposes them is either dead or on their side."

A chill skittered from the base of my skull to the small of my back.

He kissed me on the forehead. "Good luck, Vivibear."

# CHAPTER 13

## *Vivica*

The kitchen staff had gone home for the night, so I grabbed a roll and a slice of ham and made myself a sandwich. I ate half of it on the way back to my mother's hospital room and tossed the other half to Commander, who gulped it in one swallow.

"No change," Melvin said when I entered. His eyes fell on the dog, but he made no comment. He'd never been an animal lover.

"Mother, I brought Commander for a visit."

The dog whined and nudged her still hand with his nose. When she didn't respond, he sat and rested his chin on the edge of the bed.

I settled in the recliner next to Commander and said a silent prayer while I stroked the dog's head.

"What made you believe the exclusivists?" Melvin asked.

I rocked for a few seconds while I thought about the term the media used to describe Christians who believed all parts of the Bible—the real one, not the government's Revised Freedom Version. "The realization that it must be true because nothing but the truth could be so divisive. Jesus even talked about how he didn't come to bring peace, but a sword. And that daughters would be against their mothers. And enemies would be members of your own household."

He shifted and crossed his legs. "I see how you related to that."

"If that part was true, then so was everything else the exclusivists believed." I hated that term, but I was trying to use words that made sense to Melvin.

"You truly believe your mother's going to Hell?"

I swallowed. "Yeah." My voice cracked. "If she's never accepted Jesus as her Savior."

"How can you believe in a God who sends people to Hell?"

"God doesn't send anybody to Hell. People choose Hell by rejecting his Son."

"Your mother is a good person."

"No one is good enough for God."

He shook his head. "God won't do that to your mother. You'd feel a lot better if you'd believe that too."

"That wouldn't make it true."

Jaxon scuttled into the room, and his eyes were wide. "Harrison escaped."

Melvin jumped up, causing Commander to rise to his feet. "How?"

"Outside help. One of his cohorts figured out what happened and found a way to hack our system so he could get away."

Relief flooded my veins. When I'd manipulated the security system, I'd tried to make it appear that help was coming from the outside. At least they'd bought it.

"How long ago?"

"About twenty minutes."

Melvin's eyes fastened on me. "I see. And you're *sure* help came from the outside."

"Yes."

"Do what you can to track him. He's responsible for Genevieve's condition."

Jaxon turned on his heel and left.

"What. Did. You. Do?" Melvin's eyes blazed.

I hesitated. How could I lie when Melvin was starting to show an interest in my faith? What kind of example would that be? I swallowed. "Nothing that won't help in the long run."

"Are you certain?"

"Just because you blame someone doesn't mean they're responsible. What's my father guilty of? Making my mother angry?"

"Oh, let's see. Abandoning you. Faking his death. Don't tell me you've forgotten that."

"No." Commander started to pant, so I ran my hand over his head.

"I should have you arrested."

"If you do, we'll never know the truth."

"We know the truth." He twisted his diamond ring. "I should never—"

"Quit blaming yourself for convincing my mother to talk to my father. Something bigger is going on." I told him my suspicions about an assassination attempt.

"But that sounds crazy." He buried his head in his hands. "It's hard for me not to blame myself because your father's presence is the most logical explanation."

For a few minutes, only the machines' beeps filled the silence.

Melvin raised his head. "If you believe someone killed your mother, then you should get out of here. You may be in danger."

"I'm not leaving." I'd stay and keep preaching a salvation message until something happened. Maybe my mother could hear me and understand. I leaned back in the recliner.

He sighed. "I hope you don't regret this."

"I won't." I put my earbuds in. I needed to hear a sermon from the pastor I'd been listening to lately. Anything to get my mind off this situation.

\*\*\*

"The people of Judah didn't know what to do." The pastor's melodic voice soothed me. "Their enemies had come to wage war against Jehoshaphat, and the people of Judah thought they didn't have the power to face the vast army that was threatening them. So they sought the Lord. They cried out in their distress."

I blinked my grainy eyes. Even though I was sleepy, I could relate to crying out to God.

"God reminded them not to be discouraged or afraid. It wasn't their battle. It was God's. They needed to take their positions, stand firm, and the Lord would deliver them."

My eyelids drooped.

\*\*\*

I awoke shaking in my mother's hospital room, so I pulled up the thick blanket someone had spread over my lap. Commander was dozing next to my recliner. Rubbing the sleep from my eyes, I took out my courier to check for messages, but a shrill blast from my mother's machines scattered my thoughts. I tossed the blanket aside, and my pulse thudded in my neck.

Melvin jumped up from the couch.

Commander awakened and whined.

My eyes fell on the machine.

Flat line.

No.

*Not now. Please, God. Not yet.*

Dr. Alstead and a nurse burst into the room and began CPR. In a trance, I took the dog, backed out of the room, and watched them work.

*Please, God. Not yet.*

Melvin wrapped his arm around me.

My breaths came in shallow gasps.

*Please, God. Not yet.*

Dr. Alstead stopped and turned toward the clock. 02:43. The nurses stepped back.

*No, God.*

*Please.*

*Not.*

*Yet.*

# CHAPTER 14

## *Drake*

"Drake, we need you for Operation Guardian Light." Liam blinked a few times and crossed his arms. "With your head in the game."

He was lucky we weren't having this conversation in person since he'd left to return to Operation Coastal Republic HQ. I was still ready to put my fist through the image of his face projected on the safe house wall. He'd been bossing me around since we were kids, and I was over it. "Don't act like you're the only one who's ever had to make a sacrifice. I've always given a hundred percent." I'd given so much that I wondered if the cost was worth it, and if what we were doing was really God's will.

Now we were planning an operation to steal the uranium from the containment facility, so our scientists could make the nukes that would protect our future country. But after scouting the building's security protocols with Liam, I knew our team had a huge challenge.

"Not lately, you haven't," Liam snapped.

So much for family loyalty. Jethro Portner stood next to my brother, chomped gum, and stared back at me. "I could gather intel at the president's funeral. If our family isn't well-represented, it'll look suspicious."

Liam rolled his eyes. "Mom and Oliver can handle it."

"Right," Portner said. "Like you're gonna be concentrating on espionage anyhow. More like you'll be busy comforting Storyteller."

I scowled. "Don't call her that." Vivica hated the Warriors code name Portner had given her after she'd had trouble lying well enough to pass a polygraph.

Portner smirked at Liam. "He's got it bad, don't he?"

"Did Vivica even ask you to come?" Liam asked.

"Not for the funeral, but I already told her I'd—"

"So you may be butting in where you ain't even wanted," Jethro said. "Look. We gotta get uranium for our nukes ASAP. You can be the one to fly the Lobo in to pick up the uranium and get it back to HQ. Can you handle that?"

"Yes sir."

"I'm counting on you. The Coastal Republic's future is at stake."

I clenched my teeth. "Fine. But then I'm going to Vivica. And that's final." I ended the call.

***

As much as I wanted to get to Vivica, I wasn't completely heartbroken that I had the chance to try out the V-32 Lobo Solitario. It turned out that it was exactly the type of aircraft we needed to get in and out of the area around the International Nuclear Containment Facility where the Peacekeepers stored the highly enriched uranium.

While I was handling the Lobo, the rest of my team was disabling security and breaking into the facility. The plan was for me to slip in, pick up the uranium, and get far away—fast.

I got out of the truck I'd driven to the hangar where the first of the Lobos had been delivered fresh from Winworth's plant earlier that day. Carolina, the grizzled pilot and mechanic who ran the airstrip, ambled out in the rain to meet me.

"Sure gettin' sick o' this rain." She pulled a pink hanky from her coveralls and blew her nose.

"No kidding. I hear it's a lot worse in the Great Plains Region. They're dealing with floods."

"Not to mention that nasty virus. How long 'til that stuff gets here?"

"No idea." I ran my fingers through my wet hair. "That's not something I want to bet on." I walked into the hangar.

Carolina shook her head and pointed at the plane. "You know how to run this thing?"

"I watched some training videos." I grinned. "Can't be much harder than the video games I used to play when I was a kid."

She snorted. "Might want to be sure if you're gonna be toting radioactive material around. Not exactly something you want to crash land."

"Thanks for your vote of confidence."

"My pleasure," she said. "But I did take it for a spin a few hours ago, and it really does pilot itself." She crossed her arms. "Makes an old flygirl like me feel obsolete."

"Not a chance. You never know when we'll need an experienced aviator like you." I winked.

She snorted and hit my arm. "You're full of it, son. Like your dad."

Carolina had flown with my dad in URNA's Air Force. Truthfully, she'd probably spent more time with him than I ever had—thanks to the grudge my mom had held after their divorce. But I'd seen Dad enough before he'd died of cancer a few years ago, and it was because of him that Liam and I'd become Warriors.

I opened the hatch and got in. When I pressed the power button, a screen lit up. "Welcome to the V-32 Lobo Solitario," a seductive female voice, a lot like Alona's, said.

Carolina stuck her head in. "You can change the voice if it's not tough enough for you. Personally, I don't like that chick's tone." She reached over and poked the screen a few times, and a menu appeared.

I picked Jake, who had a North American accent. I didn't need the distraction of a female voice—worrying about Vivica had already taken enough out of me.

Carolina gave a few more pointers and showed me how to program the destination and sync my courier to the system. Then she slammed the hatch and saluted. When she stepped back, I steered the aircraft out of the hangar, but I could feel it propelling itself, so I let go.

It rolled out into an open space, the rotors began to spin, and the Lobo shot upward. Then, it converted to airplane mode and sped through the night sky toward the containment facility.

I drummed my fingers against my legs. I was probably being paranoid, but I had this feeling that something—I didn't know when or where—was about to go very wrong.

I prayed God would keep Vivica and my team safe, and then I turned my thoughts to something that'd been bothering me for a while. Was Operation Coastal Republic the worst kept secret in North America?

Several months ago, I'd argued with my stepdad about the operation's security.

"How do you expect to keep this from an entire region of people?" I said. We were at the governor's mansion in the private bowling alley he'd had installed after becoming governor years ago.

Oliver released his bowling ball, and when he got a strike, he faced me. "The alternative is publicizing it. Then what would you expect from President Wilkins? Even though she's a Nationalist at heart, she has to keep the Peacekeepers happy, so she'd be forced to retaliate. The Peacekeepers would be there to assist." He shook his head. "We must do this quietly and then announce our independence. It's the best way."

"What if the citizens don't support secession? Shouldn't they get a vote?"

"How do you propose a vote without the Peacekeepers finding out? Normally, I'd agree with you, but in this case, tipping our hand would be disastrous." He took his bowling ball from the return. "If you want out, I understand."

"No." I was the one who'd helped drag him into the mess.

"Good. Then keep working with the Warriors." He stepped forward and sent the ball down the lane. I'd walked away, feeling worse than before our conversation had started.

"Cavalier, this is Night Hawk. What's your twenty?" My teammate's voice boomed through my cramped space.

I glanced at the radar. "ETA five minutes."

"Circle around. Team's having some problems on the ground and hasn't extracted the package yet."

Great. "Be specific."

"We think the Peacekeepers caught wind of our mission and beefed up security. We're not aborting yet, but it may come to that."

I drew a breath and took manual control of the Lobo. "Keep me posted, Night Hawk."

"Will do."

My shoulders tensed. If Operation Guardian Light went south, it definitely put Operation Coastal Republic in jeopardy. Without nuclear weapons, we were at the Peacekeepers' mercy. As I circled, I considered how the Peacekeepers would react to secession. Zahedi was a smart guy—he hadn't seized power to lose control of an entire region in North America. Letting us go peacefully could cause a chain reaction if other regions joined our country.

Our revolution hadn't been the success we'd hoped. The Warriors had made some gains, but we still didn't have all of the freedoms we'd started fighting for. My mind wandered back to the doubts I'd had for a long time.

Maybe none of this was God's will and we should give up, stop fighting, and submit to the authorities he'd given us.

"Cavalier, this is Night Hawk. Turn back. We're under fire."

"Did you get the package?"

No response.

I restarted the navigation, and the aircraft sped toward the facility. I didn't take orders from Night Hawk. The International Nuclear Containment Facility appeared on the screen, and when I pressed some buttons, the Lobo's rotors began working. The aircraft set itself down—like a helicopter. No need for a runway. As soon as it landed in a soybean field, I checked my holster for my Diablo 87 and jumped out. Rain soaked through my uniform.

A fence surrounded the facility's perimeter, and I ran to it, stopped, and listened. Nothing but the splatter of rain. Walking the length of the fence, I kept an eye out for any of my team members. A flash caused me to crouch behind an empty truck. A door stood open, and light poured out. Three of my team members marched forward while six security guards held them at gunpoint.

I gritted my teeth and bit back a curse.

Spotting some storage barrels that could provide cover, I sprinted forward and ducked behind them. We'd sent in five guys. Where were the other two?

I pivoted when a second door screeched open, and Night Hawk and Blackbird darted out. Night Hawk clutched two metal suitcases while Blackbird held two Demonio 57 machine guns—that weren't ours.

Blackbird split off toward the barrels where I waited. I half expected someone to bolt out of the doors behind them, but no one did.

I raised my hands. "It's Cavalier," I said as Blackbird approached. He nodded and handed me the other Demonio 57. "I'll help you pick these guys off. Anybody chasing you?"

A stricken expression settled on his young face. "We shot 'em. Took their weapons."

"And Night Hawk has the package?"

"Yes sir."

I touched my earpiece. "Night Hawk, this is Cavalier."

"Go ahead, Cavalier."

"Take the Lobo and get the package to the Mine."

"That's your job, sir."

"Got to help Blackbird free our guys. Standby for the Lobo's coordinates." Shielding my courier from the rain, I used GPS to locate the aircraft and sent the location to Night Hawk's device.

"Got the coordinates. That thing easy to fly?" He was trying to sound confident, but doubt crept into his voice.

"You'll do fine. It flies itself." I clutched the machine gun. "We'll take care of things here."

"Yes sir."

Blackbird and I exchanged glances. The guards had lined our men up against a wall. I couldn't believe they were going to kill them without interrogating them.

Unless our enemies already had everything they needed.

The men drew their weapons.

"Now." My pulse hammered my neck.

Blackbird and I aimed at the factory guards, letting loose a spray of bullets, and they began dropping. Our men careened toward the fence. While they were scaling it, a second batch of guards swarmed out of the facility. We continued shooting while our men hotfooted it for cover.

As we slogged through the mud toward the SUVs parked on the

edge of the factory property, the men we'd rescued returned fire.

A bullet grazed my arm, and I almost lost my footing on the slick ground. I wavered and propelled myself forward. One of the SUVs edged closer, and the door opened. A bullet pinged the side of the vehicle as I dove in. The SUV bounced away over uneven terrain, and I ignored my throbbing arm.

"Night Hawk, it's Cavalier. What's your twenty?"

"In the air. About ten miles out."

I blew out a breath. Blackbird put pressure on my arm while two other guys continued to shoot at the guards.

"The Lobo took a few shots to the fuselage, but you'll never believe what happened," Night Hawk said.

I thought of Sexy Alona's presentation. "The fuselage healed itself?"

"It was totally crazy, man. Never seen anything like it."

I glanced over my shoulder at the rest of the team. They'd stopped shooting but remained at attention. "Let me know when you deliver the package."

"Copy that, Cavalier."

# CHAPTER 15

## *Vivica*

I stayed for my mother's funeral.

Though my father's warning pulsed in my mind, I couldn't abandon Melvin—even after he'd insisted. My mother had been his entire world, and now he was lost. For years he'd worked, planned, and schemed with her.

Now Melvin and I stood side by side at the national cemetery. My mother's funeral had been a state event, but the service dedicating her monument had been invitation only. Her body wouldn't be buried at the cemetery. Instead, Dr. Alstead had prepared it for cryopreservation, and her earthly shell would remain in a warehouse with other wealthy citizens who hoped to be revived someday when technology advanced.

Why had she put her faith in science's empty promise of eternity when God had already made it possible?

The crowd had thinned. I wasn't ready to leave, though I roasted in a proper and stylish black suit. I reached over and squeezed Melvin's hand. Drake tightened his grasp around my shoulders, and I let him. He'd arrived shortly after my mother's death and had refused to leave me except when I went to bed.

His support and loyalty had been lifelines.

We needed to return to the presidential mansion for a formal state dinner, yet leaving carried a finality I wasn't ready to accept.

Taking a quivering breath, I donned sunglasses and walked with Drake to the executive car. My hand rested on the vial of my mother's blood concealed in a pouch that fastened around my waist and remained hidden under my clothes. Since I'd drawn the blood, I hadn't let the container out of contact.

I'd find answers soon.

The car drove us back to the presidential mansion. Governors, representatives, and members of the Council of World Peacekeepers waited.

Still in the trance that hadn't abated since my mother's passing, I greeted guests and accepted their condolences. Navid crossed the room and clasped my hands. I forced myself not to flinch when he kissed my cheeks.

"Please accept my deepest sympathies for the loss of your mother. The world has lost a beautiful gem. We can be thankful that part of her lives on in her exquisite daughter."

Out of the corner of my eye, I noticed Drake stiffen. "Thank you for coming." It was my automatic response.

"Have you given any thought to what your future holds?"

I tucked a stray hair behind my ear. "I—"

"Secretary General," Drake said as he stepped forward, "Now is hardly the time to grill Miss Wilkins about her future."

Navid raised his chin and turned toward Drake. "And you are?"

Drake offered his hand. "Drake Freeman. I'm a friend of Miss Wilkins's. I'm also Oliver Matheson's stepson."

Navid's eyes narrowed as he surveyed Drake and ignored his outstretched hand. "I see. I spoke from a position of concern, since Miss Wilkins will not be able to stay here." He turned to me with determination blazing in his eyes. "My offer remains if you decide you need employment."

"And my answer is the same, though I appreciate the offer." I fought the grimace that battled to emerge on my face.

He smiled, revealing perfect teeth. "Very well. Again, please accept my condolences."

When he was out of earshot, I turned to Drake. "Thank you."

"That guy is a creep, but try a little harder to disguise your disdain," he whispered.

"You've always told me I'm a terrible actress."

"Until Navid came along, you were showing vast improvement," he said.

I closed my eyes. "I don't want to be at this dinner."

"Then leave."

"I can't. I have a duty to fulfill." My heart kicked in protest. That was something my mother would've said—and done.

Drake chuckled softly, but it held a note of sadness. "My dear, you're no longer obligated to play games with these people or abide by their social constraints."

I knew that, but leaving the dinner before it ended seemed disrespectful to my mother. When the party was over, she was gone for good.

It was a stupid sentiment. She'd been gone for five days. But with her eternal future uncertain, I wasn't ready to let go of this final remnant of her life. I hoped and prayed that she'd heard me while she was unconscious.

Or that sometime in her life she'd asked Jesus to forgive her.

But it wasn't likely.

What about Melvin? I couldn't leave him to take care of everything. Yet my father's warning echoed in my memory.

"Vivica?" Concern etched Drake's face. "If you want to leave, I'll support you."

"How?"

He clasped my hand. "We'll go right now, and I'll take you anywhere you want to go that's safe. Just say the word."

"No." I squeezed his hand. "Thank you, but it's only a few more hours." I squared my shoulders. "I can make it."

\*\*\*

Later that night, I sat in my office staring at the computer screen, rocking in my chair, and pondering my future. Commander rested by the door—he'd been my other loyal companion since my mother passed. Drake had insisted on staying one more night to make sure I was okay.

Financially, I was well off. I'd inherited a substantial sum from my mother but wouldn't gain full control of the trust until I turned twenty-one. However, the current payments were generous. If only everything else had worked out so neatly.

I swallowed hard when I thought of the kind message I'd received from Ben—and his wife—earlier that day.

```
Vivica,

Ally and I were both saddened to hear about
your mother's death. Please know that
we're praying for you in this difficult
time.

In Christ,
Ben and Ally Lagarde
```

Why had he felt it was necessary to include their last name? Was I so far removed from his thoughts that he assumed I'd forgotten him? I squeezed my eyes shut. Not now. Ben had moved on and had to be part of my past. Besides, I only had the energy to dwell on one heartbreak at a time.

I propped my head against my fist. Where could I start to prove my mother's death hadn't been natural? Tears bit my raw eyes. Proving she was murdered wouldn't change her eternal destiny. I buried my head in my hands and sobbed. I should've tried harder to help her see how lost she was.

Two months ago, I'd tried to bring the matter up while we'd been on the jet traveling back from an official visit to Europe—one of the few times she'd deemed it safe for me to leave the compound. Melvin had been snoring, and my mother had been conducting official business on her MD3.

She slammed the device against the table and groaned.

I pulled myself out of my novel and let my doc fall into my lap. "What's wrong?"

"Nothing." Her lips drew into a thin line.

I surveyed her and started to pick up my doc.

"I had a message from my security director."

"What's wrong?" I asked again.

She clicked her nails on the table. "He suspects the Warriors aren't abiding by the treaty and are still scheming ways to force their religion on all of us."

"That's never been their mission. They fought to restore a government that protects religious freedom. Not to mention other liberties."

"The exclusivists have freedom to worship," she said.

I cringed at the term *exclusivist*. "Freedom of worship doesn't guarantee a person's right to live according to her conscience—even if that choice offends people."

Her eyes narrowed. "Don't lecture me. The rebels signed a treaty, and if we don't keep peace, the Globalists will take over this country."

"I'm sorry. Being able to share the truth about Jesus is important to me."

She crossed her arms. "Why? How can you believe all that? I didn't raise you that way. Being a good person should be enough."

"But it's not." I gave her a quick example of why it wasn't, according to the real Bible—not the government's edited version.

"Vivica, you can keep trying to convert me, but I've made up my mind about what I believe. Be grateful that I'm tolerating your need to take comfort in these exclusivist beliefs."

Then she'd picked up her MD3 and started to work.

I hadn't had another opportunity.

"Why didn't you give me more time, God?" I pounded the desk. "Why?" My voice rose. "How could you?" I shoved my fist against my mouth and stifled the scream I'd suppressed for five days. Commander jumped up, ran over to me, and nudged my elbow.

"Vivica?" Melvin slipped into the room, gently pushed the dog aside, and knelt to wrap his arms around me. "Sweetie, go to bed."

"I won't sleep. I have to find out who did this to my mother."

He flinched and released me. "Your mother had a ruptured aneurysm. Accept that, and stop looking for trouble." He shook his head. "You should've listened to your father and gone into hiding."

"I had to say good-bye." I couldn't just walk away when we'll be separated for eternity.

He cleared his throat. "I understand. But—"

"Don't you see?" I clutched his arm. How could he give up and accept an edited version of reality? "Her biochip should've indicated something was wrong." I swiped tears with the back of my hand.

He rubbed the place on his upper arm where his own biochip rested. "You're right." Melvin's face darkened. "But your father could've been the one who used nanobots to cause the aneurysm."

"The nanobots wouldn't have worked that quickly. Plus, my gut tells me he isn't involved. Deep down, you agree. You thought it was okay for my mother to talk to him."

He put his hands on his face. "A decision I'll regret every day for as long as I live. Your mother was my world. And because of me, she's gone."

I couldn't meet his eyes. I didn't want him to see the pity I knew would be lighting my eyes like a beacon. Instead, I rested a hand on his shoulder. "She's gone because Navid murdered her, and I'm going to prove it."

He nodded. "Do what you have to do."

\*\*\*

I sat up in bed and whipped my head from side to side. What had awakened me? Tossing aside the covers, I leaped from my bed. Sweat dampened my neck and forehead.

A chill swept my body like a demon lurking, teasing, waiting to pounce and devour me.

"Commander?" He snored in his bed next to my door.

If the threat were real, wouldn't the dog have barked?

Peering through the window, I searched for an intruder, but the lake's placid surface reflected the night's stillness. My reaction must be the aftermath of a forgotten nightmare that had taken root in my fertile imagination.

No, something was wrong.

I lunged for my courier, searched for a message, and found nothing. The newsfeed showed no major developments. Neither did my doc.

Clutching my courier and crossing the room, I stopped at the door that led into the hallway. My hand rested on the knob. I turned it and inspected the hall through the crack.

Empty.

Moving into the hallway, I crept toward the guest room where Drake was staying. If he could reassure me this was all in my head, then I'd have a chance to sleep. And I desperately needed rest.

A faint buzz interrupted my stride. The persistent hum urged me toward the bank of windows that lined the right side of the hallway. It sounded like a drone. But why would—?

A burst of fire slammed through the window. Glass spewed.

Commander barked and charged out of my bedroom.

I screeched and jumped away as a second fireball blasted through the gaping hole, narrowly missing the dog. Flames licked the carpet and walls.

Commander moved toward me with a yelp. Raw skin showed on the tip of his tail.

"It's okay, boy." Bending to grab the dog's collar and breaking into a run, I neared Drake's room on the left as the door swung open. He burst into the hallway and coughed at the smoke that assaulted him. "They're firing on both sides of the house!"

"The bunker," I yelled and pulled my top up over my nose and mouth as I led Drake and the dog down the hallway toward the bunker entrance.

We rounded a corner, which took us away from the windows, but the smoke's choking grip continued to drain us of oxygen and clarity.

Another explosion roared behind us, and Commander strained against my grasp on his collar.

The bunker entrance had to be close.

*Please, God.*

A flash of lime appeared, and Melvin, in bright pajamas, stumbled toward the bunker door and waved his biochip in front of the scanner. The light next to the scanner blinked red.

Someone had changed his access level already?

Melvin pointed frantically at the screen's error message. And tried again. And again.

I coughed but opened my courier to access the security system I'd hacked when I'd helped my father escape. "Take the dog," I said to Drake.

He gripped Commander's collar.

I glanced over my shoulder. The fire roared closer. I made a few adjustments on my courier. "Try it again."

Melvin held his arm in front of the scanner.

The fire danced within a few feet. With our enemies taking out both sides of the house, this had to work.

*Help us, God.*

The scanner's light stayed red.

We raced to the nearest window. Melvin pushed the curtain aside and fiddled with the latch, but it stuck. With one hand, Drake grabbed a lamp from a nearby table and tossed it through the glass.

"Go, Vivica." Melvin pushed me toward the shattered window. It was a single step out of the tall, narrow frame to the ground.

"What if they—?"

I didn't need to finish.

A drone buzzed into my line of sight, stopped, and blinked victoriously in a wicked, verdant glow.

# CHAPTER 16

## *Vivica*

Melvin threw himself in front of me.

The drone buzzed up several inches to scan his eyes, and the light changed from green to yellow.

"It's recalibrating," Drake muttered.

I grabbed Melvin's shoulder to move him aside, but he held fast. The fire marched closer. "Don't do this," I said. "That drone will shoot as soon as the light turns green."

"Don't let it capture your retinas," Melvin said, "and duck out the window."

Drake nudged me, yet I froze. Melvin couldn't die without Christ.

"Vivica, go now," Melvin said. "Or we're *all* going to die.

"I—"

"I believe," he said. "Everything you told your mother about Jesus. It has to be true, and I accept it. You've changed." He patted my shoulder. "And I love you."

My throat thickened. "I love you too." I couldn't let him do this. What if he was telling me what I wanted to hear?

Drake grabbed my waist and pulled Commander and me through

the window as the drone fired.

I knew I shouldn't look back, but I did—as Melvin collapsed, clutching his chest.

"Keep your head down!" Drake yelled. "Get to my car."

We sprinted away from the house toward the garage where the valet had stored Drake's car. Behind us, the high-pitched whine intensified, and I lunged toward the garage's side door.

Locked.

"Take the dog," Drake said.

I clung to the collar and patted Commander's head.

Drake shoved his fist up under his shirt, drove it through the glass, reached inside, and unlocked the door. We ran for the car, and Drake placed his thumb on the trunk latch until it scanned and released. Behind us, the drone tried to fit through the window, and when it couldn't, it backed up, rotated forty-five degrees, and prepared to try again.

"Get in the driver's seat." Drake grabbed a Demonio 57 from the trunk and threw open the passenger door.

I hurried around to the other side, shoved Commander into the back seat, and climbed in. I'd rather drive than shoot. The car started as the drone zipped through the garage window.

I flipped the car's override switch so I could drive it myself. When I backed the car up, the garage door sensed movement and swung open. I hit the gas pedal, and the car screeched out and onto the driveway. A drone hovered on my side of the car.

Drake popped up through the sunroof and fired a quick spray of bullets at the drone.

It plunged from the air.

He twisted around and targeted the second drone. It glided into the earth and crashed.

Commander barked, maneuvered his front paws onto the console, and raised up.

Pressing the accelerator to the floor, I clutched the steering wheel as we neared the gatehouse. I slowed the car's speed and hoped the sensors embedded in the pavement would trigger the iron gate to open, but it held fast.

A third drone rose from behind the gatehouse.

"Don't stop, Vivica."

"The gate should be open by now. We drove over the sensor!"

Drake leaned out his window and aimed at the drone, but this one must have received communication from the other two on the type of threat because it dodged when Drake fired.

"Open!" I screamed.

The barrier held.

Drake took another shot, but the drone dodged again, and this time a fiery blast burst from the drone and streaked toward our car.

I swerved, slammed on the brakes, and threw the car in reverse.

The fireball whizzed over us and slammed into the gate.

When the blast demolished the gate, Drake gave me a high-five over Commander's head. We passed through, turned onto the highway, and escaped the chaos. Then, we dodged emergency vehicles and traffic cameras on the way to a safe house in the southern part of the Great Lakes Region.

***

When I awoke around noon the next day in the safe house bedroom, the memory of the night's terror lingered. I stumbled into the apartment's small living room, where Drake slumped on the couch watching TV. Commander rested at his feet. I pointed at his arm where his T-shirt had bunched up. "Didn't realize you were hurt."

He glanced at the bandage on his upper arm. "Not from last night. Bullet grazed me on my last mission."

I swallowed. What had he been doing that was so dangerous? "Ouch."

"It's fine. I'm tough." He motioned toward the TV screen. "Guess who's about to get the blame for the attack on the presidential mansion?"

I groaned. "The Warriors." My voice sounded raw.

His jaw tightened. "Yep. Now Zahedi has the perfect excuse to stop withdrawing the Peacekeepers. His press conference is starting in a few minutes."

"Oh, yay." I tried to process this information as I rubbed my eyes to rid them of sleep—and of the memory of Melvin's bullet-riddled body falling into the blazing mansion.

What if he'd lied about believing to get me out of the house? Had he sacrificed his own eternity to save my life? I prayed that wasn't the case.

The scene on the TV changed, and the camera zoomed in on Secretary General Navid Zahedi as he began speaking in front of a trio of white hyperboloid skyscrapers. The tallest stood in the middle and had spires reaching toward the heavens. The words on the screen indicated he was at the new headquarters for the Council of World Peacekeepers in the Middle East Region of the Republic of Asia.

"Recently," he said, "I had the privilege of announcing that the Council of World Peacekeepers would reduce the number of officers in the United Regions of North America. Due to the efforts of the Wilkins Administration, and because of the treaty between the URNA government and the rebel group known as the Emancipation Warriors, peace reigned throughout the continent."

Navid paused and gazed into the camera, and his magnetic eyes displayed a faint trace of glee. "However, an attack on the presidential compound has made it necessary to halt the removal of our officers. President Sanders agrees. This senseless attack resulted in the death of Melvin Powers, the personal assistant of the late President Wilkins. Evidence points to the involvement of the Emancipation Warriors in this attack. My investigators believe President Wilkins's daughter Vivica was involved in staging the attack, because she had yet to vacate the compound, her body was not found, and she has a history of involvement with this rebel group."

I gasped.

"You've got to be kidding me," Drake muttered.

Navid wasn't finished. "It is imperative that we locate Ms. Wilkins immediately, and I am prepared to offer a substantial reward for information that results in this fugitive being brought to justice."

My mind spun. Had we been careful enough last night? Had traffic cams caught our faces? How long would it be before they found me?

"We cannot allow the rebel group to disrupt the peace in this nation," Navid said. "World peace and improving quality of life for all citizens around the globe is my mission, and I shall not rest until I see this dream fulfilled. Thank you." He turned, refusing questions from the reporters.

Drake removed his courier from his pocket. "I'm calling Ophelia. We need a new alias for you ASAP."

***

"Where're you two headed next?" Ophelia asked that evening at the safe house, as she finished dyeing my hair a coppery red. She had created all of my aliases.

"I have no idea. Drake's kept that to himself."

She set to work trimming my hair. "Just wondered 'cause Liam didn't say."

"How *is* Liam?"

"He's fine. Busy as usual. Don't see him as much as I'd like." She worked without speaking and paused only to step back and inspect her work.

"Are you okay? You seem extra quiet today."

She smiled. "I have a lot on my mind." She paused, glanced at her courier, and went back to work on my hair. "Now, we'd better brainstorm a new name for you. The doctor will be here soon to work on your retinas."

***

Late that night, after Ophelia and the doctor had finished my new disguise and left, Drake arranged a flight to the Coastal Plain Region where we would visit a research facility. After the pilot left us at an airstrip, we piled into a car and drove for several hours through a rural area. Commander was with us and would be until I found a place to leave him while I worked. It wasn't as if I had a home.

Just as the sun was rising, we arrived at a gate that protected a single building.

"I thought you said this was a research facility. I expected it to be bigger," I said.

Drake grinned. "Wait." He opened the car window and allowed the scanner to read his retinas. "Let the scanner on your side do the same, or the gate won't open."

I complied and hoped it would recognize me. After all, I'd changed my identity multiple times, and the doctor had updated my retinas to match my new alias a few hours ago.

It took a few seconds to register, but the gate opened.

Drake parked next to the building, and we faced additional security cameras to enter. Inside, a yellow room was lined with wooden benches. Two armed guards stood on either side of an elevator.

"Good morning, gentlemen," Drake said.

The guards nodded in unison.

Drake took his courier out of his pocket and handed it to the guard. "Give them yours."

I obeyed, and the guard put our devices in a small metal container and closed the lid. The other took out a wand and scanned Commander, who wagged his tail and nipped at the wand.

"Easy, boy." I pulled on the leash—that Drake had slipped away and purchased while I'd been sleeping—and glanced around. "We're going underground, aren't we?"

"Right. We're standing above an abandoned salt mine. It's over six hundred feet down," Drake said. The guard returned our couriers. Facing one more scanner, we each allowed it to read our retinas. Then, an elevator opened and beckoned us to the bowels of the Earth.

Swallowing my protest, I entered, tapped my foot, and stroked the dog's head when the door enclosed us. The downward journey reminded me of the elevator at the National Archives—the building where important documents were stored below ground.

I scratched the itchy mask clinging to my face.

"Go ahead and take it off," Drake said. "You're safe here."

I ripped it off, thankful for the reprieve and cool breeze that flowed over my irritated skin. I was tired of constantly changing my identity. I wanted to be Vivica Suzanne Wilkins.

Not Penelope Diane Fisher.

The elevator door slid aside, revealing a cavernous, gray room supported by thick pillars of the same pale gray material. Tunnels led to the left and right, as well as straight ahead.

The cool, dry air was a welcome relief to the summer humidity that swelled at the Earth's surface. Lights had been added to the ceiling, and every so often, minerals in the walls and ceiling caught the light and sparkled.

"After you've been here awhile, you'll taste the salt," Drake said.

"This is incredible."

A young man in an open, four-seater cart sped toward us, and when he came closer, I gasped.

"Nathan?"

"In the flesh." His olive-colored eyes gleamed, and he grinned.

Nathan Worth was the handsome young man I'd almost been forced to marry in Fortune City. His sandy hair, which had been trimmed into partial submission during our time as prisoners, now curled wildly. He wore a pale blue lab coat.

"Welcome to Emancipation Clandestine Research Lab, also known as the Mine." Nathan stopped the cart, leaped out, and shook Drake's hand before giving me a quick hug. "I was very sorry to hear about your mom. You look good though. The red hair's sassy."

"Thanks." After everything I'd been through, I wasn't sure how he could compliment my appearance. "You look good too."

Drake eyed Nathan but made no comment.

I pointed to the dog. "This is Commander. He was my mom's."

"Nice to meet you, buddy." Nathan smiled and scratched Commander's head. He stood on his back legs and tried to lick Nathan.

"Down, Commander!"

"He's all right. I can have one of our hospitality coordinators take care of him while you and Drake get a tour."

"Thanks."

He took out his courier and sent a message.

"What all goes on here?" I asked.

"How about I just show you?" Nathan said. "It's much easier."

A young woman with cornrow braids zipped around the corner in a two-seater cart. When she got out, she fished a dog treat from her pocket. Commander pulled toward her, and she grinned when he swallowed the treat. "I'm Ciara. I'll take care of him, and he'll be waiting in your room later," she said.

"Thanks." I handed her the leash. Evidently, I was going to be staying for a while.

Ciara led him to her cart, and he sprang onto the seat next to her. Nathan motioned us onto his cart. "Hop on."

I took the seat in the cart next to Nathan, and Drake sat behind us.

Nathan sped down the tunnel to our right. Though lights illuminated the tunnel, it was narrower, and the ceiling was lower than the room where we'd entered. He stopped next to a metal door, got off the cart, and swiped his badge on the keypad. Then he motioned us into a laboratory where several scientists worked at different stations. If I hadn't known we were in a salt mine, I wouldn't have been able to tell based on this room that'd been finished with cinder block walls like a building on the Earth's surface.

"I'm an apprentice," Nathan said. "I work with your father and—"

"Wait." I held up a hand. "My father's here? In this lab?"

"Yeah. Ever since Fortune City."

I glared at Drake. "You knew about this, didn't you?"

"Yes. I'm sorry I couldn't tell you."

I could tell he regretted it, but that didn't subdue my irritation. "I'm going to need a little more detail on how that happened." I crossed my arms. "And why you're all willing to trust him."

"Sure." Nathan took a breath. "During the liberation at Fortune City, after you and I split, I started working with the forces who were getting ready to destroy the city. I was with a group of guys when we found a man wandering around near the train station the regulators used to get inside."

I shuddered at the memory of the prison and how heavily my life had been controlled.

"When we got closer," Nathan said, "I recognized him as your dad, but it was obvious something wasn't right with his mind. We got him medical help."

"What was wrong?" I asked.

"Concussion. The doctor thought there was something else wrong with his brain and did a bunch of tests, but he never figured it out. The problem seemed to pass after a while. Anyway, we finished our work and blew up the city. On the flight back home, I started talking to your dad. Turns out, he'd been planning an escape for some time, but he'd never had a chance to pull it off. Then, we met the same recruiter who brought us to the lab, and we've been living and working here ever since. My new work is a departure from engineering, but I love science, so I'm a happy camper."

"Do you trust my father?"

Nathan's face grew thoughtful. "He's never given me a reason not to, but I understand why you're asking." He pointed, and I saw my father, dodging lab tables to get to us. He'd trimmed his shoulder-length hair into a crew cut, and his gold stud earring was missing.

"Vivibear! Are you okay?" My father gathered me in his arms. "I'm so sorry about your mother." He stepped back and looked me over.

My chin trembled, and I nodded.

"I heard what happened at the presidential mansion. Why did you stay when I told you to leave?" He didn't wait for me to answer. "I have something I need to tell you about your mother's blood sample."

I gripped the side of the table and glanced at Drake, who smiled sympathetically. "Did you find nanobots?"

"No." He sighed. "Your mother's blood was clear."

# CHAPTER 17

## *Vivica*

"That can't be right," I said. "It's too convenient. Navid killed my mother. I *know* it."

"I'm sorry, Vivibear," my father said. "I ran tests. And three other scientists analyzed the same blood sample—in case I missed something. None of our results showed nanobots."

"What if the tests weren't good enough?" I wailed. "I have another vial." I pulled it from underneath my shirt. "Run more!"

Drake rested his hand on my shoulder. "My dear—"

I jerked away. "What? You believe the results?"

"I have no reason to think otherwise," he said.

I dropped the vial in my pocket and buried my face in my hands. I couldn't expect anyone to understand everything I'd been through. Now, I couldn't even blame Navid for killing my mother.

But I wasn't going to let them see me break down any further. I lifted my head and looked at Drake and Nathan. "What now?"

Nathan smiled sympathetically. "I'll help you get settled."

"Thanks." I didn't have the strength to argue.

***

The next day, I relaxed in my room in the Mine and licked away the fine dust of salt that had settled on my lips. Actually, *room* was a generous description. It was really a cave-like closet with a nook hollowed out of the wall for a bed. A mattress, toilet, sink, shelves, and a bar for hanging clothes completed the accommodations. The shower room was down the hall.

Commander sprawled beside me, and I stroked his back and wondered about my next step. Now that I was Penelope, or Penny, I could continue my work as an agent. I didn't know what the Warriors had for me, but I longed for the freedom to wander around in the sunshine.

A stroll through the salt mine might help.

I put on Commander's leash, grabbed a bag from the container that Ciara had provided in case he decided to do his business, and sauntered down the narrow passageway that led out to the wider thoroughfare, which was the path for carts.

A few minutes later, Nathan's vehicle skidded to a stop, and he whistled. "Lookin' good, Viv. Or should I call you Penny? Love that nickname."

Commander strained against his collar and greeted Nathan.

"Hey, boy." Nathan patted the dog's head and grinned at me. I smiled in spite of my lousy mood. Nathan always had that effect on me.

"I was looking for you. I have something you'll be interested in, and Freeman said to let you in on it since he's tied up." He patted the seat next to him.

Commander and I hopped on. "What's that?"

"How much has he told you about the Warriors' independence plan?" The cart buzzed through the tunnel. Every so often we passed metal doors marked only with numbers. Some had empty carts parked next to them.

"You mean the plan to secede, form a new country, and deter global retaliation with nuclear weapons?" I rubbed my arms and wished I'd grabbed a sweatshirt. My room had climate control, but the passageways didn't.

"That's the one." Nathan chuckled. "I take it you have doubts."

"I might not if I knew more details."

"Freeman knows you well. That's the whole point of our little tour." Nathan took a quick right turn, causing me to slide in to him. "Anything you see needs to be kept on the down low."

"Got it." I scooted back, and the corner of his mouth twitched.

We approached strips of plastic sheets hanging from the ceiling, and Nathan batted them aside and drove through.

He stopped the cart next to a door. After I tied Commander's leash to the cart, we entered a room with rows of computers. I did a quick count and determined at least forty people were working at individual stations. "What's this?"

"Just one part of Operation Coastal Republic. These workers are helping URNA citizens all over the country relocate into the Coastal Plain Region without the government getting suspicious."

"Like what they did for me when I was hiding out during my pregnancy? They created a false trail for my doc, so the government wouldn't track my real position."

"Exactly."

"What about the people who live in the CP but don't want to be part of the new country?"

"They can leave, but if they stay, they'll have the same rights as everyone else."

I frowned. "That's great if GPV doesn't get everyone first."

"Your dad's working on a biochip that gives a signal to stop the virus from attacking the body, but it can't be used to gather health data."

"Here?" No wonder this place had such heavy security.

"Yep. Want to see?" He headed back to the cart, and I followed. "It'll take a while to get there since it's on the other side of the mine, so get comfortable."

I relaxed against the seat and tried to get Commander to do the same, but he squirmed between Nathan and me. "Do you think the Warriors can pull off the operation?"

"Well—we'll never know if we don't try." He tapped his thumb against the steering wheel. "Frankly, short of rocketing out of here and colonizing Mars, I don't see any other great options if we don't want to live under tyranny."

"I know." I drew my knees to my chest and wrapped my arms around them. Anything to block the wave of cold settling over me. "Drake said something a while ago that I've been thinking about." I bit my lower lip. "That we should look forward to Heaven. If that's what we're supposed to do, then why bother fighting? If people know the truth about Jesus, does it matter what our country's like? What if the Coastal Republic isn't God's will?"

"Then our plan won't work," Nathan said quietly. "Honestly, I've had the same thoughts. But God puts governments in place, and if we want to honor him by fighting for a government that protects the inalienable rights that he gives, it's okay. If it's a part of his plan, it'll happen."

"Right." Nathan's point made sense.

He grinned. "This probably isn't the best time to ask, but I'm curious."

"Oh boy."

"What's the deal between you and Freeman?"

"We're friends, so I care about him. But there's no deal. Why?"

His eyes twinkled. "I'm nosy. That's all. Although, part of me is sad that the liberation forces showed up when they did. Otherwise I might've had you for myself." He winked.

"What can I say? It's fate." My face burned.

We rounded a pillar, stopped, and got out of the cart. I tied up Commander.

Nathan paused next to a scanner and let it read his retinas. "Come in." He held the door open. Crossing to a lab table, he held up a vial of amber liquid.

"It looks like the all-natural cough syrup my nanny, Ana, used to give me."

He grinned. "I had the same stuff growing up, but no, this is the serum our scientists developed to help boost the immunity of those of us who haven't been exposed to GPV."

"Have you tested it?"

"On myself and a couple of coworkers. We've not gotten sick. Or the virus hasn't made it this far yet." He pointed to a package of vials and syringes lying on the table across from us. "We're getting ready to send doses out to our agents in the Great Plains region. I'll give you some if you want."

"I'll think about it." It was kind of weird seeing Nathan in his mad scientist persona.

"It'll also boost your immune system."

"Fine." I rolled up my sleeve, and he injected the serum. A burning sensation traveled my arm, and I rubbed it.

"Does your arm feel like it's on fire?"

"Yep."

"Sorry, I forgot to mention that. It's completely normal." He pushed up his lab coat sleeves and rubbed his hands together. "Now we've got to figure out how to mass produce this stuff and distribute it."

"What about the biochips my dad is creating?"

He shook his head. "Those are taking longer to get right, but we think they'll be more effective than the serum." He motioned for me to follow and pushed open double doors. "Harrison?"

We entered the smaller lab, but there was no answer. Nathan pointed to an office with a darkened window. "Guess your dad's off doing something else, but ask him to show you the chip technology sometime. It's pretty cool."

My courier buzzed with a message from Drake.

Meet me in Lab 24.

"Where's Lab 24?" I held up my courier.

"I'll take you. It's back near the Operation Coastal Republic HQ."

We detoured to my room to drop off Commander, and he barked a few times after I closed the door. The poor dog probably wanted a normal life too.

"So," Nathan said when we were on our way, "since there's no deal between you and Freeman, I might have a chance?"

I smiled. "If you're prepared for a fight. Drake intends to marry me."

"Do you plan to marry him?"

I laced and unlaced my fingers. "I don't know." I didn't want to think about marriage.

"Do you love him?"

I scowled. "That's none of your business."

"Either you do or you don't."

"That's not true. There are different kinds of love."

"You know the kind I'm talking about."

"Did Drake put you up to this?"

"Nope. I'm looking out for my own interests. Well, sort of. I want what's best for you, and if that's Freeman, then so be it. If not, then it might be me."

I closed my eyes. How much more stress could I take?

The silence ballooned between us.

"I'm really sorry," Nathan said. "I didn't mean to upset you. I'll back off." He pulled up next to the lab door.

"You don't have to back off of being my friend." I rested my hand on his shoulder.

"Good to know."

The door swung open, and Drake barreled out. I quickly removed my hand from Nathan's shoulder. "Thanks." I faced Drake as Nathan drove away. "What's going on?"

"Maybe I should ask you that." There was no mistaking the edge in Drake's voice.

"Nathan was giving me a ride."

"Is that all?"

"And what if it wasn't?" I put my hands on my hips. "Didn't you ask him to give me a tour?"

Hurt flickered in his eyes, and he turned away. "I have news." He motioned for me to follow him into the lab. "One of our agents recovered drone wreckage from the presidential compound, and our scientists were able to pull information from the ones I shot down." He swiped his courier and projected a picture of Melvin on the wall.

I thought of his sacrifice, and tears stung my eyes.

"According to the data harvested from the drones, Melvin was targeted for assassination." Drake paused and tapped his courier, projecting a picture of Drake and me together at the state dinner. "But until I started firing on the drones, someone had only planned to incapacitate and capture you and me."

# CHAPTER 18

## *Drake*

Vivica took a deep breath. "Can we prove Navid is behind this?"

"Not directly." I tried to concentrate on work instead of Vivica's friendship with that Worth kid. "But the drone technology is consistent with what we know the Peacekeepers have available." I studied her. "Given the fact that the Peacekeepers want you in their custody so badly, I strongly recommend you don't leave the Mine."

She put her hands on her hips. "I can't stay here forever. I'll go crazy if I don't see the sun."

"I'm sorry." I hated the distress in her gorgeous face. "Have you tried the artificial light room? Eat your lunch there. It's what some of our scientists and hackers do because they don't have time for anything else." It wasn't a perfect solution, but it might help.

"Why do you always tell me what to do?"

I furrowed my brow. "My dear, I'm well aware you have a mind of your own. I'm merely making a suggestion for your own safety. Feel free to disregard it like you usually do." She always had to have her way. Must be an only-child symptom. Why didn't she realize I loved her and wanted to protect her?

She bristled and her eyes sparked. "What am I supposed to do?

I'm not trying to disregard your advice. I've been sitting down here stewing. I need a purpose!"

I rested my hand on her shoulder. "Let me set you up with our hackers who are helping people relocate to the Coastal Plain Region."

"Fine. As long as I'm doing something to help."

***

After getting Vivica to work with our hackers, I took off on foot through the mine. I could've taken a cart, but I needed to walk and had plenty of time before my meeting with Liam, Jethro, and the rest of the Operation Coastal Republic's leadership team.

We met in a hollow cavern with furniture that belonged in a company boardroom. I took a seat at the round table and scrolled through the news feed on my courier while I waited for the others.

Jethro, my brother, and five other guys filed in. Once, a couple of men had commented about the lack of women on the team, but Jethro had given them a death stare, and they hadn't mentioned it again.

Jethro called the meeting to order. "Drake, give us a report on Operation Guardian Light."

I cleared my throat and told them about the ambush and how Night Hawk had brought highly enriched uranium back to headquarters. Our scientists were now working on weapons.

"And you're okay with how the mission turned out?" Jethro chomped his gum.

"We achieved our objective and retrieved the uranium," I said.

"But now the Peacekeepers know we're up to something."

"Like they didn't before? Could we stop pretending they don't have a clue about what's coming?" I held up my courier. "Have you not bothered to read the news? President Sanders asked Zahedi to send even more Peacekeepers into the country."

"Because of GPV," Liam said.

"You think the Peacekeepers are going to stay in the Great Plains Region?" I crossed my arms. "Hang out? Help the sick? Ignore their intelligence officers who are reporting strange things happening in the Coastal Plain Region?"

Jethro's mouth settled into a thin line. "GPV's spreading fast. Our agents have reported cases in all of the regions. The Peacekeepers'll have their hands full."

"They're the ones transmitting it!" I shouted. "They're using GPV as one more excuse to take over!"

"We don't know that," Liam said. "We still need proof."

"Which is why I'm pulling you off Operation Enduring Light and putting you back on the GPV investigation," Jethro said to me. "You wanna waste time believing a conspiracy theory, then you're gonna waste your time investigating it."

I crossed my arms. "You don't trust me to help with Enduring Light?" That mission would ensure that the nuclear warheads were ready to go.

"I need someone I can count on," Jethro said. "For whatever reason, you've gotten soft."

"You define soft as saving a team of men who were being ambushed? I'm fascinated. Why don't you tell me what your definition of tough is?" I didn't wait for his answer and charged ahead. "Something else is going on here." I looked around the table. Two of the guys ducked their heads and messed with their couriers. "Why don't you clue me in?"

Jethro and Liam exchanged glances, and Liam cleared his throat.

"Tell him," Liam said.

Jethro rolled up his sleeves and exposed the snake tattoo that wound up his arm. "Someone hacked your courier."

"When?"

"Before Operation Guardian Light, but we didn't figure it out until after the ambush when one of our guys reported the guards at the nuclear containment facility were specifically looking for you."

I swore and pounded my fist on the table. "You're just now telling me?" I took the device out of my pocket and tossed it on the table. "How long were you going to let me walk around with a compromised courier?"

"Our people secured it remotely," Jethro said.

"No one thought to tell me?"

"Maybe you already knew." Jethro narrowed his eyes.

"And now I know what's really going on." I stood and backed away. "This isn't about believing GPV is some conspiracy theory. Thank you, gentlemen. I get the blame for the ambush because unbeknownst to me, someone hacked my courier. That's it—I'm working with the enemy. Never mind I've devoted the last five years of my life to this cause."

"Drake, enough," Liam said.

"You're right. It *is* enough." I slammed the door and headed to my room. I was halfway there when I saw Vivica and that Worth kid laughing. I clenched my jaw and charged forward.

"Hey." I stopped. "It pains me to interrupt your flirting, but I need to speak with Vivica on a business matter."

Worth smiled. "No problem. Catch you later, Vivica." He hurried away in his cart.

"We weren't flirting," Vivica said.

"Really? It looked like flirting. Sounded like flirting. It's funny how you can use Ben as an excuse when it comes to avoiding a relationship with me, but it doesn't seem to be a problem with Nathan." I told myself to stop, but the words kept coming. "Oh no, you're fine having a relationship with him."

Hurt flashed in her eyes. "Not that you deserve an explanation, but Nathan and I bonded in Fortune City. We're friends who went through a traumatic experience together. That's it."

I shrugged and crossed my arms. "Whatever."

She stepped closer. "No. It's not whatever. Nathan's always been good to me. And you know what? He doesn't pressure me to be in a relationship I'm not sure about."

"My dear, being sure has never been your problem. It's being brave enough to do something about the feelings you don't want to admit you have." I sounded more confident than I felt.

She stared at her feet. "You said you needed to talk to me, or was that a lie to trap me here?" She looked up, skepticism in her expression.

I ran my hands over my face and took a deep breath. I needed to cut the out-of-control jerk act immediately. "Jethro asked me to look into the GPV matter again." Though if I found anything important, they might not believe me.

She gave a curt nod.

"Would you mind passing along any information you've gathered?"

"Fine." Her features relaxed. "I haven't done anything since my mother died, and I've been busy helping citizens relocate." She took her courier from her pocket. "I'll send you the file I worked on."

"Thanks." I shifted. "I'm sorry. I've had a bad day, and taking it out on you is wrong. You have the right to be friends with whomever you want."

She didn't look up from the courier. "I understand." She pocketed the device. "File's on its way." As she turned and walked down the gray corridor, my heart dropped.

I'd completely blown it—and had no one to blame but myself.

# CHAPTER 19

## *Vivica*

For the next few days, I settled into a routine of helping create false documents for people who were leaving their home regions for the CP, and my father gave me a tutorial on his biochips. I visited the Mine's artificial light room, which helped, but I was still looking forward to the day when I could leave.

After our fight, Drake had vanished, and even Nathan had kept his distance. I relished the peace. One night, I was pulling back the covers on my bed when my courier buzzed. Commander lifted his head.

"Agatha!" I projected her image onto the stone wall. The uneven surface distorted her face but didn't hide her red eyes, and my heart flipped. "What's wrong?"

"Chad's sick."

I sank onto my bed. "GPV?"

She nodded.

"Didn't the Warriors send you the serum?"

"Yes. But it wasn't enough or it was too late or it's not effective." She dabbed her eyes. "But the doctor thinks Chad *might* pull through because he has enough immunity from the serum."

"How long has he been sick?"

"Three days. The doctor's optimistic because he's not hemorrhaging yet. Most people start bleeding after two days..." She sniffed. "If we can stabilize him, the Warriors are going to pull us out of the field and bring us to the Mine."

I clutched a pillow to my chest. "Well, that part would be wonderful."

"Yeah." She swiped her face with a tissue.

"I'll be praying, and I'll spread the word to my friends."

"Thank you. That's the best thing we can do." She fidgeted with her hair. "There's another reason I called."

"Whatever it is, I'll help."

Agatha raised her eyebrows. "You might rethink that offer in a minute."

"If it'll get me out of this hole in the ground, I'm in."

"You're in luck. I got a tip from a baker in our region a week ago—before Chad got sick. Anyway, this baker isn't a Warrior and has always been loyal to the government until he noticed some weird things with the flour that the government provides for his bakery." She twisted a tissue. "I can't leave Chad to check it. Will you do it? I could ask somebody else, but I trust you. I just don't want you to get sick."

"I'll be fine. I'll load up on serum."

"Are you sure?"

"Absolutely." I *could* pass the information on to Drake and let him handle it now that he was working on GPV. But Agatha had requested me. He'd have to get over the fact that I'd be leaving the Mine.

***

"You're not mad?" I asked Drake half an hour later. I stood in the narrow passageway outside his room and couldn't quite meet his eyes.

Why hadn't he put on a shirt before he'd answered the door?

"Nope." He leaned against the doorframe, his well-muscled chest on display. "Why would I be? I was the jealous idiot who got upset with you, and for that, I'm sorry."

Stupid physical attraction. *Focus.* "Then you don't have a problem with me going to check out the tip Agatha gave me. In the Great Plains Region?" I held up my courier.

"*We* can go first thing tomorrow morning." He turned away. "Get some rest."

I frowned. "I can do it alone."

He scrubbed his hands over his face. "I know, but it's safer if you don't. Plus, it may be the break we've been looking for."

I gaped at him. "But you 'strongly recommended' that I not leave the Mine."

"That's what your alias is for."

"But—"

"Good night." He closed the door.

***

"What's our story going to be?" I asked Drake the next day as we made our way to Brent's Bakery in the Great Plains Region. Before we'd left the Mine, my father had insisted that Drake and I take the biochip prototypes he'd created to give us another layer of protection against GPV. After a pilot had flown us to the region, we'd borrowed a car at an airfield the Warriors managed.

"We'll claim we're from Health Management doing a random inspection," Drake said. "You can snoop and get the samples while I chat with Brent."

"I'll check public records to see if his bakery's been inspected lately. If it has, we'd better have a good excuse for being there." I was thankful for a task. As long as we focused on work, we were fine. The rest of the trip had been spent in awkward silence.

I used my courier to find the inspection log for Brent's Bakery. Cars and trucks clogged the streets, and people, clad in masks to protect them from GPV, hurried down the sidewalks. Rush hour. I prayed the bakery didn't close early.

It took several tries, but I found the bakery's record. "Perfect. They haven't been inspected for two years."

Drake chuckled. "So much for government efficiency."

"Or…he's working with the government, so they've agreed to leave him alone." I tucked a stray hair behind my ear.

"Then you'll just have to use your acting skills to be convincing." His voice held a note of sarcasm.

I ignored the barb.

We found an empty parking space a few shops down from the bakery and walked to the brick building with a red awning. The sign in the window was dark, and the cases were empty.

"Place hasn't been open all day." A woman closed the door to the salon next to us and edged closer. The cloud of hairspray around her reached us first.

I groaned. "I'm so disappointed. I love the bread." I'd read on the website that bread was Brent's specialty.

"Me too. I was hoping to pick up a loaf after my appointment." She patted her fresh hair do. "Brent makes the best whole grain bread this side of the Mississippi."

"Have you heard why they're closed?" Drake asked.

She put her hand to the side of her mouth and leaned closer. "Rumor has it government inspectors shut them down." She glanced from side to side. "Don't know how that could be, because every time I was in there, the place was spick-and-span."

I frowned. There should've been a record of the inspection that shut the bakery down.

"I tell you," the woman said, "I sure wouldn't want to own a bakery and navigate all the government regulations on sugar and fat. Maybe Brent stopped following the rules, and they shut him down."

Interesting. "Did he side with the rebels during the revolution?"

Her mouth gaped. "Absolutely not."

"Perhaps he got sick with that GPV virus that's going around," I said.

"Could be." Her hand dropped to her side. "That stuff is nasty. The worst part is, no one can figure out how it's spreading."

Drake stepped out of the way of a man who whizzed by on a bicycle. "Heard any rumors about that?"

Her hand went back to its place at the side of her mouth. "Creepiest rumor I heard was the water supply. Lot of us aren't drinking tap water now." She pointed at the bakery. "I kept buying bread from him 'cause he assured me he wasn't using tap water either. But you didn't hear any of this from me." She clutched the handle of her purse and shuffled down the street.

Drake and I exchanged glances. "Let's check out the back door," he said.

We found the alley and, dodging trash that littered the pavement, followed it around to the back of the building where there was a metal door with *Brent's Bakery* written in orange.

Drake tried the handle, and it turned. The door swung open, and I gasped.

A man lay in the middle of the kitchen floor.

Dead.

# CHAPTER 20

## *Vivica*

Drake knelt next to the man's body. "It's Brent." He held his courier next to the man's face for comparison. "Matches the picture Agatha sent us. Poor guy. Looks like GPV got him."

I closed my eyes and tried to forget the grotesque sight of the dried blood caked around his nose and mouth. Then, I pulled a mask from my bag and put it on. Drake did the same.

He pointed to a scab on the man's upper arm. "His biochip is gone."

"Weird."

"I wonder if he took it out himself."

"Surely he would've heard the rumors about the chip protecting people from GPV." I glanced around. "Does he have a doc?"

Drake headed for a box of serving gloves on a shelf. He gave me a pair and put some on before he poked around in Brent's pocket and held it up.

"I'll clone it."

Drake motioned toward a desk in the corner. "Better clone his computer hard drive too."

I nodded and went to the desk.

Resting my courier on top of the computer, I copied its contents to my device. I'd comb through it later. Then I downloaded information from Brent's doc.

I'd just put my courier back in my pocket when I heard voices outside. I stiffened.

"Get in the refrigerator." Drake jumped up, yanked open the stainless steel door, and I followed him in. The door closed, encasing us in cold. A wheeled shelf laden with crates of apples, pears, strawberries, and eggs stood next to us. Drake pushed the shelf away from the refrigerator wall and motioned for me to join him behind it.

I shivered and rubbed my bare arms. Of all days to be wearing a tank top and shorts. Drake put his arm around me, and I was too cold to protest.

Footsteps sounded outside the refrigerator. "Hey, Willis. Who called this in?" a female voice asked.

"The neighbor reported the bakery hadn't been open, and the owner hadn't been seen for a couple of days. Neighbor thought that was weird. I did a little poking around and noticed his biochip blacked out a week ago," Willis said.

"Why would his chip have blacked out?" the woman asked. "This guy's been dead for hours—not a week."

"Maybe he took it out himself." The faint click of an MD3 indicated one of them was snapping photos.

Drake and I exchanged glances.

"Looks like GPV got him," the woman said. "Say, you worried about it yourself?"

"Nah," Willis said. "Got no reason to. I'm loyal to the government."

"What's that got to do with anything?" she asked.

"I hear they're…"

The refrigerator kicked on, and the buzz sounded like a plane readying for take-off. "Seriously?" I whispered. Drake and I crept closer to the door.

"…to cull the ones who aren't loyal."

"I didn't know that was possible."

"Sure is."

My stomach flipped as our suspicions were confirmed.

The refrigerator's buzzing stopped, and we returned to our place behind the shelf. The man and woman were quiet as they finished removing the body.

The chill iced my fingers and toes, so I clasped my hands together and blew on them. Drake pulled me closer, and I didn't protest as I relaxed against his chest—only because I was cold.

The refrigerator door swung open, and I pressed my back against the icy metal as if it could protect me from the light streaming in.

"Anything good in there?" Willis yelled.

"Just fruit."

"Might as well take some home to your kids," he said.

I held my breath. Drake's heart thudded against my arm. One of the crates slid forward and tipped downward. If she took it all the way out…

"Nothing here my kiddos like. But I'm gonna take a couple of pears for the road."

She replaced the crate and slammed the refrigerator door. I slumped against Drake and started breathing again.

"Let's wait a few minutes," he said.

"Fine." I swiped my courier and searched the data that had been on Brent's doc. When I found a secure communication from the government dated last month, I knew I might be on to something.

I pointed at the screen. "Drake, look." We huddled over my doc and read.

Dear Mr. Carson:


Health Management would like to thank you for your loyalty throughout the years you have been in business. Your bakery's practices have been exemplary, and you have no citations from the government for violating rules that ration sugar and fatty substances.


Beginning August 1, all government-subsidized bakeries will be required to use our special vitamin-enhanced flour in all of their baked goods. This flour contains a blend of vitamins that will boost the immunity of the populace. Your next shipment of flour will contain these special vitamins, and we ask that you cease using regular flour immediately upon the receipt of the vitamin-enhanced flour.


Sincerely,
John A. Palomoni
Health Management, United Regions of North America


"I'd be willing to bet the flour does more than boost immune systems." I chewed my lip. "It might even do the opposite."

"Then let's get samples." Drake pushed the refrigerator door open, and I peeked out. It was clear, so we began opening cabinets and found some small storage bags.

"Get several. I want backups." Drake removed his backpack. "I'm going to send some ahead to Nathan using a delivery drone." He took out the small machine that looked like a remote control airplane, but it had a hollow space in the center. I picked the smallest bags that would fit inside the drone.

I'd heard about the government using delivery drones, but I didn't know the Warriors had them. "That's cool."

"We just started using them. They're designed to dodge government drones, and they move fast enough that they're hard to detect."

Narrow white containers rested under the stainless steel table. One was labeled all-purpose flour. The other was cake flour. I filled four containers with cake and all-purpose flour, snapped on the lids, and handed two of the samples to Drake. He tucked them in the drone, programmed it with instructions for Nathan, and put the machine in his backpack.

"Let's get out of the city before I release it," he said. "The last thing I want is the government knowing we're on to them."

After I stowed the extra samples in the pocket of my cargo shorts, we slipped out of the bakery and back to the car.

\*\*\*

Once we were in the air on our way back to the Mine, Drake napped while I looked through more of Brent's emails, but I found only ads. However, a paper journal that had been on his desk had caught my attention, so I'd grabbed it. I skimmed through most of the entries. Mundane life details. A few tidbits about family. Then, there was the interesting part.

I'm starting to have my suspicions about that vitamin-enhanced flour the government is making me use. It shouldn't have messed with my bread recipe, but it did. I don't want to say anything, though. I can't have the government question my loyalty or think that I suspect them of anything shady.

Had Brent been able to find proof? I flipped further, but there was no other mention of the flour or the bread recipe.

We'd have to wait for the test results.

# CHAPTER 21

## *Vivica*

My courier rang, and my eyes flew open. I rubbed my stiff neck and sat up straighter in my plane seat. Surely we had to be close to the Mine.

"You're up early," I said to Nathan as I projected the call.

"Never went to sleep. I got your drone delivery and couldn't wait to dive in. This is too exciting, and Freeman's not answering."

"Glad I could be your back-up plan." I glanced over at Drake, who was still sound asleep, and turned my courier so Nathan could see him.

He winked. "You're always my first choice, but Freeman was the one who sent the flour samples, so technically, I should wait for him to wake up. But he did mention you in the instructions, so you can get the results too."

I nudged Drake, and he flinched but didn't open his eyes.

"He's out. Please tell me."

"Just sent the official report to your courier."

I opened the file, and the projected image replaced Nathan's face. I skimmed. Hypnotic properties…mind control…violent behavior…death. My tired brain swirled, so I closed the file, and

Nathan's image reappeared. "Give me the summary, please."

"No problem. Basically, that baker was right. The flour contained more than added vitamins. Fortunately, when we tested it, our system recognized it. I don't know how many times we test a chemical, and it shows up as an unknown substance."

I massaged the bridge of my nose. "What is it?"

"Joy dust."

"What's that?"

"It's a nickname for a drug that was discovered about twenty years ago by a pharmaceutical company that was looking for a safe and effective mood enhancer, but it didn't work as advertised. Well, at first it did. Gave people a high, but after the stuff built up in their systems, yikes. It made people susceptible to hypnosis, mind control, erratic behavior—even death. Joy dust got pulled from the market and landed on the government's list of banned substances."

"But now they're using it."

"Right. The thing is, this new chemical's basic composition is joy dust, but they've tweaked it. Joy dust 2.0." He waved his hand dramatically.

"That's sick." But I smiled in spite of myself.

"Sorry." His cheeks tinged pink.

"How's it tweaked?"

"They've added properties that weaken the immune system, which could keep people from fighting off the smart virus—if they don't have a chip. But the basic composition is still the same as before. If joy dust builds up in somebody's system they can be easier to control—at least after enough doses."

I massaged my temples. "So people are either going to die from GPV or be subject to mind control?"

"You got it."

"And the flour doesn't contain GPV?"

"No, I'm sorry. I wish it did, so we could stop the epidemic."

I blinked my grainy eyes and didn't dare wonder if there could be more bad news, because the answer to that question was always *yes*.

"There's something else," Nathan said.

Of course there was. "I don't want to know."

"Yeah you will," Nathan said. "It's not that bad. I promise."

"You'd better be right."

He swiped his hand over the stubble on his face. "Remember how I told you there was something wrong with your dad's mind when we picked him up outside of Fortune City?"

"Let me guess. Joy dust?"

"Ding, ding, ding. For a long time we thought his problem was the nanobots, but I looked back at your dad's test results. The basic drug tests didn't look for joy dust since it's a banned substance. But, they stored blood samples because no one ever conclusively diagnosed him. I got a hold of a sample and did another test. Sure enough, his blood tested positive for large concentrations of joy dust. Well, joy dust 2.0."

I sighed. "That explains his erratic behavior in Fortune City and why he's back to normal now."

"Yep."

"What if they used it on the rest of us in Fortune City? That would've been easy to do. They controlled everything we ate."

"True," he said. "When I got here, they did some tests on me, so I'll check to see if my blood samples are in storage. If they haven't been destroyed, I'll test my blood for joy dust." He cleared his throat. "My original tests showed traces of the nanobots they used to track us."

A chill iced my body. "Will those hurt us?"

"Honestly, the more research I do, the less I'm convinced that nanobots are our biggest problem. Your dad's been thinking the same thing lately."

My mind was whirling with these new revelations. "Thanks for the update."

"You're very welcome." Nathan grinned.

We disconnected, and I gazed out the window at the angry, swirling clouds beneath us. Rainfall had pelted the Coastal Plain region for weeks and seemed to show no sign of relenting.

Drake stirred and opened his eyes. "How long was I out?"

I held up my courier. "Long enough to miss some huge news." I filled him in.

Drake rubbed his chin. "Sounds far-fetched, but I know it's probably not." He shook his head. "I'll be glad to get you back to the Mine."

"Really? You didn't seem that concerned when I asked to leave."

His jaw twitched, and he looked out the window. "If you say so."

I steeled myself for what I needed to say next. Now was as good a time as any. "Drake, I have to talk to you about something." I wrapped my arms around my waist.

He raised his eyebrows. "That sounds ominous."

"After we're done today, we shouldn't work together anymore."

His jaw tightened. "Why?"

"Because we don't have a future. This whole trip has been painfully awkward. I think I'm called to be single, and I don't want to lead you on. I know you care about me, and I'm not in the same place."

"I see."

"Nathan's just a friend, and Ben's part of my past. Please don't blame them. I take full responsibility, and I don't want to hurt you."

"It's far too late for that."

"I'm sorry."

I wished he'd say something. Anything. But a vacant look replaced the mischievous spark in his blue eyes, and he turned and gazed out the window.

# CHAPTER 22

## *Drake*

"Someone hacked my courier." I couldn't take the excruciating silence, and Vivica and I had at least an hour left in the flight.

Vivica sat up and stared at me. "Any theories on who did it?"

"Nope. But Jethro blames me." I still couldn't believe he'd suspect that I'd betray the Warriors.

"Well…" She bit her lip and twirled her stylus.

"Well what? You think it's my fault too?" If she did, she should spit it out and finish off what was left of my heart.

"No. That's not it." She sighed. "It's possible that Navid could be targeting you."

"Why?"

"He seems to have a thing for me." She cleared her throat. "What if he feels threatened by our relationship?"

"You mean yours and mine?" I bit back a cynical laugh. "And what relationship would that be, my dear? The one where you refuse my attention except for when you're in trouble? The one where you ignore my feelings for you? Or wait—" I held up a hand. "Maybe it's the one where we work together, trying to pretend there's nothing between us other than lukewarm friendship."

"You're not being fair," she said. "Do you have any idea what I've been through? How many people I've lost?"

"Don't try to blame it on losing people you love. You were pushing me away before your mother and Melvin died."

Tears filled her eyes, and I wished I could cut off my tongue.

"I'm trying to figure out what God wants with my life," she said. "What if I'm called to be single? Why do I have to make a decision about us right now?"

"I never said you did." I massaged my temples. "You put that pressure on yourself. I simply made my intentions clear and told you I'd wait." My courier vibrated, so I unbuckled my seat and walked to the back of the plane—which wasn't far. But I needed the space. "Hey, Liam. What's up?"

Silence.

I held out my courier. We were still connected. "Hello?"

"Bad news," he rasped.

"What?" I gripped the back of my scalp and braced myself. Mom? Oliver?

"I can't—" He choked back a sob.

Ophelia. "What happened?" I closed my eyes.

"Someone killed Ophelia…and stole her identity."

\*\*\*

After I told Vivica the news, she buried her face in her hands and wailed. I fought flares of rage while I knelt beside her. During the last year, she'd lost more than I had, so I needed to be strong. When she didn't pull away, I wrapped my arms around her.

"God help us all," I whispered.

"It feels like God doesn't even care."

I started to protest but stopped. I didn't feel like defending God.

She lifted her head. "How's Liam?"

"Devastated. Angry." I swiped tears from her cheek with my thumb.

"When was Ophelia killed?" she asked.

"A couple of weeks ago. The woman impersonating her fooled everyone but Liam. He and Ophelia had been working separately for about a month, and he started to get suspicious when she kept putting off coming home. So he tested her. Asked something only Ophelia would know. Got a reply that was way off. But the woman vanished before Liam could get to her."

She drew a shuddering breath. "Have they found Ophelia's body?"

"Yeah." My fingers clawed the armrest on Vivica's seat. "In the woods behind their house." My beautiful sister-in-law didn't deserve that. She'd always looked out for me. Been honest with me—even when I didn't want to hear it. Ophelia had been the one to make me own up to my feelings for Vivica.

She winced. "I knew something wasn't right the last time I saw her—when she created Penny. I thought she wasn't feeling well. Or she was worried. She told me she had a lot on her mind, but I'd never seen her so quiet...and cold."

Cold was exactly right, and I mentally throttled myself for not noticing the difference in the woman's demeanor. But we had another problem. "Who knows how many of our agents' aliases have been compromised?"

It would take incredible skill to impersonate Ophelia. Not only would the person have to know her quirks and habits, they'd have to have her ability to create disguises. Plus, the woman would've had to know to target Ophelia in the first place. There weren't many options—and only one good possibility.

My stomach dropped like a missile.

Vivica was staring at me. "Drake, do you think...?" She bowed her head. "Never mind."

"Say it." We had to be thinking the same thing. Vivica fidgeted with the seatbelt flap.

"Look at me." I put my hand over hers. "And tell me what you're thinking."

She met my gaze. "Faith?"

I nodded. "But I can't believe she'd do that to Liam—and me."

"She already betrayed you and the rest of the Warriors. What would stop her from taking the next step?"

"Decency? Her conscience?" But Faith had apprenticed with Ophelia and knew how to make disguises. I pinched the bridge of my nose. "I'm afraid you're right. But don't say anything to Liam until we have proof, okay?"

She squeezed my hand. "I won't."

***

Because Ophelia had never been to the Mine, and Liam had never told her about it, the Warriors' leadership team determined that location hadn't been compromised. However, when Vivica and I landed in the Coastal Plain Region, we traveled to the Mine in the trunks of two separate cars.

Vivica had already disappeared to her room by the time my car arrived, but I checked with the guard to make sure she was there. He assured me she was, so I took a cart and went to Liam's apartment.

Liam was sprawled on his couch with several empty beer bottles. "Go away."

I pushed the bottles aside and sat next to him.

He lifted his head enough to glare at me. "Get out."

"I'm sorry." I rested my elbows on my knees and cradled my head.

"You should be."

I straightened and stared at him. I'd never seen my brother drunk.

I'd hardly even seen him drink. "Why wouldn't I be sorry? Your wife was an amazing woman. I'm sick about this."

Liam sat up and jabbed a finger in my chest. "This is *your* fault."

I stood. "We'll talk about this in the morning." I walked to his refrigerator and took out the remaining beer bottles. He didn't need any more tonight. As I turned to leave, Liam plowed into me, slamming me against the wall. The uneven surface jabbed my back, and I lost my grip on the bottles. They shattered.

Liam swung at my face, but I ducked, and his fist smashed into the wall. He swore, charged after me, and swung again. This time I was ready, and I knocked him off balance and wrestled him to the ground.

He stared up at me, his eyes cold and full of hate. "You want to know why I blame you? Why this is your fault? Why I'll never know my child?"

"Ophelia was pregnant?" I loosened my grip.

"Found out from the autopsy report." Liam let out a hollow laugh, sat up, and narrowed his eyes. "Your ex-girlfriend did this."

"Do you have proof?" For months, I'd tried to come to grips with the idea that the Faith I'd known—the Christian person she'd pretended to be—had never existed. But after we figured out she betrayed the Warriors by becoming a mole, she'd disappeared. Part of me hoped she'd regretted betraying her family—and me. I'd prayed that God would change her, and that she'd ask him for forgiveness.

Now, even though my gut said she was responsible, I wanted to believe she was innocent and someone else had killed Ophelia.

"I'll find proof," Liam said. "And when I do, I'm holding you responsible."

"I didn't do this. She fooled me too!"

"You were an easy target. You brought her into our lives."

"Faith's parents were connected to the Warriors for years," I said. "As far as we knew, they were loyal. Ben is. It's not our fault Faith went bad."

Liam shook his head. "How do I know you're not working with her now? Someone hacked your courier. You let someone get close enough to do *that*. Everyone thinks you're so into Vivica, but maybe you're seeing women on the side."

"That's crazy. I spend all my time working." I backed away from him and held up my hands in surrender. "I'm done talking until you sober up."

"What about your little trip to the Caribbean Region?"

"To buy the Lobos?" I scowled. "What about it?"

"Our tech nerds figured out that's when your courier got hacked."

I considered all the people I'd interacted with during the trip—and there weren't many.

Except…Vanessa. At the beachside restaurant. She was the right height and weight to have been Faith in disguise.

I was such an idiot.

"Have something you need to confess?" Hate spewed from Liam's eyes.

I set my jaw. "No."

"I'm never going to forgive you."

I swallowed and reminded myself Liam was drunk. "Good night." I turned to leave.

He shoved me toward the door. "Stay away from me. Every day I look at you, I'm going to think of my wife and baby—dead in the woods behind my house. All because you fell for Faith Lagarde."

He slammed the door in my face.

I wanted to blame the alcohol, but it didn't change the truth.

This situation was at least partly my fault.

# CHAPTER 23

## *Vivica*

It was almost noon the day after Drake and I returned to the Mine when Agatha tore into my room and woke me up. Commander launched off the bed and greeted her.

I sat halfway up and rubbed my eyes. "Hey. Nice to see you."

"Sorry." She patted the dog's head. "Couldn't wait any longer."

"What's going on? Is Chad okay?"

She perched on the edge of my bed since she was short enough to fit in the little hollow without ducking. "He's still weak, but they gave him massive doses of serum." She clasped her hands. "It's working. We got here a few hours before you and Drake."

"Thank you, God," I whispered, thankful for a bit of good news. "I need to eat. I'm not hungry, but I'm a little light-headed." I got up and rested my hand on the rough wall to support myself.

We went down the passageway to the shared kitchenette where she started rummaging through cabinets. She removed a box of crackers and retrieved grapes and spray cheese from the refrigerator. "Looks like this is the best we can do."

"I love spray cheese." The edge of my mouth crept upward as I sat on a stool at the bistro table.

"No one loves spray cheese."

I unwrapped a cracker and coated it with the yellow paste. "Hungry people do." I popped it in my mouth. "I need every ounce of strength I can get." I grabbed a bunch of grapes and told her about everything that had happened—including Navid's offer.

"Wow. That's a lot to take in."

"No kidding."

Agatha sat at the bar and leaned on the counter. "How're things with Drake?"

My heart flopped. "Over. I told him we can't work together anymore."

"Why?" She frowned and lowered her voice.

"Singleness is best for me, and I don't want to give Drake the wrong idea."

"Really?" Agatha crossed her arms. "How is God leading you?"

"I don't know."

"That's what I was afraid of. If you've surrendered your life to Christ, then shouldn't he get a say in the matter?"

I opened my mouth to protest but clamped it shut.

"I almost lost the love of my life because I was being stubborn and not letting God lead me." She stood. "I don't want you to make the same mistake. If God's will is that you stay single, I'm with you. But don't use singleness as a cop out." She paused and searched my face.

I examined the ingredients on the spray cheese. How had the government not outlawed it? Probably because the politicians had investments in the companies that produced it.

"Maybe God wants you with Drake." Agatha lowered her voice. "Or someone else will come along. Either way? Don't leave God out of this decision." She stalked from the room and then turned back. "And so we're clear, I *am* certain Navid isn't God's will, okay?"

I launched a cracker at her.

\*\*\*

That afternoon, I reported to my cubicle to work on moving people into the Coastal Plain Region. I'd just taken a break to stretch when Agatha rushed in.

"I need to talk to you. Now." She pulled me out of the room and into the hallway.

Blood drained from my face. "Is Chad okay?"

She nodded and wound a red curl around her finger.

I grabbed the rough wall for support. "Please tell me no one died. I can't take any more death."

"It's nothing like that, but—"

"But what?" My voice was a hoarse whisper.

"It's Drake." She bit her lip. "He's abandoned the Warriors."

# CHAPTER 24

## *Vivica*

"What?" My mind churned. No way. Drake would never do something like that. He'd recruited me. "How do you know?"

"He left a message."

I shook my head and thought through the possibilities. "It's the joy dust. Someone's contaminated his food and gotten to his mind. Or he's upset about Ophelia dying."

"I thought the same thing about the joy dust." Agatha clasped her hands and rested them in her lap. "But Drake made certain to address that in his resignation letter."

I leaned forward. "Let me see it."

She swiped her courier and handed it over. "He sent this to Liam and the rest of the leadership team this morning. Liam forwarded it to me—so I could tell you."

```
Dear Emancipation Warriors Leadership Team:

It is with sadness that I resign my
position in the Emancipation Warriors. I
can no longer fully support the direction
this group is taking, and I believe the
```

```
current plan to secede will result in a
catastrophic loss of life, for which I do
not wish to bear responsibility. It's time
for me to submit to the authorities God
has given us.

Additionally, I do not intend to side with
the United Regions of North America or the
Council of World Peacekeepers but intend
to live a life of strategic neutrality.

Sincerely,
Drake R. Freeman

P.S. I've had my blood tested, and results
indicate my blood is free of joy dust. You
have my permission to confirm the results
with the Emancipation Clandestine Research
Lab.
```

I scowled. "*Strategic neutrality?* You've got to be kidding me. That's a fancy name for being a coward!" I stood and paced. "How could he do this? He's never been a pacifist!" I handed Agatha her courier before I hurled it across the room. "Where'd he go? Is he dumb enough to think he'll survive if he doesn't fight back? And what about obeying God instead of man?"

"I'm sorry, Viv." Agatha leaned forward and rested her head in her hands. "I wish I had an answer. We're all shocked. Frankly, I never dreamed Drake would do something like this. The only consolation is he's not switching sides."

"For now." I stopped and put my hands on my hips. "But who knows? I've got to find him. This is my fault. I thought I was protecting him when I said we shouldn't work together."

Agatha lifted her head. "Viv, I don't think—"

"There's more to this. I know it." And it probably *was* my fault. Had I caused this when I'd refused to say I loved him? I thought back to the night of the state dinner at the presidential mansion. Drake had alluded to his doubts about Operation Coastal Republic. He could've been ready to give up then.

She sighed. "Truthfully, yes. There's probably more to it than we realize."

"I can help him—convince him to come back." I'd had my own doubts and had worked them out. Maybe Drake would too.

Agatha raised her eyebrows. "He didn't tell us where he was going."

"I'll find him."

***

I spent a few hours combing the Emancipation Warriors' databases, hoping to get a clue as to Drake's new identity and where he could be, but I couldn't find anything. I leaned my head against the coarse wall in my room and tried to think like Drake. He might not change his identity at all. He wouldn't need to if he were going to remain neutral.

I hacked URNA's Population Management database and found the doc issued to Drake Freeman.

He was at his stepfather's beach property on the Atlantic coast.

# CHAPTER 25

## *Drake*

Five years of my life gone. And for what? I'd given everything for the Warriors, and now my sister-in-law was dead, my brother hated me, and the woman I loved didn't love me and probably thought I was a coward. As night came, I loafed on the deck overlooking the Atlantic Ocean at my stepdad's cottage.

The Warriors' fight wasn't worth it, and where did we ever get the idea that it was okay to start a revolution? Form a new country? After all, the Great Commission was to go and preach the gospel, not go and make war.

I shuffled inside. I'd need to find my own place soon. For one, too many ocean-themed knickknacks cluttered the place for my taste. But the main reason was Mom and Oliver used this house for entertaining, and I had zero desire to stick around and socialize with the wealthy businessmen and politicians who'd funded the Warriors and were probably plotting a way to get rich during the economic upheaval that was sure to follow secession.

I flicked the kitchen lights on and jumped when I saw Faith, gorgeous as ever, sitting on the couch in the living room. Her black tank top was low-cut and tight. She smiled, and her brown eyes sparkled. "Hey, stranger."

I stood at the edge of the living room and crossed my arms. "You kill my sister-in-law, then have the nerve to sneak into my house like nothing happened?"

She flipped her dark hair over her shoulder. "I didn't kill her."

"But you know who did." I narrowed my eyes.

She stared at her bare feet. Certainly had made herself at home.

My chest burned. "You impersonated her. Manipulated people you supposedly used to care about!"

She studied her manicured fingernails.

I pointed to the door. "Get out."

"I need to talk to you." She rose from the couch and slinked into the kitchen.

"Unless you want to apologize for impersonating my sister-in-law, who was one of the dearest women I've ever known, save it." I leaned against the counter.

"It's important, so you need to listen."

"Why's that, darling?" I sneered.

"Because I loved you once, and I still care about you." She rested her hand on my arm. "I work for the Peacekeepers and have a lot of influence with Secretary General Zahedi."

I wrenched away, and her hand dropped to her side. After seeing the way that pervert Zahedi had eyed Vivica, Faith's statement about having 'influence' with him made me want to hurl. "Spit it out."

"Fine." She lifted her chin.

It was pretty stupid of her to act offended. Surely she hadn't thought I'd be glad to see her.

"URNA and the Peacekeepers know about the Warriors' secession plan," she said.

I went to the cabinet, removed a glass with some anchors on it, filled it with water, and took a drink. "Secession plan? Sounds intriguing, but I don't know anything about it."

She chuckled softly. "I doubt it, but that's not why I'm here. I want you to come with me."

"Why?"

"Because I asked."

"How compelling," I said. "Where would we go?"

"You'll see."

"And I don't get any more details? Just 'come with me.' Like you never pretended to love me or never betrayed your entire family—and me."

She tilted her head. "Yet you don't protest nearly as much as I'd expected."

"What do the Peacekeepers plan to do about this so-called secession plan?"

"I can't tell you," Faith said. "Until you agree to come work with the Peacekeepers. The Warriors' secession plan will never succeed."

I set the glass down on the counter, and water slopped over the edge onto the granite.

"I know you, Drake Freeman. You have doubts about secession. You can't help it. It's how you think."

I should never have gotten close to this woman. "Any reservations I *might* have about this alleged secession plan are far outweighed by my certainty that joining the Peacekeepers and their quest for global domination is wrong."

"How can you not care about peace? Secretary General Zahedi wants everyone to live in harmony. No more wars."

"Faith. Do you understand how far the Peacekeepers are willing to go to ensure peace? You're selling your soul to a life of government control."

"I am *not!*"

I'd never realized she was so naïve. "Let's say I throw my

convictions out the window," I said. "Come with you. Then what?"

Tears filled her brown eyes. "I'll know you're safe."

"From what?"

Faith shook her head. "I can't tell you. Please just believe me."

For a second I was flattered that she cared enough to warn me, but I couldn't let her get in my head. "It wouldn't be so bad to die in a nuclear blast. *Boom!* It's over." I shrugged. "Of course, it's the radiation sickness that's the doozy."

Tears were streaming down her cheeks.

"Good grief, Faith. Knock it off. Someone did a bang-up job of teaching you acting."

"They're not going to use nuclear weapons."

"Okay. GPV then. It won't take long for it to spread here." My sleeve covered the biochip that Harrison had created.

"The Warriors have figured out a serum to prevent GPV, and there aren't many new cases," she said. "But then, you already knew that."

"How'd it spread in the first place?" I couldn't seem to stop myself from gathering intel.

Her eyes clouded. "I don't know. I really don't. I'm sorry." She ducked her head. "Please. I'm recruiting for a project the Peacekeepers are working on. I can find a place for you."

"No. Thank you. I'm going to remain neutral." I refused to meet her eyes, but I could feel her gaze.

"Okay then. Just…don't stay here. It's not safe." She stood on her tiptoes and gave me a kiss on the cheek. Then she grabbed her sandals and bolted out of the house.

# CHAPTER 26

## *Vivica*

Two days after I discovered Drake's location, I found him walking the beach at dawn. His hands stuffed in his pockets, he strolled while waves surged over his feet. I paused behind a clump of sea oats and watched. Gray clouds drooped toward the horizon and announced impending rain.

I kicked off my shoes and charged through the sand. When I drew closer, our eyes met. "Drake, it's—"

"I know it's you, my dear."

"How?" Karen, Ophelia's replacement, had created a new mask and alias for me. Though it wasn't the same as having Ophelia make my disguise, Karen was sweet, and the Warriors had done a slew of tests to make sure she was legitimate—and loyal.

"I recognized your walk."

"I didn't know it was so distinctive," I said.

He shrugged. "Never said it was."

A seagull screeched overhead, and the Atlantic Ocean roared.

"Why'd you *really* leave?" I asked.

"You're here to clear your conscience because you're afraid it had something to do with you." He ground his toe into the sand.

"That's not true." I bristled. "I care about you."

"But you don't love me." He shook his head.

"I—"

"Faith was here," he said. "To recruit me."

"You've got to be kidding. Did she confess to killing Ophelia?"

"No." He pressed his lips together.

"Did you ask her?"

"Yes."

I rolled my eyes. "What did she want?"

"She wants me to work with the Peacekeepers on a special project."

I closed my eyes momentarily. I'd had more experience with special projects than I'd ever cared to endure.

He gazed out at the waves. "She was devastated when I told her no. I'm staying here and remaining neutral."

*Devastated?* Why? "How can you walk away after everything you've fought for?" I'd wrestled with my own doubts and had come to the opposite conclusion.

He tilted his head. "The country we dreamed of is never going to exist."

"Not if everyone gives up like you have."

"The Peacekeepers and URNA know about our secession plan."

I winced. "That doesn't mean we quit."

He turned away. "A while ago, you asked me if I thought freedom was worth the cost. Remember?"

"Yeah." It was after I'd decided to join the Warriors. I envisioned us driving away from the governor's mansion I'd shared with my mother in the Great Lakes Region. Then my breath hitched. "You never answered my question that day." I shook my head. "You had doubts and still recruited me?"

"You didn't want to return to your mother."

"Whatever."

"We're both telling ourselves lies to feel better," he snapped.

"How does that solve anything?"

"It doesn't."

My fist clenched. "You think this is what God wants for you?"

"God's more interested in people finding freedom through salvation than our earthly fight for liberty." He started walking.

"Why can't we have both?"

"Because we can't." He stopped and faced me. "Not this time. I was at this a lot longer than you, my dear, and that gives me a better grip on reality."

I laughed. "Hiding in a beach house waiting for everyone else to fight for you is a grip on reality? What happened to you? You're the one who taught me that the rights of life, liberty, and the pursuit of happiness come from God—not a government. You're the one who convinced me we have to fight to create a nation where people are free to live those rights out." The salty wind slapped my hair against my face.

"I did well, didn't I?" His face twisted. "The Warriors are about to fail miserably, and Faith's desperation for me to get out of this region only bolsters my conviction. Then what? We'll have caused the loss of life for nothing. Eternal souls—lost because we thought our pitiful organization could take on the world."

"If we do nothing, the Peacekeepers may kill them anyway."

He started walking again. "I'm not sure that what the Warriors are doing is God's will. Which is why I'm not convinced we'll— you'll—succeed."

I hurried after him. "It's never wrong to take a stand against evil. If God wants me to die fighting for our freedom, then so be it. If God doesn't want the Coastal Republic to exist, then it won't. But I've never sensed God telling me I shouldn't fight."

"I'm sorry to disappoint you." He stopped and faced me. "But I'm not in the same place anymore."

My throat swelled, and I reached for his hand. "Then I guess there's nothing left to say, because I know what I have to do." I'd never imagined it'd be without Drake.

He squeezed my hand. "I wish you well, my dear." He turned and trudged through the wet sand.

The water lapped around my toes, pulling the sand underneath my feet with it as it returned to the ocean.

"I love you," I whispered.

# CHAPTER 27

## *Vivica*

The flight back to the Mine seemed to drag on forever, but I said a silent prayer of thanks for the time to pray and think in the privacy of the small cabin.

I'd endured too many losses in such a short amount of time. My mother, Melvin, Ophelia, and now Drake. I curled my fingers around a damp tissue. How could Drake do this? I should've run after him and told him I loved him.

Minutes passed as I stared out the jet's window at the landscape. Life was going on for thousands—millions—of people. Flying across my country was another reminder of how big the world was and how God had so many difficulties and people to manage.

Did my problems matter?

I'd read enough of the Bible to know that God cared. My head understood, but my heart was too broken to absorb that truth. In a way, I understood why Drake had given up—especially if he truly believed the fight wasn't God's will.

Drake had lost a lot as well. Faith. Ophelia. Me.

A tide of despair had rolled in and consumed him.

Why had I ever thought I should be single? Drake needed me,

and I needed him. Yet our stubbornness and the pressures of life had killed our relationship before it had even started.

"God, what do you want? Am I on the right path? Are the Warriors doing your will by fighting? Show me how I can reach Drake. Give us another chance to be together. Help him find his way. I love him, God."

I waited for an answer but heard only the drone of the jet's engine.

***

As soon as I returned to the Mine, I requested a meeting with Liam and Jethro. They'd agreed, and the next day, my stomach churned as I stood outside of their meeting room and rapped on the door.

"Enter," Jethro said in his gravelly voice.

Liam sat at a table with Jethro. I closed the door and joined them.

"I'm very sorry about Ophelia, Liam. She was a special lady." Tears welled in my eyes as I thought of how kind and encouraging she'd been.

"Thank you." He cleared his throat and stared at his hands. "Your trip to see my brother was unsuccessful."

"Yes, but—"

"No surprise." Liam drummed his fingers on the table. "He's a stubborn idiot. We'll carry on without him. Unless he gets more of us killed because Ophelia wasn't enough carnage for him."

I tried not to gape at the hard edge in Liam's voice. He blamed Drake for Ophelia's death?

Unbelievable.

"Storyteller, what were you saying before Liam interrupted?" Jethro regarded me with his gunmetal-colored eyes.

"Faith visited him."

Liam slammed his fist onto the table, causing me to jump. "I knew he was working with her." He shoved his chair away and stormed out of the room.

"That's not what—" I started to get up.

Jethro held up a hand. "Let him go." He pulled a pack of gum from his pocket and popped a stick in his mouth. "Want some?"

"No, thanks."

"Liam blames Drake for Ophelia's death."

"Yeah, I got that." I crossed my arms. "It's not Drake's fault."

"I know. But Drake helped recruit Faith." Jethro shrugged. "Grief can make a man crazy, and Liam didn't think about how he'd make his brother feel by blaming him and all. Still, I'd have bet Drake was tougher than that. Guess you never know what's brewing inside a man's head."

"No sir."

"Look. You got any useful information, then spit it out. I ain't got all day."

"Faith told Drake the Peacekeepers know about Operation Coastal Republic."

Jethro muttered a curse under his breath and cracked his gum. "Won't stop us."

"Faith's also recruiting for the Peacekeepers. Some special project. I need to find out what it is and why she's so desperate for Drake's help."

Jethro appeared to weigh my request. "Got any credible leads?"

"Not yet."

"Talk to our tech people who figured out Drake's courier got hacked." He steepled his fingers. "They might have a clue on how Faith found him—and how to track her. You get a lead, I'll let you sniff it out." He stood. "Get busy."

"Yes sir." The mission should be simple enough.

As I walked out of the room and thought about Drake's courier being compromised, an unrelated idea slammed into me like an out-of-control-vehicle. *Hacked*. Why hadn't it occurred to me before now? Someone with my expertise should never have missed something so obvious.

My mother's biochip had been hacked.

*** 

I jumped in a cart and drove through the mine's tunnels toward my father's lab. I'd been so focused on the nanobots causing my mother's death that I'd missed another possibility.

The cart skidded to a halt, and I threw open the lab door and rushed in. A few scientists I didn't recognize looked up. "My father— Harrison. Is he here?"

A man with a shiny scalp pointed his thumb over his shoulder. "Go on back to the office."

I hurried through the maze of lab tables and knocked on the doorframe.

"Vivibear!" My father grinned. He stood, ushered me into the office, and closed the door. "What's wrong?"

"Mother's chip was hacked."

He let out a low whistle. "We should've thought of that sooner." He leaned against his desk. "How can we prove it? The chip alone wouldn't have the capability of killing her, even if someone hacked into it."

"Right. But when I asked Dr. Alstead why Mother's chip didn't report an impending aneurysm, she brushed me off. What if whoever was monitoring her data saw it and ignored it? Or changed the chip so it wouldn't report a health problem? Or what if someone changed the data so it showed she was fine—but wasn't?"

My father tapped his chin. "Maybe. Especially since the Global Health Organization helped distribute and implant the chips."

"And GHO is a branch of the Peacekeepers."

"And the Peacekeepers weren't thrilled when your mother made the treaty with the Warriors."

"Because they wanted to take over URNA." I buried my face in my hands. "I have a new mission, so I can't look into it."

"I'll take care of it. Go do your thing." He gave me a hug. "Be careful."

***

Nathan waved me into his lab. "Viv! You doing okay?"

"Define *okay*." I went in, leaned against a table, and fiddled with some empty glass vials.

Concern flashed in his eyes, and he walked away from his computer. "That good, huh?" He put his arm around me. "Can I help?"

"I need to track Faith Lagarde, but I have to find her alias first." I chewed my lip. Maybe I should call Ben and ask if he knew anything. She may've tried to contact him.

"Heard she's the one who killed Ophelia."

"At the very least, she impersonated Ophelia."

He blew out a breath.

"I've got to figure out what Faith's up to." But I wouldn't disrupt Ben's perfect new life. "Who are some tech people I could talk to?"

"Daniel and Danielle."

"Tech twins or a cutesy couple?"

"Twins. They'll fix you up. In fact, you'll probably get along great. You can bond over hacking." He took off his lab coat and tossed it over his desk chair. "How about I give you a ride to their office?"

"Perfect," I said.

"And, Nathan?"

"Yes?"

"When I leave, will you watch Commander for me?"

"You betcha."

***

After Daniel, Danielle, and I brainstormed, we figured out how to track Faith by using the window of time during which she'd visited Drake at the beach house. Once we determined she was in the Desert and Pacific Region, I headed to see my father before I left.

"I've got news about your mother's chip," my father said as soon as I entered his lab.

"Did you find proof that Navid killed her?"

"I hacked the Health Management database since that's the branch responsible for monitoring citizens' biochips." He paused. "Someone changed your mother's data—and did a poor job of it. I was able to uncover the original data." He bowed his head. "Your mother's health started showing signs of deteriorating months ago."

My chest tightened. "If she'd been treated…" My breathing turned shallow. "I could've had more time to reach her."

"What do you mean?"

"Convince her that she needed Christ in her life."

"Oh. That." He looked away.

Obviously, I needed to keep praying for my father. "Were you able to figure out who changed the data?"

"Not yet. I'll keep working." He gave me a hug. "You sure you want to go after Faith?"

"Someone has to."

"I don't like that it has to be my daughter." He bristled. "It should be Drake, but he's too busy being a coward."

I couldn't argue.

# CHAPTER 28

## *Vivica*

My face sweltered underneath my mask in the Desert and Pacific Region's heat, and I longed for the cool dryness of the Mine where I could be Vivica and not Julianna Marino. But my desire to locate Faith drove me forward through a bustling market toward my hotel. I dodged a small child and listened to women barter for fruits and vegetables.

Faith had remained at Hotel Harmony for the last several days. The majestic building boasted marble columns, and holographic images of prominent members of the Council of World Peacekeepers were projected in front. Navid's image was the largest of all, and his hypnotic gaze seemed to follow me as I climbed the steps to the entrance.

The door glided open, and a blast of air conditioning beckoned me inside. Thankful for the reprieve, I squared my shoulders and strolled to the front desk.

"Good afternoon, ma'am. How may I help you?" Behind the front desk, a teenage girl's face stretched into a robotic smile, and she tilted her head a few degrees to the right. Oh. She was an android—an older model that wasn't as lifelike as the newer ones. Her nametag read *Sally.*

"Reservation for Julianna Marino."

Sally processed the information, and her eyes lowered to my upper arm and fixated on my fake biochip. It would've been much cooler if her eyes glowed while they read my chip.

*Please, God. Let it work.*

Sally met my eyes, and her head gave a mechanical tilt left. "It will take a moment for me to confirm your identity and reservation. While we wait, may I provide you with more information about hotel services?"

"No, thank you."

"Very well. I have confirmed your identity and reservation, and your room number is 523. Swipe your biochip on the access portal next to your door." She blinked and smiled. "Enjoy your stay."

"Thanks, Sally."

"You're welcome. Have a nice day."

Once I was locked in my room, I swept for bugs and hidden cameras. The room was clear, so I opened my courier and hacked the hotel's records and security cameras.

Faith hadn't registered under her real name, so I searched for guests who'd stayed more than a few days. Only one was a female name—Tarla Veldman in 814. I accessed the cameras outside of her room and looked for footage of the woman coming in and out until I got a perfect view of her face.

Now, for step two.

\*\*\*

That evening, I waited in the lobby and pretended to be engrossed in a game on the doc that was issued to Julianna. My courier was stowed in a sequined clutch, ready to clone Faith's MD3—if I could get close enough.

Faith, disguised as Tarla, entered the lobby. She wore a yellow sundress that showed too much cleavage. A man who was seated across the room rose, hurried over, kissed her on both cheeks, and held her hands while they chatted. Then he pointed over his shoulder to the bar. Faith nodded.

Arm in arm, they sauntered toward the bar. I decided I needed a drink too, so I stopped in front of the entrance while the scanner read my ID. The gate slid aside, admitting me.

I took a seat at a table in a corner not far from where Faith and her friend sat in front of a big-screen TV with a soccer game blaring.

A freckled waiter strolled over. "Would you like a drink, Miss?"

"Sparkling water."

He bowed slightly and hurried away.

I pretended to rummage through my clutch and activated the cloning program on my courier while I strained to listen. But I could only hear Faith's honeyed tones—not actual words—over the conversation noise and the soccer game.

Sneaking a peek at my courier, I discovered it was doing its job. I breathed a sigh of relief that I was close enough to them.

Faith rested her hand on top of her companion's and then slid it away. Was she being flirtatious, or had that been some sort of exchange?

A cheer chorused through the bar, and a few men high-fived each other. One of the teams on TV had scored a goal. Out of the corner of my eye, I caught a flash of yellow.

Then, Faith stormed by my table and flounced out of the bar with her fist clenched at her side. Her companion sat frowning and staring toward the exit.

I stifled a groan but checked my courier.

Download complete.

*Whew. Thank you, Lord.*

\*\*\*

When I returned to my hotel room, I sprawled on the plush bed and combed through the data from Faith's MD3 until my eyelids drooped. Hours later, I awoke, and my neck hurt. I stood, stretched, opened a bottle of water, and considered what I'd read the night before.

Reading Faith's flirtatious messages to several different men wasn't my idea of fun.

I still wondered why she wanted to make sure Drake left the Coastal Plain Region, and the thought of him being in danger made my chest ache.

I plunked on the edge of the bed and tried to focus. A nuclear attack was the most obvious but least likely. The Coastal Republic would have the capability of firing back and destroying URNA. There had to be something that the new country wouldn't be able to defend against.

I stood and stretched as my courier dinged.

"Vivica, it's Alma." The alarm in my son's adoptive mother's tone immediately weakened my knees, and I switched the call to video mode.

*Isaac.*

Tears streaked her face, and her hair stood on end. "Someone's kidnapped Isaac."

My heart clenched. "What? Are you sure?" Maybe I was still asleep, and this was a nightmare.

"I went to wake him up—we had to be somewhere this morning—and he was gone." She buried her face in her hands and sobbed. Her husband, Gabe, appeared and put his arm around her.

Dizziness submerged me.

"Then we found the ransom note on each of our docs," Gabe said.

My hand flew to my throat. The ransom had something to do with me. Why else would Alma call? "What did it say?"

"Your son is safe, and he will be returned unharmed if his birth mother, Vivica Wilkins, reports to the Council of World Peacekeepers Headquarters in the Atlantic Region within twenty-four hours. If she does not, the child will be killed."

# CHAPTER 29

## *Vivica*

Navid's nationwide plea for information on my whereabouts had been fruitless, and now he'd resorted to drawing me out by exploiting my weakness. But how had he known where to find my son?

Faith. She'd known about the baby—her nephew.

Panic rose, but I squashed it. "Did the ransom note leave any other instructions?" I collapsed on the edge of my bed.

"No," Gabe said.

"What time was the message sent?"

"Ten hours ago."

"He was gone all night, and I didn't know." Alma sobbed.

I took a deep breath. Fourteen hours. But there was the time difference. And a flight across the country. *God, you have to fix this. Isaac is innocent.* A wave of hope rushed over me. "Did Isaac have a biochip? A real one or a counterfeit the Warriors made?"

"All of us have counterfeits—just got them last week." He held up a bloody chip. "But the kidnappers left this in the crib."

Bile rose in my throat. Whoever kidnapped Isaac would have to have drugged him to get the chip out. I tried to focus, but my thoughts scattered. "I'll turn myself in. I have to. There's no other way."

"Now hold on a minute," Gabe said. "There may be another—"

Alma's face reddened. "He's your son. We can't take a risk like that!"

"Honey, calm down. It's not good for you."

I knit my brows.

"Alma had surgery yesterday and is supposed to be resting," Gabe said.

"How do you expect me to rest when our son is missing?"

"I'll turn myself in," I said.

"Vivica, you can't give yourself to the Peacekeepers."

Alma glared at her husband. "Why not? She's willing."

"Not until we've tried to find Isaac first," he said. "We still have fourteen hours."

"Don't you want him to be safe?" Alma asked.

"Yes. I love him as much as you do, but—"

"It sure doesn't feel that way!" Alma turned her back to the camera, and her shoulders shook.

"Please," I said. "Don't fight. I'll turn myself in."

"Look," Gabe said. "You understand the Peacekeepers' end game, right?"

"Yes."

"If they want you, they're going to exploit your technological skills and get you to help their cause. We can't let them."

"The Warriors' fight is more important than your son?" Alma shrieked and hurried out of the camera's view.

I couldn't believe what Gabe was suggesting either. "But what if—?"

"Come here. We'll plan. We've moved into the Coastal Plain Region. I'll send you our new address."

"No," I said. "There's not time. But I'll try to track the kidnappers first. Take care of your wife."

I disconnected before he could protest and sat frozen. Gabe called two more times, but I ignored him.

Finally, I came out of my trance and started to call Drake, but when I remembered he'd abandoned the Warriors—and me—I fell face-down on the pillows and smothered a scream.

Who could I turn to for help? Nathan and my father were busy developing counterfeit biochips to save people all over the country. Liam and Jethro were planning secession.

Agatha was taking care of Chad.

That left one other person I'd trust with my life.

Could I ask for his help? After everything? But surely he'd want to know since it involved him too.

I took a deep breath and tapped in the number. "Ben? It's Vivica. Our son needs your help."

*** 

While I waited for Ben to fly to the Desert and Pacific Region to pick me up, I combed through the data from Faith's MD3, praying I'd find a clue that she knew about the kidnapping—and where they were hiding Isaac.

Most of the messages were cryptic, but one possibility stood out. It'd been sent the day before.

`Are we still on for tonight?`

I bit my lip. Faith *had* met a man at the bar the night before. Still, it was my only lead at the moment, so I went to work tracing the number and figured out it belonged to a Pauly Greenwood. When I found his ID profile and picture in URNA's Population Management database, my heart gave a little flutter of hope.

He wasn't the same man Faith had met the night before.

Now I had to track Pauly's doc and figure out where he'd been during the past twelve hours.

\*\*\*

Three hours later, I checked out of the hotel and drove to an airstrip in the desert where a small jet waited on the runway. Ben got off the plane and greeted me with a quick hug, and I stepped back and looked into his chocolate eyes. He'd grown a goatee that made him look more mature.

"Thanks for helping." I didn't know what else to say, and that seemed appropriate enough.

"You're welcome. He's my son too." Ben set his jaw. "Where're we headed?"

"I think the kidnappers are holding Isaac at a house in the Atlantic Region about fifty miles from Peacekeepers' Headquarters." I handed him my courier with the coordinates for the airstrip closest to the house. "A man named Pauly Greenwood has been in and out of there during the past several days—and it's not his home." I hesitated. "I hacked into the Pop Management database and traced him because he's been in communication with your sister." I showed Ben Pauly's government ID photo.

Pain flickered through Ben's expression as he gazed toward rock formations and the twisted, spiky trees in the distance. "I can't believe she'd hurt her own nephew."

"I can't either." The intense sunlight blazed down on us.

"Let's roll. It's ridiculously hot out here." He turned toward the plane. "Ally's on board and will help you plan. She's been itching to get in on some action."

I tried to keep the shock from registering on my face as we boarded and Ben headed for the cockpit. Ally sat with her hands resting on her swollen belly. Her fingernails were painted cobalt with white polka dots. Her shiny black hair was cut in a pageboy, and she surveyed me with curious dark eyes.

I extended my hand. "Nice to meet you."

She smiled and shook my hand. "Likewise."

"When are you due?" I forced myself to sound pleasant, but my voice came out an octave higher.

"Next month."

"Boy or girl?"

She beamed. "Boy."

My heart twisted. Just a little. Ben had a son to replace the one who would never be his. Not that there could ever be a replacement. Why had I thought of it that way? I should be happy for them.

"We were very sorry to hear about your mother," she said.

"Thank you for the kind note you sent." I glanced at Ally's abdomen. "Are you sure you should be flying?"

Ally's eyes flashed. "I'll be fine."

"Okay, then. Let's make a plan."

\*\*\*

After Ally and I figured out the best way to rescue Isaac, a heavy silence engulfed the cabin, and my thoughts turned to all that had happened during the last several weeks. I felt as if someone had picked me up and transplanted me into another person's life.

My repressed sobs edged to the surface and threatened to break out. But now wasn't the time to collapse. Not in front of Ben and Ally. At least Ally was asleep.

"Please, God. I need you to speak. Show me what to do."

*You will not have to fight this battle. Stand firm and see the deliverance I will give you.*

I blinked. After months of silence, was God speaking?

Or was I making things up? It seemed like a lifetime since I'd listened to the sermon about King Jehoshaphat—right before my mother had died.

I stared at the patchwork of fields below. Could I trust God enough to fight for me, especially when I'd fought my own battles for so long?

***

Ben came out of the cockpit. Ally stirred, awoke, and smiled at him. His eyes lit up, but his face remained serious. "There are severe thunderstorms, and it's too dangerous to land at Smith Airfield."

Ally and I exchanged glances, and I looked at my watch. Two hours until my deadline.

"Is there another airstrip?" I asked.

"Diverting would put us at least an hour and a half away by car." He projected a radar image from his courier, and I groaned. The band of storms was huge.

A chill rushed over my body as I studied the map. Could I turn myself in to Navid for my son's sake? "It looks like we can land near Peacekeeper Headquarters."

Ben grimaced. "Yes, but you're not—"

"I don't have another choice." My stomach roiled.

"We can see if the weather clears and land at Smith," Ben said.

"He's right. Let's wait out the storm and stick with the plan to get Isaac back." Ally's forehead creased in concern. "You can't turn yourself into Zahedi."

"Yes, I can." I took a deep breath. "And that's exactly what I have to do."

***

After we landed, Ben drove me into the city while Ally waited at the airfield. With trembling fingers, I worked on transferring the information I'd downloaded onto my courier from Faith's MD3 to a hidden file on my government-issued doc. It was a risk, but I definitely couldn't take my courier.

"I haven't finished going through the data, so I'm not sure what Faith is up to—besides betraying her nephew's whereabouts to one of the most evil men in the world." I handed him my courier and pocketed my doc. "This has all the information I snagged from her MD3. Get it to Jethro. We're worried about a project she's recruiting for and are afraid it'll interfere with Operation Coastal Republic."

Even though the car was driving itself, Ben kneaded the steering wheel. "I hate that you're doing this. I should be going in your place."

Tears pricked my eyes. "Except they didn't ask for you."

"Does Drake know?"

"No." My voice trembled, and I blinked back the moisture. "He left the Warriors—permanently."

"You've got to be kidding me."

I read the message Drake had left.

"I never would've pegged him as a deserter." Ben shook his head. "Well, that explains why you contacted me. You would've called Drake if he were still around."

"It shouldn't surprise you that he'd be my first choice." I picked a hangnail. "You have a wife to take care of."

"How could Drake give up on you?"

"It's not about me."

"It's more about you than you realize."

My heart thudded. I hadn't wanted to admit it, but Drake had not only abandoned the Warriors, but he'd given up his fight for me.

"I saw the way Drake looked at you. How he tried to play it cool, but he's loved you for a long time." He blushed. "I wanted that kind of love, and when I met Ally, I got it."

"I'm glad." My heart should've been aching, but numbness had taken over my entire body.

"I know it was hard for you to understand why I was so willing to marry Ally in Fortune City, but that was the reason."

"It was always missing in our relationship," I said. And it was true.

The car stopped next to a curb, and the headquarters loomed ahead. The compound consisted of a lower level that took up an entire city block and two rotating towers, which each made a full circle every two hours. Ben rested his hand on my shoulder. "Are you sure?"

I took a deep breath. "No."

"Viv?"

"Yes?"

He stared at his hands. "I'm sorry."

"I know." I gazed at him. Ben would always have a special place in my heart. "You'll never know how much I appreciate you and Ally being willing to help." I held out my hand, and he squeezed it.

"I'll be praying."

"If you don't hear from me within the hour, go after Isaac," I said.

"I know. We can handle it."

I nodded. "Take good care of him. His parents' new contact information is in my courier."

As I walked toward the building, sweat broke out on my upper lip. Just a few more steps. A doorman greeted me. I took a deep breath and stepped up to the security desk where a strong-jawed woman kept watch. Her eyes narrowed as she looked me up and down, and I wished I'd changed out of my rumpled shorts and faded T-shirt.

"May I help you?"

"My name is Vivica Wilkins, and I've come to turn myself in."

# CHAPTER 30

## *Drake*

Running in humidity was like trying to propel myself through a vat of the baked potato soup my mom used to make for Liam and me. I burst into the beach house and took a deep breath. Every night after the sun set, I jogged along the beach, trying to outrun my guilt. But it never worked, and tonight was no exception.

Truth was, I was obeying the authorities, so my conscience shouldn't be messing with my head. But it was, and I was a worthless chicken.

Not even God wanted to bother with me.

After I hit the shower, I threw a steak on the grill. The meat sizzled, making my stomach roar. When the steak was finished, I sat down at the table on the deck and had the passing thought that I should pray. I picked up my utensils and sawed into the steak, but the thought didn't go away.

Fine. I'd bless the food. It might help my conscience.

"God," I muttered. "Bless this food."

*You can do better than that.*

My knife and fork clattered against the plate, and conviction assaulted me. I couldn't disagree. I could do better—and needed to

165

if I was ever going to have any peace.

I rested my head in my hands. "God, I'm sorry. I haven't been acting like you're in charge, but you are. And you're good at it. Please clue me in on what to do."

***

I'd just finished cleaning up from dinner when my doc buzzed. Lately, I'd been ignoring the thing and letting calls go to voicemail since Faith had been relentless—almost stalker-like—in contacting me. But a secure call was coming through, which meant that someone from the Warriors was taking a huge risk by using their courier to contact me. I looked more closely at the number.

Ben Lagarde.

"Freeman."

"Vivica turned herself into Zahedi an hour ago."

I blinked. What? "Well, my friend, you get right to the punch line, but I'm not much of a fan of your sick jokes."

"You ought to know me well enough to realize I'd never joke about this."

I switched the call to video mode. "How do you know?"

"I was with her."

"And you let her turn herself in to that maniac? Why?" Lagarde was lucky he wasn't standing in front of me, or that pretty-boy nose of his would be flattened.

"How about instead of being ticked at me, you take some responsibility," Lagarde said. "What happened to your convictions about obeying God instead of people? If you weren't off feeling sorry for yourself, then Viv would've gone to you for help, and I wouldn't have had to drag my pregnant wife across the country."

Ouch. Ten points to Lagarde for an on-target jab. And I had it coming for all the times I'd made fun of the guy for being a wimp.

Turns out the real wimp was me—projecting my worst qualities onto him. He'd been out fighting for justice while I'd been sitting around trying to excuse the government's atrocities with scripture.

I exhaled. "Bring me up to speed."

As Lagarde explained what had happened, my chest started to burn.

"Zahedi won't let the kid go," I said. "He'd lose his leverage."

"No kidding. Viv's afraid of that. That's why Ally and I were only supposed to wait an hour before moving on to plan B and going after Isaac."

"So the hour's up and you need help?"

"Yep."

At least God had answered my prayer—I knew what I had to do. I clenched my fist. "Tell me where to meet you."

# CHAPTER 31

### *Vivica*

Because my eyes had been surgically altered and my hair was dark brown, they didn't believe I was Vivica Wilkins and made me wait all night in a sweltering prison cell while they confirmed my identity.

At last, a guard with bushy eyebrows appeared and led me to a suite of offices on the top floor of Tower One. Spacious windows gave Navid a panoramic view of the city, and because the headquarters were on the edge of downtown, no skyscrapers obstructed his view. From his perch, he no doubt felt as if he were a god looking down on his minions, who raced to and from the suburbs to work while he pretended to be busy in his fortress.

A secretary wearing a dress cut to her navel escorted me to the inner sanctum, where she pointed to a leather chair. "May I offer you a beverage?"

"Water."

She trotted away and came back with an unopened bottle. I took it, and she sauntered out.

I pressed the cool bottle against my neck and face.

A panel next to a bookcase slid aside, and Navid appeared. A slow smirk spread over his face. "Vivica, it's nice to see you, though you aren't up to your usual standards. I have never seen you so disheveled, but the shade of your hair is lovely."

I stood and bit back the urge to tell him what to do with his standards. "Sorry to disappoint you, sir. A prison cell that's as hot as an oven isn't conducive to grooming." I glanced at my stained and wrinkled cargo shorts. I should've at least combed my hair. But I wasn't going to give him the satisfaction of knowing his comments affected me.

"It can be remedied." He motioned to the chair. "Please, have a seat." He settled at his desk. "I apologize for your wait in the prison cell. You understand why we had to confirm your identity. In addition, I am in the process of moving our headquarters to the Middle Eastern Region of the Republic of Asia, which has kept me very busy."

"Lovely. Now let Isaac go."

Navid stroked his chin. "It is not that simple."

"Why?" I prayed Ben and Ally had already taken him back.

"If I return the child, what assurance do I have that you will cooperate with my demands?"

My heart skipped a beat. "You have my word."

He laughed. "You have no idea what will be expected of you. How can you possibly give your word?"

"You always intended to hold Isaac hostage? Even though the ransom note said you'd let him go?" I feigned shock.

He stood, crossed the room, and poured some brandy. "Would you like some?"

"No."

"Suit yourself." He took a drink.

"How did you find him?"

Amusement flickered in his expression. "I have a very talented officer who investigated the events that occurred on the night you gave birth and simply followed the trail."

"Faith Lagarde?"

His amusement turned to admiration. "You hid the child well. And then his parents moved. An average person with limited resources would never have been able to locate him."

"You're certainly not average." It sounded more complimentary than I intended.

"No, and neither are the people with whom I choose to surround myself." He sipped the brandy and eyed me over the glass. "By the way, how are you coping since the loss of your mother?"

I folded my arms. "I'm devastated. Her death was completely unexpected."

"I certainly hope the malady is not genetic."

"I'm a lot like my father." Goosebumps dotted my arms. Was this his subtle way of letting me know he was responsible and threatening me?

"Indeed." He tilted his head. "In some ways. However, not in the ways I am presently considering."

I didn't want to think about what that meant. "Could we get back on track and talk about my son?"

"Interesting you insist upon claiming him as your son when you gave him away."

My fists curled, and my fingernails dug into my palms. "If I didn't want to claim him, I would've terminated him."

"That is why you will be such a marvelous fit for the task I have in mind." Navid smirked.

My stomach roiled. "What do I have to do?"

He leaned against the edge of his desk. "My sources tell me that you oppose the Posterity Protection and Self-Determination Act."

Hearing the name of the law that required terminations of certain pregnancies made my chest tighten. "Your sources are correct."

"Excellent. I have been studying that law and have determined that it is wasteful."

"Really." How had he come to that conclusion when my mother hadn't even been able to convince URNA's Council of Representatives to repeal the law?

"Yes. Do you not see? Human potential wasted simply because of the age of a mother or a child's birth order."

"Of course I see that."

"I am sure you do, though for different reasons."

I arched an eyebrow. "What other reasons could there be?"

His MD3 buzzed, and he glanced at it. A smirk flitted at the corners of his mouth when he returned the device to his pocket. "Reasons that compel me to ensure you are on my team."

"Even though I don't want to be?"

His smirk grew into a wolfish grin. "Vivica, your skills as a hacker are impressive, and your work on Cater was remarkable."

Cater was the automated system that delivered meals to prisoners, and I'd been forced to upgrade it during my imprisonment in Fortune City. "I didn't have a choice."

"Which is why I know you work well under adversity." He rested his empty glass on his desk. "I had originally intended for you to work in another capacity that would help me maintain my position as secretary general. However, when you refused, I had to find another person to fill that role. Now I see that it is serendipitous. My current proposal is a better fit for you."

"What?"

"I would like you to develop an algorithm that evaluates the DNA of the unborn and determines the child's value in relation to the rest of the population."

I blinked and tried to process the consequences of such a program. "How is this determined?"

"The Peacekeepers will set the standards."

I frowned. "Why is that necessary?" I had a few ideas, but playing dumb would make him believe he had an advantage.

"If we can assess the DNA of the unborn, and the child has superior genes, then we will spare him or her from termination."

That's what I'd thought. "And the others?"

"We shall terminate them, of course."

"If you're still requiring some mothers to terminate, then you've not improved the law."

He shook his head. "I thought you would be delighted with the opportunity to save more children."

I leaned forward. "Your ability to regard them as children and so casually dismiss the lives of the ones who don't meet your standards is disgusting."

"Surely you can acknowledge that some human beings are superior to others."

"No. I can't."

"That viewpoint is astonishing, especially from a woman who possesses such intelligence and beauty."

"None of that makes my life more valuable in God's view."

He narrowed his eyes. "You would bring your god into this matter. I suppose you will tell me that human beings are not valuable because of what they do but because they are made in the image of your god."

"Since you're already acquainted with my beliefs, I see no reason to rehash them, even though they're true."

"Truth is relative. Your mother was not able to impart this to you?"

"Wait. All truth is relative? Isn't that an absolute truth?" I laughed.

Navid's eyes flashed. "Sparring with you is most enjoyable. We shall have a very intriguing work relationship."

I did my best to ignore the desire blazing in his expression, and I fixed my gaze on the window behind him. "What guarantee do I have that if I cooperate, you'll let Isaac go? How much work do I have to do?"

"You will work until I am fully satisfied." He reached out and brushed his hand over my cheek. "Do we have a deal?"

My throat constricted. What was my limit? What was I willing to sacrifice to save my son? What did God expect?

*Trust me. Stand firm.*

Knowing I needed to trust God and practicing trust were two different matters.

*I will deliver you.*

"Perhaps you need some additional motivation, though I had hoped it would not come to this." Navid walked to a screen and brushed his hand across it. "This is a live feed. Your son is with one of my officers now."

Isaac sat in the middle of a floor surrounded by toys. Reaching my hand out, I touched the image of his face. Because he sat in front of a plain white wall on a wooden floor, I couldn't determine where he was. He crawled toward a toy tractor, picked it up, and aimed it at his mouth.

"Officer," Navid said. "Please motivate Miss Wilkins."

Holding a knife, Pauly walked on camera. "Thirty seconds until your son dies." He pulled Isaac into his lap.

My pulse throbbed in my neck. Trust. I wanted to argue with God that I could fix the situation if I complied with Navid's wishes. How bad could it be? I wasn't innocent.

*This is not your battle.*

The words thrummed over and over in my mind. How many times had God asked me to endure things I never thought I could?

Too many. But somehow he'd always brought me through.

And now he was testing me again.

My life wasn't my own.

Neither was Isaac's.

I stood on wobbly legs and faced Navid.

"No."

Navid stared at me. "Perhaps you misspoke."

"No. I did not." I held his gaze, but my heart thudded. *God, this is too much. Don't ask me to do this.*

"Very well. I misjudged you and will need to implement a different strategy." He smirked. "A guard will be here shortly to escort you to your quarters. Officer, kill the child."

"No!" I screamed. "Don't. Please!"

The feed went black as Navid strode from the room and locked the door behind him.

My knees weakened, and I pitched forward, bowing my head. I wanted to call after Navid and surrender.

*I will fight for you.*

"Please spare my son, God," I whispered.

# CHAPTER 32

## *Drake*

Prior to turning herself in, Vivica had tracked Pauly Greenwood to a split-level house on a tree-lined cul-de-sac. I'd flown to meet Ally and Ben Lagarde, and the next morning, we'd started implementing our plan to rescue Isaac.

Ally had dropped Lagarde and me off a street over from Pauly's house, and while we were wearing disguises, we pretended to be two buddies going for a run down the trail that snaked through the woods behind the house. Exercising in the midday heat wasn't very believable—especially since we'd both pitted out our shirts and would've normally taken them off.

But we had to hide our Diablo 87s and tranq guns somehow.

*Work is good.* It gave me something to think about other than the woman I adored being trapped with Zahedi. I clenched my jaw and took longer strides. *God, please protect her. Help us get Isaac safely back to his parents.*

We rounded the bend in the trail, stopped, and watched the house through the gap in the trees. A few minutes later, Ally parked in the driveway and got out. She wore a disguise, clutched a pink tote bag, and waddled up the uneven sidewalk.

"Are you sure about letting her do this?" I asked Lagarde as we veered off the trail and moved closer to the house.

"It's a little late now." He paused behind a tree. "She's tough." His voice had a slight tremor, but he steeled his expression.

Ally rang the doorbell. When no one came, she rapped on the door. "Hello? Anybody home?"

I grinned at her convincing drawl.

We knew Pauly was there, and Ally had to get him to come to the door. Earlier that morning I'd called Harrison, who'd hacked into Pop Management and tracked Pauly's doc for us. Like father, like daughter.

"I'm moving in," I said. "Keep an eye on your wife."

He nodded, and I ran toward the house and pressed up against the bricks.

"Whaddya want?" A man said in a throaty voice. Too many illegal cigarettes.

I poked my head around the corner. Ally smiled at the thin, bald man who hadn't shaved for a few days. He leaned against the doorframe.

She held up the tote. "I'm selling—"

"Not interested." He started to slam the door, but Ally blocked it with her foot.

"My jewelry is perfect for the special lady in your life. I use only the finest materials."

"I ain't got no lady."

"No one? Not even your mother? Or sister? An aunt. How about a cousin?"

"I said no one. Youse got a hearing problem?"

I bolted toward the deck that had weeds growing through the wooden slats. When I peered through the patio door, I could see Isaac on the living room floor, surrounded by a bunch of toys. I slid the door open, tiptoed inside, and almost choked at the dirty diaper smell. Isaac crawled toward a red truck, oblivious to his stench.

"Look, I ain't got time to waste on whatever spiel youse got for me. I'm busy." Pauly clutched a knife behind his back.

"Please sir, I need the money for my little one."

He sighed. "If I transfer a few bucks to your cash card, will you scram?"

"Yes!" Ally clasped her hands. "Thank you, sir!"

I unloaded a dart from my tranq gun and closed my hand around it. *Forgive me Alma, Gabe, and Vivica.* I leaned over, pricked Isaac's back with the dart at the same time I put my hand over his mouth. Fearing an overdose, I yanked the dart out quickly. He squirmed for a few seconds but went limp. I checked his pulse—steady.

"Oww!" Ally shrieked and doubled over.

Pauly used several curse words as verbs, nouns, and adjectives.

My heart stopped but started beating again when I realized Pauly had shoved the knife in his back pocket—and not in Ally.

I pressed Isaac to my chest, stepped over the toys, and headed for the door.

"Sorry. I'm okay," Ally said. "Probably a false alarm. Been having contractions for weeks."

As I closed the patio door, Pauly was frantically transferring money to a cash card. I sprinted off of the deck, through the woods, and back down the trail.

A few minutes later, Lagarde caught up with me. "She hit Greenwood with a tranq dart when he wasn't looking and is on the way to our rendezvous point."

I blew out a breath and slowed my pace. "Thank God."

"Told you she was tough."

I stopped and held Isaac out to Lagarde. The kid was cute and not heavy, but the smell was killing me. "He looks like you."

For a second, Ben stared at the sleeping boy. Then he took him and kissed the top of his head. "Nice to meet you, little buddy." Isaac's eyes fluttered open. Lagarde gave me a sideways glance, but I didn't miss the tears.

We started down the trail, and our couriers vibrated in unison. I read the message. "Looks like we'd better get across the border ASAP. The Warriors are declaring independence tonight."

# CHAPTER 33

## *Vivica*

After several agonizing minutes that dragged like hours, a short man with wispy hair that barely covered his scalp opened the door to Navid's office and looked me up and down. "Let's go." He motioned for me to follow, and I stumbled after him, tears blurring my vision.

My son was dead because of me.

We left the office area and took an elevator into the lower level. Then we passed through an arched doorway and into a hallway with mosaics on each side. A staircase with wrought iron railing gave the room an imposing and cold appearance.

"Did they really kill my son? Please. Tell me. I have to know."

Wispy Hair stopped and turned. "I have no idea what you're talking about."

I stifled a whimper. *Please God, come through for Isaac.*

We took the stairs and passed through two doors the guard unlocked with his biochip. Each time the door closed behind us, a frisson traveled my spine. Our footsteps echoed on the tiled hallway that led to a massive wooden and iron door at the end.

Wispy Hair withdrew an old-fashioned skeleton key from his pocket and unlocked the door that lacked exploitable technology. He shoved me inside and when the lock clinked, I wished I could die.

My eyes adjusted to the darkness.

A canopied, four-poster bed stood in the middle of the room. My legs shook, but I propelled myself across the room where a sliver of sunlight peered through the curtains. I pushed aside the gray curtains that coordinated with the bed's canopy.

As if I were wading underwater, I crossed to the table next to the bed and turned on the lamp.

*God, help me.*

I entered the adjoining bathroom and inspected it. A cluster of white-wicked candles sat next to a soaking tub along with various perfumes and lotions.

Checking the bathroom window, I discovered more bars. I returned to the bedroom and searched for cameras and listening devices—and found both.

Gathering lotion bottles from the bathroom, I knocked the remaining ones into the bathtub, and they rolled and scattered. I rushed into the bedroom and lobbed a bottle of Vanilla Dream body lotion at the camera in the corner. The first time I missed, and the bottle spurted open and left a dent in the wall. Lotion slithered downward and gathered in a scented blob on the wood floor. I chucked a second bottle and made contact. The camera sparked, quelling my death wish.

I did the same for the camera that monitored the bathroom. Then, I removed a listening device from the lamp beside the bed, stalked to the toilet, tossed it in, and flushed.

I returned to the bedroom, unplugged the lamp, tossed the shade on the bed, and felt a sting on the back of my neck. I slapped my skin, but when I inspected my hand, I didn't see a mosquito body smashed in a smear of blood.

Gripping the lamp like a baseball bat, I stood at the door ready for anyone who entered, but my knees wobbled, and my breath came in short gasps. A curtain of darkness began to obstruct my vision, and I pitched forward on my knees. The lamp hitting the floor barely registered above the buzzing in my ears.

One thought pummeled my mind.

It wasn't a mosqui—

# Chapter 34

### *Vivica*

I awoke under a canopy of gray. My parched tongue was pasted to the roof of my mouth. I sat up and breathed slowly, fighting the suffocating hopelessness that threatened to overtake me. I could *not* let the man who'd ordered my son's death defeat me.

No one had changed my clothes, though someone had replaced the lamp and camera. And cleaned up the lotion. I swung my feet over the side of the bed, but when they hit the floor, I had to grab one of the posters to steady myself. The bathroom had been cleaned with the same precision. The lotion bottles had been replaced in their spot by the tub.

The message was clear. I had to comply, or they'd drug me. What I'd thought was a mosquito had probably been a miniature drone.

My pulse raced in time with my throbbing head, so after lapping water from the faucet, I returned to the bed and reclined against the soft pillows.

Though light streamed in through the window, I wanted to sleep again, but I had to think of an escape plan. There had to be a way out of here. Some sort of weakness. But what could I do with cameras monitoring me or without access to technology?

My doc—or rather, my alias's doc. I reached into my back pocket and removed the device, but I groaned when I realized all service was blocked. No incoming or outgoing calls or messages.

Of any kind. No wonder they'd allowed me to keep it.

I squeezed the bridge of my nose. A wave of despair choked off my breath, and I grabbed two handfuls of hair. I had to think about anything but a madman butchering my son—unless Ben and Ally had found him in time.

Clinging to that hope and gritting my teeth, I vowed to keep fighting—for Isaac's sake. So, I turned my attention to the information from Faith's MD3 that I'd transferred to my doc from my courier.

She'd saved an article on the best vacation spots in the South Pacific, an article on rhinoplasty—like she needed a nose job—and an article from an obscure research journal by Dr. Colin Gates entitled, "The Use of Nanobots in Weather Modification."

My heart thudded. Weather modification? I skimmed the article. Had Dr. Gates found a better use for nanobots than in medicine?

"…Recent breakthroughs in nanotechnology that allow weather modification…scientists have moved beyond the days of cloud seeding…nanobots give the government the power to prevent large-scale disasters…reroute tornadoes and hurricanes to minimize destruction…weaponize weather to deter enemies…"

My heart somersaulted, and I stood and paced.

Weaponized weather would be perfect, wouldn't it? A massive hurricane or tornado, controlled by nanobots, engineered by humans, and designed to cause massive destruction and casualties—in a newly formed country with vast coastlines.

One well-timed natural disaster would be enough to make the new country surrender and beg for global intervention. No wonder Faith wanted Drake off the beach and out of the region. It was hurricane season.

A storm was brewing, and I had to find a way to stop it.

# Chapter 35

## *Vivica*

My stomach roared in spite of the horror that surrounded me. How could I be hungry? My eyes fell on the minibar across from my bed. I stood and fought a swell of dizziness. Staggering to the snack bar, I opened the refrigerator.

Empty.

I searched the cabinets surrounding the refrigerator, and they were mostly empty—except for several jars half filled with dark leaves.

I picked up a container and examined it. Tobacco. My appetite vanished. I hadn't misread Navid's lustful gaze. If part of his tobacco collection resided in this room, then he expected to spend time here with me.

I returned the jar to the shelf, flopped back on the bed, and battled nausea. My hand bounced against the pocket of my cargo shorts, which made a crinkling sound.

It couldn't be. I still had the samples of contaminated flour that Drake and I had taken from Brent's Bakery. I froze when an idea pelted my brain. Could I pull it off without the camera catching me? Would there be a high enough concentration of joy dust in the flour to mess with Navid's mind so he'd willingly let me go? Would inhaling joy dust make a difference in how it influenced a person?

I stumbled into the bathroom for another drink. When I returned to the bedroom, I shut off the lamp, curled up in a fetal position under the covers, and worked my hand into my pocket. Removing the pouches, I rubbed the bag between my fingers to see if the flour was still powdery. It was. Giddiness bubbled in my chest.

Perfect.

\*\*\*

I'd have to be quick. I lay still in the bed, pretended to nap, and rehearsed the plan. When I'd knocked out the camera before, it had been about thirty seconds before the drone found and sedated me. It had taken another thirty seconds for the drugs to take effect.

At most. That was probably a generous estimate.

I prayed sixty seconds would be enough to contaminate Navid's jars of tobacco and get away from the cabinet. I tried to picture how many jars were in the cabinet. At least five.

I chewed my lip. This plan could take time—days of the drug accumulating in his body, and I suppressed a shiver when I imagined what I might have to endure while I waited.

But I didn't have a better idea.

I sat up and closed my hand around the wide candle sitting on the nightstand. I left the lamp off. The lack of light might confuse the miniature drone.

And it might not.

Leaping off the bed, I tossed the candle at the camera in the corner. It fell from the ceiling, and I rushed over and stomped on it.

I raced to the cabinet, wrenched it open, and unscrewed the first jar. I dug a bag of flour from my shorts, dumped part of it into the tobacco, and stirred it with my finger.

I moved on to the next jar.

And the next.

Then I heard the buzz.

Moving from side to side in hopes of confusing the drone, I grabbed another jar and another packet of flour from my pocket.

A sting pierced my neck.

*Please, help me God.*

I replaced the jar and grabbed the last container. My fingers shook as I unscrewed the lid.

Not now. I would *not* pass out.

I emptied the remaining flour into the tobacco and replaced the lid as a black curtain encroached upon the edge of my vision.

No.

I shoved the jar back toward the shelf, but my grip weakened, and the container slipped from my grasp, shattering against the marble countertop. The curtain neared the center of my vision. As I swiped the broken glass and tobacco, a sliver sliced my palm.

I swayed and stumbled toward the bed and then reached for the post. My bloody fingers curled around it, and I swung myself onto the bed as darkness engulfed me.

\*\*\*

I opened my eyes, sat up, and looked around the room. Twilight gave the room a ghostly glow. The broken glass and tobacco leaves had been removed. Someone had bandaged my hand.

My head throbbed. Rubbing my temples, I gazed at the camera that had been replaced. Its red light blinked in victory. I stumbled to the bathroom and splashed cold water on my face. When I came out, I opened the cabinet door.

All of the half-empty tobacco jars had been replaced with full, sealed containers.

My heart skidded.

"God, why are you doing this to me?" I hissed and stumbled back to the bed.

Falling face down, I sobbed into the pillow. The contaminated flour had been my last hope of defeating Navid. Now what did I have?

*Stand firm. I will deliver you.*

"How? Like you delivered Isaac?" Another round of tears flowed, and my swollen throat ached so badly I couldn't breathe. Navid had killed my child and would never pay for what he'd done. I slammed my fist against the mattress.

*Trust me.*

Drawing a shuddering breath, I clamped my hands over my ears, as if that could somehow shut out God's voice. Did God expect me to let my enemy have his way?

*** 

A little later when the drugs' effects had lessened and my anger had dissipated into numb acceptance, I faced the camera. "I'm hungry. Could someone send food...and some books?"

I collapsed on the bed and fought drooping eyelids. Allowing myself to be drugged again had been a stupid idea, especially since I needed to be alert.

Twenty minutes later, the door opened, and Wispy Hair wheeled in a cart that appeared as if it belonged in a fine hotel with room service. A bud vase with a red rose sat next to a silver tray, a pitcher of ice water, and a stack of novels. He left, locking the door behind him.

I staggered to the cart and lifted the lid. Vegetable stir-fry, rice, and a fruit salad. I took the tray to my bed, and after a moment's hesitation, I took the food to the bathroom. I rinsed the fruit and vegetables and devoured them but left the rice untouched because I couldn't let them contaminate *me* with joy dust.

I'd just replaced my tray on the cart and started to read when the door opened. Wispy Hair stepped in. "His lordship will be visiting in one hour. You are to shower, and the beauty team will be here in twenty minutes to prepare you."

The fruits and vegetables nearly made an appearance, and I clutched the book to my chest.

"If I refuse?"

Wispy Hair paled. "I don't recommend it."

"Be specific."

"His lordship expects his women to comply, or they will find themselves in much more deplorable circumstances—where they will be used to satisfy *many* men."

I tried not to flinch. But I did. "Okay then. I'll be ready."

# CHAPTER 36

## *Vivica*

A man with a half-shaven head styled my hair that he'd dyed my natural golden color, and a woman with lavender hair and a tongue piercing did my makeup. What was most remarkable to me was that they did their work silently and efficiently without bumping into each other.

"You're both good at this. I'm impressed." I longed to curl up in a ball and hide, but instead, I sat rigid and tried to forget what was about to happen by making insipid comments.

Silence.

My stomach churned. "How many women do you do this for on a regular basis?"

The woman dabbed some blush onto my cheeks. "We've been a team for many years. This is our first assignment at this location."

"Do not ask any more questions," the man said. "We have been instructed to keep our communication minimal."

"Okay," I whispered. I didn't care to see a poison drone disguised as a mosquito take them out.

Looking around the room, I searched for anything I could use as a weapon. My eyes fell on a pair of tweezers. If I could steal them without the cameras noticing, I could jam them into Navid's neck. Yet that plan could go horribly wrong if Navid overpowered me—something I guessed would be easy for him.

Before I could make a move, she secured the tweezers in a bag and opened a tube of crimson lipstick. After they finished, the makeup artist paused at the door. "You'll find clothing choices in the wardrobe." She glanced at her watch. "Per our instructions, we have left you ten minutes to dress." She averted her eyes. "Good luck."

Luck wasn't what I needed.

I went to the closet and picked the most modest thing I could find—a black sequined dress that would fall several inches above my knee but was cut too low. The only shoes were high heels. I chose a pair of silver peep toes that had the lowest heels, at about three inches.

While standing at the closet with my back to the camera, I tried to remove the metal hook on one of the hangers, but I couldn't detach it from the wood. With trembling hands, I replaced the hanger. It was too risky anyway.

Once I dressed, I sat in the chair next to the closet and waited. My skin grew clammy, and my breaths came in short gasps.

*Please, God. Help me.*

The door opened, and Navid entered. A slow smile spread across his face when he saw me. "Good evening, sweet Vivica."

"Good evening." My voice caught.

"Stand up. Let me look at you."

I obeyed and even did a twirl, and when I did, my breath hitched. Drake had always told me I was a terrible actress. Would I be able to keep my composure?

"Wonderful. My team did an excellent job. Though when they have a beautiful canvas to begin with, it is not difficult."

I clenched my teeth and sat back down.

"You have nothing to say? You cannot thank me for the

pampering? I find that a pity. I was hoping for a stimulating conversation."

"You kill my son and expect stimulating conversation from a grieving mother?"

He chuckled. "It is interesting you still consider yourself the child's mother."

"Giving him up for adoption doesn't mean I stopped loving him." My voice cracked. I should never have refused Navid. I bit the inside of my cheek and focused on that pain instead of the ache ripping my heart in two.

He sat in the chair next to mine, then reached over and stroked my cheek. "Sparring with you is always most enjoyable. Perhaps it will provide a distraction for you."

I took a deep breath. If he wanted to spar, then we'd spar. Anything to keep *him* preoccupied was an answer to prayer. "Did you assassinate my mother?"

He rested his elbows on the chair's arms and steepled his fingers. "How could I have done that? The beautiful Genevieve died of an aneurysm."

"You didn't have someone tamper with her biochip's data?"

"That is a farfetched and fascinating story, but it would be difficult to prove, since I do not have the power to cause an aneurysm. Even if you could verify someone tampered with the data, I doubt the Council of World Peacekeepers, or the media, would be interested." He stood and walked to the cabinet that contained his tobacco jars.

I hated to admit to myself he was probably right—since the media only reported what URNA's government and the Peacekeepers allowed.

Navid opened the cabinet door. "I have some news." Tapping his chin, he scanned his options. "May I interest you in some of the world's finest tobacco?"

"No, thank you."

"Ah, yes. How could I forget that you do not enjoy such indulgences?" He selected a jar. "This blend is my favorite." He filled a pipe that had a snake coiled around the bowl and moved back to his chair. "Errol tells me that you attempted to contaminate my tobacco."

I bit my lip and forced humility into my tone. "My apologies." *That it didn't work.*

"My security team is constantly on guard because I have faced many assassination attempts." Amusement flickered in his eyes. "However, this is the first time anyone has tried to control my mind. I trust you will abstain from such nonsense from now on."

"Of course." I bowed my head. "Rebellion is fruitless." I'd meant for my words to appease Navid, but when I heard them spoken aloud, the truth blindsided me.

Rebellion—against God—*was* fruitless.

"It may comfort you to know that your plan, while extremely clever, would not have worked." He smiled. "The concentration of joy dust in the flour was simply too low and the amount inadequate."

I gritted my teeth while he lit the pipe.

"Now then, have you heard the news?

"How would I?" Grateful for a new topic, I raised my head and gazed into his dark eyes. "My doc doesn't have incoming or outgoing service."

"Of course." He removed his MD3, swiped his thumb over the screen, and projected an article onto the wall.

I skimmed the headline. "Coastal Plain Region Declares Independence from URNA."

My heart thudded. The Warriors had done it. That bit of news bolstered my waning hope.

"You have nothing to say?"

"I don't know how to respond. You could be trying to trick me with a fake headline."

"I am not deceiving you." He swiped his MD3 again and revealed another newspaper headline, "Coastal Plain Region Becomes Independent Coastal Republic." He showed me several more.

"That's quite a blow to the Peacekeepers." I crossed my arms and shifted into agent mode. "What're you going to do?"

His eyes gleamed. "Let nature take its course." He took a draw on the pipe.

Was that his way of admitting to weather modification? "What does that mean? You're not concerned you've lost control over part of URNA?"

"It is nothing you need to worry about because ultimately this so-called republic will fail and beg for my council's help. You are safe with me, because I always protect my treasures."

"From what?"

"All manner of danger. Natural disasters. Weapons of mass destruction. While I enjoy discussing this subject with you, this cat and mouse game is growing tiresome. Ask what you want to ask."

"Do the Peacekeepers have the power to modify the weather?"

He laughed. "Sweet Vivica, I am flattered that you think I possess such god-like powers."

*Ugh.* "Answer me."

"So demanding." He narrowed his eyes. "Yet I suspect you already know the answer, so there is little to be gained by continuing this conversation." He stood. "It has been most enjoyable visiting with you. I will be back tomorrow."

He strode to the door, knocked, and waited for the guard to open it. Navid glanced back over his shoulder. "I hope you will not concern yourself with what we have discussed. I would hate for the burden of worry to mar your beauty."

He closed the door, and I gripped the bedpost.

*Thank you, God.*

# CHAPTER 37

## *Vivica*

The next afternoon, my beauty team visited again in anticipation of Navid's visit, and the makeup artist battled with my puffy eyelids and red eyes. I'd spent the day sobbing and praying for the strength to let God fight for me.

Once I was dressed and ready, Navid entered. "Good evening." He looked me up and down. "That dress is stunning."

I hated the way the hunter green material clung to my body. "Thank you." I met his gaze.

"Are you still angry with me, Vivica?" A smile spread across his face.

My pulse whooshed in my neck. "Strange that a man of your intelligence has to ask." I did nothing to hide the coldness in my tone.

He chuckled. "I have some news that might change your attitude and make you more cooperative."

I doubted it. "What's that?" My voice shook, and my pulse thumped.

He swiped his MD3, and the feed with Isaac that Navid had shown me a couple of days earlier projected on the wall.

"No." I covered my eyes and backed away. "I will *not* watch my son be slaughtered." My legs weakened.

"Sweet Vivica, I am not a barbarian." He gently pried my hands from my face and held them at my side. "Watch."

I focused on the footage and didn't allow myself to recoil at his soft touch.

A doorbell rang. Pauly, who was holding a knife to Isaac's throat, froze and let go of my son. Then someone pounded on the door.

"Hello? Anybody home?" a woman yelled in a thick drawl.

Isaac crawled away as Pauly stood, shoved the knife in his back pocket, and walked out of the camera's view. "Whaddya want?"

The woman tried to sell him some jewelry while Pauly grew more and more annoyed. Could the woman be Ally? I wished the camera had been placed differently.

My hand flew to my mouth when a man I didn't recognize crept into the room, jabbed something in Isaac's back, and slapped his big hand over my son's mouth. I cringed when Isaac went limp and prayed the man was Ben in disguise, but he seemed too tall and muscular.

The woman shrieked just before the man took Isaac and left.

"Sorry. I'm okay," the woman said. "Probably a false alarm. Been having contractions for weeks." So the woman could've been Ally. Hope began to grow inside me, but I wasn't ready to let myself accept it.

Navid stopped the video. "I hope this will lessen your burden. Your makeup artist told me how hard she had to work to make you presentable, and my heart broke when I saw the camera footage of you grieving so heavily."

His heart *broke?* No. I couldn't think about Navid being capable of compassion. My thoughts raced. "Did the people who took my son get away?"

"Yes." Navid lifted his chin. "We have lost track of the child."

I prayed it was true—though I was afraid to believe it. Still, relief persisted and pulsed through my body.

"In spite of this setback, I believe I will be able to convince you to work on my DNA project without using your child as leverage."

God had asked me to trust him, and now I needed to believe he had come through with an answer to my prayers—and that he'd continue fighting for me.

Which meant it might be wiser to work *with* Navid—or pretend to do so without compromising my principles. "If—I'm going to work for you, I'd…well, would you consider letting me work on your weather modification program?" I leaned closer and rested a tentative hand on Navid's arm. "I'd like you to share the details with me."

His black eyes sparkled. "Of course, if this will make you happy, it would give me great pleasure to show you. However, I must take your request to work on the project under consideration."

"Thank you." I smiled. "Weather modification is fascinating."

When the guard answered Navid's knock, he spoke in low tones and then motioned for the guard to enter. The man had a swastika tattooed on his neck, and when he stepped close to handcuff me, cigarette smoke emanated from his entire being.

"Please forgive the handcuffs and the fact that Errol must accompany us," Navid said.

"I understand."

We entered the dark hallway, and Navid led the way into a wood-paneled elevator. "As you will remember, I am in the process of moving the Council of World Peacekeepers Headquarters to the Middle Eastern Region of the Republic of Asia. I feel much more comfortable being near my home. North America simply is not to my liking." The elevator began to ascend. "You will be making the trip with me to my new home, and you will find the luxurious accommodations pale in comparison to what my current residence offers."

I stifled a gasp and tried not to allow dread to creep into my expression. "When?"

He eyed me with amusement. "Soon."

The elevator door slid open.

"Welcome to the command center for the Strategic Weather Enhancement and Engineering Program," Navid said. "Or as our scientists affectionately know it, SWEEP."

Two rows of computers were arranged in stadium style seating in front of a large radar screen of North America and South America. In spite of the multiple workstations, only two men and a woman sat at computers. I studied the radar. The Coastal Republic's new border was highlighted in orange, and a gigantic green cell, indicating rainfall, hovered over most of the new country.

"More rain," I said.

"Flooding has become quite the problem throughout URNA, has it not?" Navid's eyes gleamed.

I stared at him. "And this command center is the cause?" We began walking down a set of stairs that led to offices.

"Of course. Cloud seeding is a technique that has been used for many, many years—even before URNA was formed after the Second Civil War. The Council of World Peacekeepers has perfected cloud seeding and added enhancements to help control the population."

I winced, and my eyes widened when I remembered the gossiping woman in the Great Plains Region who had told Drake and me that people suspected the virus was spread through water. "The Peacekeepers are using *rainfall* to spread GPV?"

"Excellent deduction. The cloud seeding has served two purposes. Excessive precipitation causes flooding and ensures maximum exposure to the smart virus transmitted through water—"

"Which means URNA needs help from the Peacekeepers because of sickness and flooding."

"Indeed." He tilted his head. "However, if citizens obeyed the law and took their biochips, they have nothing to fear from GPV."

"What about the flooding?"

He rested his hand on my arm and stroked the area over my fake biochip with his thumb. "Errol has informed me your chip is a counterfeit. We must remedy that situation as soon as possible, because I could not bear the thought of losing you to such a violent illness."

I gave him a wobbly smile.

A door opened at the top of the stairs, and a woman wearing a short skirt sauntered toward us. When she came closer, I drew in a sharp breath.

"Faith?" My mind swirled with all of the things I wanted to scream at her, but I had to stay focused on gathering information.

She flipped her bottle-blond hair and smiled at Navid. "I have an update for you whenever you have a chance to meet."

He looked her up and down, but his face remained expressionless. "Contact my secretary, and schedule a time."

Her face fell. "I will." She turned to leave without even a glimpse in my direction, and I couldn't restrain my fury.

"How could you put your own nephew in danger?" I shouted. "And impersonate Ophelia?"

She froze, slowly turned, and wrapped her arms around her waist.

"Shall we carry on?" Navid put his hand on the small of my back. "Ms. Lagarde is very busy, and I have more to show you."

I bristled but softened my tone. "Please. I *need* answers."

She looked straight at me with hollow eyes. "Nothing—not even family—should get in the way of peace." She ducked her head as if she expected Navid to retaliate, but instead, he gave her an indulgent half-smile, showed her his back, and guided me toward an office. Faith scurried up the stairs and out of the command center.

Pity replaced my anger. *God, help her.*

Through the office window, I saw a woman sitting in front of a computer. Navid tapped on the doorframe, and the woman stood and bowed. Her shoulder-length white hair was tipped with black. Two copper spikes dangled from her earlobes. "Jillian, please explain the finer details of SWEEP to Miss Wilkins."

"Yes, your lordship." She closed her office door behind her and motioned up at the screen with the radar. "As you can see, we have a map of URNA."

"And the Coastal Republic." It seemed like a small victory that the Peacekeepers were forced to acknowledge my new country.

"For now," Navid said.

"Of course." I lowered my eyes.

"Anyway," Jillian walked up the stairs to an empty computer station, made a few strokes on the keyboard, zoomed in, and displayed the east coast of URNA and the Atlantic Ocean. "We're in the middle of hurricane season, and so far it has been an extremely active one. Part of my job is to monitor storms and assess their potential for destruction."

"The larger the storm, the better?" I asked as Navid and I moved closer to her.

"Correct." She pointed to a cell in the Atlantic. "I've been watching the data on this storm all day."

"Where does the data come from?" I asked.

"The Azar 646 drone collects data from the hurricane's eye."

"The drone is named after my late mother." Navid's eyes shone with pride.

Jillian flashed him a smile before continuing. "Our scientists fly planes through the storm and into the hurricane's eye. Then they release the Azars to collect data inside the storm." She turned to Navid, and regret filled her expression. "I've been studying the data and don't think this is the storm we want, but you'll be the first to know if something changes."

Navid pursed his lips. "That is not what I want to hear."

The color drained from Jillian's face. "Your lordship, I apologize, but we want a storm that will have the most impact, so patience is critical."

He lunged for Jillian, and I sucked in a breath. *Thwack.* She hung her head and rubbed her cheek.

"It is not necessary to lecture me on patience." His eyes flashed.

"Yes, your lordship."

"Continue," he said.

Jillian raised her head. "When I find a storm that has the most potential of becoming a Category 4 or 5 hurricane, we'll release another Azar into the eye of the storm. This drone will be filled with millions of nanobots that will be released and programmed to steer the storm in the direction we desire."

"The Coastal Republic." I bit my lip and avoided looking at Navid.

"Yes." She bent over her keyboard and made a few strokes. "We can even cause the nanobots to spawn and guide tornadoes once the hurricane makes landfall."

"This is all fascinating." And extremely horrifying.

"Thank you, Jillian." Navid rested his hand on my shoulder and guided me up the steps.

As we neared the top of the stairs, I noticed a loose tile on one of them, and within seconds, a plan formed in my mind.

When I crossed over the step, I caught my foot against the tile and tripped. I pitched forward and crashed onto the floor, making sure to land hard on my wrist. I clutched my wrist and moaned.

Navid's face reddened, and he snapped his fingers. Errol came running and knelt beside me.

"I hope I didn't break it," I wailed. "I need a doctor."

Errol looked up at Navid, who scowled. "What are you waiting for? Fetch my physician." Errol hurried away, and Navid fixed his gaze on Jillian, standing at the bottom of the stairs. "Why is this tile loose?" He pointed at the offending tile, which was now even farther out of place.

"I-I don't know, your lordship." She motioned over her shoulder. "My office is that way, and I rarely go upstairs or use that exit. I'm sorry, but I hadn't noticed."

"Do you not care about safety?" Navid stomped down the stairs, and Jillian darted toward her office. *Protect her, God.* I should've anticipated he'd take his wrath out on someone else before I'd pulled my little stunt. Shoving away the guilt, I removed my doc from my pocket and checked for outgoing service.

It was working.

A door slammed, and Navid pounded it. "How dare you hide from me?" He let loose a string of curses while I worked as quickly as I could to make the message I wanted to send secure. I didn't want the government to be able to find and censor it. My courier would've been safer, but the doc was better than nothing.

Navid jiggled the doorknob and then continued to pound and swear.

```
Strategic Weather Enhancement and Engineering
Program at Peacekeepers' HQ is weaponizing
hurricanes and tornadoes with intent to destroy
CR. V. Wilkins
```

I signed my own name because if the government or Peacekeepers intercepted it, they'd already know it was me. Thinking quickly, I sent the message to as many people's docs as I could because I couldn't risk compromising their couriers. Then, I deleted all traces of it.

Navid turned as I stuffed the doc back into my pocket. When I saw his stormy eyes, I wanted to shrink through the tile floor.

I swallowed and clutched my wrist. "It's not Jillian's fault that I'm clumsy."

"She should never have run into her office like a naughty child."

"Someone can fix the tile."

He strode out into the hallway. "Errol should have returned by now." He came back and knelt beside me, and his angry expression melted away. "How is your pain?" My stomach knotted as he brushed the hair back from my face, and it took every ounce of self-control I possessed not to recoil at the tender look in his eyes.

# Chapter 38

## *Drake*

I burst out of my room in the Mine and sprinted down the corridor. Though Jethro had given me a hard time about wanting to return to the Warriors, he'd let me back in after I'd passed three separate polygraphs—but I still had to prove myself if I wanted back on the leadership team.

Vivica had sent a distress message to my doc, and adrenaline pulsed through my veins. Communicating had to have put her in danger, and thinking about what Zahedi might do to her made my blood pressure spike.

*God, keep her safe.*

I thought about her message. Weaponizing weather was far-fetched. But it had to be why Faith had wanted me to leave the beach house.

I rapped on the door of Harrison's private quarters. "Open up. It's important."

The door swung open, and Harrison gaped at me. "What's wrong?"

With a shaking hand, I shoved the doc at him. He took a pair of glasses from his pocket, read the message, and frowned.

"Is it possible?" I asked.

"I think so." He stared into space for so long that I was about to scream at him to look alive when he answered, "Nanobots could be used in weather modification." He handed back my doc.

I took out my courier and started typing a message. "I'm calling Jethro."

***

"The way I see it," Jethro said to the leadership team a half-hour later in the Mine's boardroom, "we got no choice but to destroy the Peacekeepers' headquarters."

Jethro had allowed me to come, but I didn't have a vote.

Harrison stood and looked as if he were about to lunge across the table and use Jethro's gold chain to choke him. "Not with my daughter in there, you're not."

"No kidding." I made eye contact with each of the men who sat at the table. "It's reckless and stupid. And could cause another war. Kill innocent civilians—"

"You got a better idea, speak up." Jethro scowled at me. Okay, not a smart move calling Jethro's idea stupid—even if it was.

"We don't even know that destroying the building would stop them," Harrison said. "They could have another command center housed elsewhere. They could even be underground, like we are. We need to know for sure. Otherwise, we tip our hand by going in."

Jethro looked at Liam. "You got an opinion?"

"I'm not sure it's necessary to provoke the Peacekeepers by attacking their headquarters. We've already done enough to upset them with secession," Liam said. "We're lucky there's been no retaliation—yet."

Two of the other guys murmured in agreement.

Even though Liam and I still weren't speaking, I shot him a

grateful look before looking around the table at all of the men. "Let me investigate," I said. "I'll get the information you all need to make a solid plan."

"How you gonna do that?" Jethro asked.

The plan forming in my mind was crazy, but I had to try. I crossed my arms. "I'll let Faith recruit me."

***

Early the next morning, I returned to Mom and Oliver's beach house, and that afternoon, I walked along the shore, praying for Vivica's safety and waiting for Faith to contact me—or show up. I'd sent her a message saying I'd reconsidered her recruitment offer.

A seagull screeched, and the sky was bright blue, making it hard to believe there was a storm out there somewhere that might be headed for us.

The foreboding I'd carried—and tried to ignore—for weeks reminded me of its presence.

"Hey!" Faith sauntered toward me and then broke into a run. Her short dress clung to her curves in the right places and showed off her toned legs. She'd dyed her hair blond, which I hated. She looked much better as a brunette.

She threw her arms around me. "I'm so glad you decided to listen." She gazed up at me like she wanted me to kiss her. "We're going to make a great team. I've missed you."

"I've missed you too." I swallowed, let go of her, and took a step back from temptation. I didn't need to go that far. "What's next?" I asked.

She smiled and took my arm. "I'll fill you in on the plane."

***

Once we were in the air on our way to Peacekeepers' Headquarters in the Atlantic Region, Faith handed me a glass of diet soda—the only kind the government allowed companies to manufacture. I took a drink and remembered why I shunned chemical-filled stuff.

I set it aside. "Tell me what I'm helping with, or are you going to keep me in suspense?" I grinned and relaxed back in my leather seat.

She winked, turned, and cracked open a soda for herself. While she had her back to me, I reached into my pocket, slipped my courier out, and turned on the record function.

"The Strategic Weather Enhancement and Engineering Program," she said, "has been in the works for several years, and Secretary General Zahedi thinks it's one of the most effective strategies for implementing peace." She finished pouring her drink and sat in the seat opposite me. She crossed her legs, allowing her skirt to edge upward.

I cleared my throat. "Since Project Harmony was a failure." I wanted to see if she knew about Fortune City.

Faith narrowed her eyes. "What?"

"Never mind, darling. Continue." Maybe *darling* was a little much, but I had to sell this act.

She tucked a strand of hair behind her ear. "Anyway, the SWEEP command center is housed at Peacekeepers' Headquarters in North America. The secretary general is planning to move headquarters overseas to be closer to his home, but SWEEP will remain in North America, because the Peacekeepers have a location on every continent." She took a sip.

"Cool," I said. "So what do you have for me?"

"Well, I'd love to have you work on SWEEP, but unfortunately, there's been a change of plans." She leveled a gun at me, and I raised my hands.

Good grief. Why hadn't I seen that coming? "Don't do this, Faith."

"Relax."

"That's impossible when I have a weapon pointed at me." Eventually, my courier would stop recording and send the file as a message to Liam—if Faith didn't find it first. But I wanted a chance for him to know what had happened. Not that he'd care.

"It's just a tranq gun. You're too valuable to kill."

"That's very flattering." I should never have fastened my seatbelt. Now I couldn't even try to overpower her.

"I did love you," she said. "But after you met Vivica, everything changed."

It had. I'd tried to fight my feelings but had failed miserably. "I never cheated on you."

"Not intentionally, but you lost interest in us."

I bristled and dropped my hands. "You accuse me of cheating when you betrayed an entire organization? Not to mention your family." I held her gaze and unbuckled the seatbelt.

"I did what I thought was right—like I'm doing now."

I lunged as she fired. When the dart pricked my chest, I yanked it free and staggered forward. But my muscles slackened, and darkness replaced Faith's smirking face.

# CHAPTER 39

## *Vivica*

When the doctor had come scrambling into the command center, he'd determined my wrist was not broken, but I'd been so convincing about the pain even Jethro would've been impressed. The doctor had wrapped my wrist and given orders to keep ice on it before sending me back to my quarters. The relief on Navid's face had seemed genuine.

The next afternoon, I lounged on my bed and iced my wrist while facing the dread that gnawed me.

Navid was crazy, drunk with power, and unstable. But the flash of caring I'd seen made me view him as a person with a soul that would spend eternity in Heaven or Hell. I hated that. I *needed* to think of him as a monster. Navid deserved to go to Hell for everything he was doing.

I drew a pillow to my chest. It was possible that Navid's servants had poisoned my food with enough joy dust that I was susceptible to mind control, but I'd been careful about what I'd eaten.

Perhaps God had thwarted my attempt at poisoning Navid's tobacco because this battle wasn't mine—it was God's. And he wanted to fight for me. Instead, I'd rebelled and tried to fix the situation on my own. I was sure it was okay to take action sometimes, but this time, God had told me to stand firm. He'd deliver me.

What if my freedom didn't come in the way I expected, and God was using Navid's fondness of me—however warped it was—as protection?

I slid off my bed and dropped to my knees. "Lord, I praise you because you're my faithful deliverer and protector. I hate this. I'm so scared. But you can change hearts. You died for Navid like you died for me." Tears stung my eyes. "Neither one of us deserves your grace and mercy, but you've offered it." I took a deep breath. "Help me be a light to Navid. And God, I'd still like to get out of here, so if you could work on that, I'd appreciate it."

\*\*\*

An hour later, Navid entered my room. "How is your injury?" He strode to the chair where I sat, grabbed my wrist, unwrapped it, and examined the bruise.

"It's fine."

"Excellent." He walked to the barred window, pushed the curtain aside, and looked out.

"Are you okay?" I rewrapped the bandage.

"Yes." He rubbed the back of his neck and cleared his throat before he strode to the cabinet and filled his pipe. "You should be thankful you are an only child."

"Why?"

"Sibling rivalry. One should never underestimate its power."

Even though most of me struggled to care, relating to Navid as one human being to another was something God would want me to do. Plus, it had the added benefit of keeping Navid focused on the issue at hand and distracted from other things. "Tell me what's happening."

"Why?" He took a seat.

"You're upset. I'm trying to be a good listener."

He narrowed his eyes. "It's more than that."

"What else would it be?"

"You could be seeking information to use against me. Perhaps my brother Bahram has gotten to you."

"How? I've never met him, and I'm a prisoner here."

While Navid smoked, I picked a hangnail and prayed.

"Sweet Vivica, do not pick your nails. You will make things challenging for your beauty team."

I dropped my hands in my lap. Obeying him didn't matter, but keeping him from getting angry did.

"Bahram is visiting," Navid said. "He is a power-hungry narcissist who has been plotting to overthrow me for years. When the Council elected me secretary general, he began a campaign to impugn my character, and he has not stopped since."

Power-hungry narcissism must run in the family. "I'm sorry."

He blinked. "Are you?"

"Why would you say that?" He cared about my motives—and sincerity. Interesting.

He leaned forward. "Because you seem different. Less afraid."

"If you want my cooperation, then my being afraid isn't helpful. It doesn't mean I'm plotting against you."

"True. Though you tried it once before." He straightened. "Do you know why I haven't touched you?"

My stomach tightened. "No."

"A light shines in you, and it mesmerizes me unlike anything I have ever experienced. I do not wish to cause it to dim." He stared at me with his hypnotic gaze. "What is it that makes you different, sweet Vivica?"

My mouth went dry. How should I respond? The truth would

anger him, but I couldn't lie. The silence grew unbearable.

I swallowed. "Jesus Christ."

"I should have guessed." Navid chuckled. "Surely you must be an exclusivist for this belief to make such an impact on your entire being."

I met his gaze. "Yes. Christ forgave my sins and has made me a completely different person, and now—"

"I see." He held up his hand. "I am glad you find comfort in your religion. Perhaps it makes this situation easier to bear." He stood. "I will be back tomorrow. Right now I must deal with Bahram."

\*\*\*

At dinnertime, Wispy Hair entered my room with a cart of food, and I looked up from the book I was reading as he rolled my meal over to me. "Please tell me your name," I said. "Since I'm probably going to be here for a while." I refused to believe that, but if I was going to look at Navid as a human being, I should do the same for his staff members.

I never knew when I might need an ally.

"Devon." He lifted the cover and revealed a tomato and mozzarella salad and green grapes.

"Thank you." I placed a napkin in my lap. "Now, I understand that I can't have outside access via my doc, but I'd like to keep up with current events. Is there any way to do that?"

"Give me your doc, and I'll find out."

"Thank you, Devon." He took the device, bowed, and left.

\*\*\*

Devon returned for the cart and handed me the doc. "With the secretary general's permission, Jillian programmed your device to have a newsfeed. Incoming and outgoing communication is still blocked."

"Thank you."

He nodded and exited quickly.

I immediately began scrolling through the newsfeed for an update of what was happening in the Coastal Republic. According to URNA's government-controlled media, officials were having difficulty maintaining order and implementing a government. Plus, large numbers of URNA citizens were attempting to emigrate to the Coastal Republic, and the media reported supposed atrocities at the new country's border.

I had trouble believing anything that came from URNA's government-run media could be objective, and while I didn't doubt the Coastal Republic was facing huge challenges, I doubted the situation was as dire as the media outlets were reporting. What troubled me more was a different headline.

```
Potential Superstorm Headed for Atlantic Coast
   Tropical Storm Sigourney has been upgraded
   to a Category 2 hurricane and is gaining
   enough momentum to become a superstorm.
   URNA's National Weather Federation has
   issued a hurricane watch for the Atlantic
   Region, but the hurricane is expected to
   make landfall in the Coastal Republic by
   Wednesday evening.
```

This had to be the kind of storm Jillian would be looking for. I glanced at the date on my doc. Today was Monday, and the article had been written hours earlier.

My heart thudded as I pictured Drake at his stepfather's beach house—in the path of the storm.

*God, please keep Drake safe, and help me figure out what to do.*

# CHAPTER 40

## *Drake*

The sharp pain in my shoulder drubbed my sleepiness, and I opened my eyes to darkness. When I stretched my bound legs, they hit a solid surface, so I paused to listen. The dull hum of tires against the road made me groan.

Faith. The tranq dart. And now a trunk. Great combo.

Riding in a trunk was never fun, but this wasn't my first rodeo. I moved my cuffed hands up and down my leg, hoping to find my courier, but Faith had probably taken it. Which meant that Jethro wasn't coming with the cavalry.

I strained, but all I could hear was music seeping into my mold-scented, coffin-like space. Someone needed to detail this vehicle's interior.

We rolled along for what I guessed was another half-hour, but I wasn't really sure. Then, the car stopped.

I tensed. How long had I been out? The car moved ahead. My limbs were heavy, and my brain struggled to process at its normal speed.

I weighed my options and didn't like my chances of a successful escape—especially with restraints on my hands and feet.

*God, I know you and I haven't been on the best of terms lately, but I could use your help.*

The car halted again, and this time doors slammed. Holding my breath, I listened for voices.

Nothing.

A few minutes later, I heard footsteps. I closed my eyes in case someone opened the trunk.

The trunk squeaked open.

"How much did you give him?" a man with a girly voice asked. Well, it could have been a chick with a manly voice. Didn't feel like risking a peek, however.

"The dose you told me to use for someone his height and weight," Faith said. Lovely girl. Would make some poor schmuck a nice wife someday.

"Go get Errol, and bring a stretcher," the girly man or the manly woman said. "We gotta get this guy inside, and we're gonna need help."

Inside where?

Footsteps pounded against a hard surface. A siren yowled in the distance. Rough hands grasped my arm and lifted me up. Keeping my eyes shut, I let my body remain limp, which considering how loopy I was, wasn't difficult. I got a whiff of curry and garlic. Had to be in the city.

Man, I was hungry.

Faith must've returned with Errol because someone lifted and tossed me onto a stretcher. Apparently, they wheeled me by a dumpster, because I almost gagged at the smell of rotting garbage. Then, the air temperature changed, and a door slammed.

"Welcome to the Headquarters for the Council of World Peacekeepers. Please allow us to confirm your identity," an automated voice said.

Good to know I'd made it to my intended destination—even if I wasn't coming in the way I'd hoped.

I'd just have to improvise.

Someone pried my eye open and scanned my retina before they started rolling the stretcher. Then, they uncuffed my wrists and unbound my legs.

When a metal door clanked shut, I waited until the footsteps died away and sat up. It was a pretty typical cell—cement block walls, bars, and a metal toilet in the corner. The worst parts were the heat and the smell of sweat mixed with human filth.

A security camera's red light blinked in the corner of the ceiling. I pressed my face to the bars and looked to the right and left but couldn't get a good view. There was nothing across from me but another block wall.

"Hello?"

When I didn't get a response, I sprawled on the stretcher. Since there was a concrete bench with a thin mattress pad, I figured it wouldn't be long until they came back for the stretcher—which was actually half-comfortable.

My hand brushed against a strap. Could be useful. I rolled up on my side to block the camera's view, closed my fist around the strap, tugged until it came loose, and secured it in my pocket.

When the drugs cleared my system, I'd have a better shot at moving fast enough to get the drop on the guard who'd come back for the stretcher, so I hoped it'd be a while longer.

Either way, I'd be ready.

\*\*\*

The one thing that I wasn't prepared for actually happened. Minutes turned into hours, until I had no idea how long I'd been shut up. I dozed, and when I woke, I stood on unsteady legs, staggered to the bars, and held on.

My words stuck, but I cleared my parched throat until I could speak. "Could I get food? Or at least water?" I rubbed my grainy eyes. "Preferably both."

The camera's red light continued to blink.

More time passed.

But still, no one came.

# CHAPTER 41

## *Vivica*

After my beauty team had left the next day, Devon entered. "Secretary General Zahedi requests that you join him for dinner in his private quarters."

Dread paralyzed me. A different venue could mean that Navid had changed his mind about keeping his hands off me.

*God, protect me.*

I forced a pleasant expression onto my face. "I'm ready."

"His lordship requests that you leave your doc in this room."

I pointed to the device resting on the nightstand.

"Very well." Devon opened the door, and Errol entered and handcuffed me. We rode the wood-paneled elevator up into Tower One, and when the door slid open, we were in a penthouse with a view of the city. Errol unlocked the iron gate separating the elevator from the living space and motioned for me to enter.

The gate clanged behind me, and Errol stood guard next to the elevator when Devon left. I clicked across the marble halls in my four-inch heels. Navid was nowhere in sight, so I took a seat on the edge of the couch, adjusted my strapless dress, and waited.

"Vivica." Navid hurried into the room, and I stood. He took my hand and examined my wrist. "I see you have suffered no permanent effects from your fall. Please, have a seat."

I returned to my perch on the couch, and he sat beside me. "Did you solve the problem with your brother?" I asked.

He frowned. "Bahram has left, but he will continue to spread lies about me. It is his way." Navid withdrew his MD3 from his pocket, tapped it a couple of times, and music began to play. First the music came from the device, and then the sound transferred to the speakers and filled the room. He crossed to a table laden with decanters of alcohol. "May I offer you some brandy?" He opened a decanter and poured the liquid into a snifter.

"No, thank you." Though I wondered if I should take a few swigs. The seductive sound of a saxophone coming through the speakers was making it hard for me to breathe.

"I received some wonderful news from Jillian this morning." He paused and took a sip of brandy. "Hurricane Sigourney is now a Category 4."

Behind my back, I drew my fist into a ball. "And you're sure the nanobots will work as planned? What if the storm takes a different path and slams into this region instead? God is still in charge of the weather."

"That would be impossible, but it's sweet that you display such faith in your god."

"There's no guarantee the Coastal Republic will beg for global involvement—even if the hurricane causes horrible destruction. You're underestimating the citizens. Most of them believe in helping each other—without government intervention."

Amusement danced in his eyes, and he took another drink. "You are one of the most optimistic people I have ever encountered. It is deliciously charming."

Ugh. We needed a new topic to steer the conversation away from me. "Why does it matter that there's a Coastal Republic? Wouldn't it be better to let that group of people live the way they choose rather than constantly battling them? If the Peacekeepers truly cared about peace, then they'd leave the new country alone."

"Global peace demands unity. Your mother would be disappointed if she could hear you talking about such foolishness."

"Why? She was never a supporter of globalism. She was a Nationalist to the core."

"Exactly." His eyes gleamed. "And she would be disappointed that her beautiful and intelligent daughter did not learn from her late mother's mistakes."

"My father and I know that someone hacked her chip and kept the real data from her doctor."

He took another drink. "Your mother died of natural causes."

"But someone prevented her from getting medical treatment. I want to know who."

"There is nothing more to be gained from discussing her tragic loss." He cleared his throat a couple of times and put the snifter on the coffee table. "Now, I've asked my cook to prepare a special dinner for you." He stood, but he swayed.

Instinctively, I reached to steady him, but he dropped to the couch. He clutched his throat, and he struggled to take a breath. His eyes widened, and he motioned wildly toward the brandy snifter. "You?" he rasped.

"No." I held up my hands. "No. I promise, I didn't do this."

Understanding flickered in his eyes. "Bahram wins…" He fell back on the pillows, drew a few more wheezing breaths, and the hand that had been clutching his throat dropped to his side.

My hand flew to my mouth, and I reached out to check his pulse. Nothing.

# CHAPTER 42

## *Vivica*

I stared at Navid's still form and vacant eyes. Though he was my enemy, watching him die was awful, and I froze, pondering his eternal destiny. I should've done more to reach him. Burying my face in my hands, I tried to block the wave of grief over my mother's death.

I hadn't done enough for her either.

Somewhere in the penthouse, a door clicked, spurring me to action.

Shaking off my horror, I pulled Navid's MD3 from his jacket pocket. I pressed his thumb to the device to gain access, opened the settings, and changed them so it wouldn't lock.

I had to use this opportunity to escape to the SWEEP command center where I could hack the drones and reroute Hurricane Sigourney.

Slipping off my high heels, I peered around the corner to where Errol stood guard at the gate. His back was to me. I couldn't assume that Errol was the lone staff member in this penthouse, though any one of them may have poisoned Navid. Loyalty might not be a problem.

Surely there was a second elevator for the staff—I found it hard to believe Navid would've shared an elevator with servants. Or I could take the stairs.

I padded across the chilled marble toward the dining room that overlooked the city. Pausing outside of the room, I listened for servants. When I didn't hear anything, I crept closer to the door that I hoped led to the kitchen.

Pressing my ear to the door, I was met with tomb-like silence. I cracked the door and peered inside.

The room was empty except for a silver cart with two plates covered by shiny domes. Navid must have planned to serve the dinner himself. I entered the kitchen, sniffed, and looked around. The food hadn't been cooked here.

My eyes fell on a butcher block full of knives, so I grabbed one and wrapped the blade in a dishtowel that hung next to the sink.

The wall opposite the cabinet, sink, and stove had two doors. I rushed to the first one and yanked it open—a pantry. The second door led to a fire exit and stairwell. The handle on the outside didn't budge. So the door would lock behind me. For a second, I hesitated, wondering if there was anything else I should take from the penthouse, but when I saw a security camera's red light blinking, I pulled the door shut and ran down the stairs.

I calculated how many floors it would be to the command center. My legs already burned, but I had to keep moving. Surely Errol would notice how deathly quiet the penthouse had become and investigate.

My feet ached, but I gripped the metal railing and kept going, and after at least ten floors, I began pausing at every stairwell to peek through the windows in each door to determine if I'd reached the command center's floor.

Finally, I found familiar surroundings, but when I grasped the door handle, it held fast.

I growled, but what else had I expected? Swiping the MD3 with my thumb, I searched the device for any kind of program that would give me access to the building's security system. I found a program called Enable and, on a hunch, opened it.

Above me, a door opened and slammed. Heavy footsteps sounded, and my heart thudded. Enable contained an electronic badge that I held up to the keypad beside the door. The lock clicked, and I blew out my breath.

After securing the door behind me as quietly as possible, I edged forward and scanned the halls. This was the right floor. I began jogging, and when the hallway came to a T, I slowed. The command center was to the left.

I gripped the knife tighter. What was I going to do when I got inside? Hold Jillian at knifepoint? She might not be alone. The Peacekeepers had other scientists working on SWEEP.

*Boom!*

The floor buckled, and I pitched forward and back as a shockwave rippled through my body. Plaster sifted down on my head. The lights sputtered and went out. The knife skittered from my grip, but I clutched Navid's MD3. A second blast crumbled the wall next to me, and I ducked as a large piece of drywall crashed into my shoulder.

Screaming, I curled into a ball and protected my head. The wall shifted again. My cheek rested against the rough carpet. I tried to move forward, but my dress had caught under a fallen beam and other debris. Water from the sprinkler system began to pour from the ceilings, and the building moaned as it settled. Emergency lights flickered on and issued a faint buzz.

I craned my neck upward, but the fallen wall blocked my range of motion and view. A chill passed over my body as I thought of the building that towered above me. Had the bomb, or whatever it was, weakened the building to the point of collapse? I squeezed my eyes shut and tried to block the image of ten stories of rubble crushing me.

I sneezed several times and coughed away the dust fighting for a place in my lungs. Who would do this? Navid's brother might be responsible. I should've pressed Navid for more details about their rivalry. Or the Warriors had gotten my message and didn't care that I was being held prisoner.

I tried scooting forward more, but again, my dress pulled. Instead of tearing free, the strapless gown worked its way to my waist. Worming forward, I wiggled out. Once I was free, I shoved the drywall aside and emerged from the debris pile. I bent and used all my weight to pull the dress out. The material ripped and gave way, causing me to fall backward. Still, enough of the dress remained to cover me, so I put it on and picked through the wreckage.

I never should've left my shoes behind. Four-inch heels would've been better than no shoes at all. While moving toward the command center, I shoved pieces of walls aside and brushed away the water that dripped in my eyes. When I reached the door, my heart dropped.

A metal beam blocked my access.

# CHAPTER 43

## *Drake*

I groaned, rubbed my head, and pulled myself up off of the concrete floor in my cell. The heaviness in my limbs had vanished, but I was weak from no food—or water. The stretcher rested on its side. The blast had thrown me off like a rodeo bull. Dim lights flickered, and dust lingered in the air.

The camera's red light had gone dark.

If Vivica was still here, I prayed she was okay. I had to get out and find her.

A floor-to-ceiling crack had formed in the cement blocks outside of my cell, so I examined the bars and found a fissure around the area where they attached to the ceiling. Gripping the bars with both hands, I gave a tug. They jiggled slightly, and I kicked myself for not spending more time in the gym lifting.

I got behind the stretcher and plowed it into the bars again and again. Then, I pulled on the bars one more time. The cement crumbled, but I groaned. The bars were welded to a beam in the ceiling.

I took the strap I'd removed from the stretcher and tied it around one of the bars. Bracing my legs, I pulled.

I'd overestimated my brute strength—the bars didn't budge. Still, I wasn't going to sit in here and wait for the building to collapse.

I knelt and inspected the lock on the cell door, and another idea hit me. I scooted over to the stretcher. A screw was holding part of the wheel in place. Using a chipped piece of concrete as a screwdriver, I took the wheel off and grasped the screw.

I maneuvered the screw into the latch on the door and shook it. The building groaned, and I glanced up, half expecting the ceiling to fall and flatten me. But nothing happened, and I kept working the lock.

When it sprang open, I raced out of the cell and down the passageway. At the end of the hall was another door, but this one had a damaged doorframe. Leaning against the door, I bulldozed it open with my weight and ran into the stairwell.

Leaping over fallen ceiling tiles, I barreled up the stairs and onto the main floor, where residents and workers were coming down from the towers to get out of the building. I hesitated, catching my breath and trying to figure where Zahedi might be holding Vivica.

Someone grabbed my arm from behind, and I tensed, ready to fight. "Relax, Cavalier. It's Sleuthhound," he whispered. We stepped out of the crowd and into a corner behind a potted plant.

Sleuthhound in a Mohawk. Wow. Never thought I'd see the day when the proper gentleman Chad Yeats would spring for that kind of style—which made it a brilliant disguise. Dust and debris stuck to his hair.

"My friend, you almost got your teeth knocked out," I said.

"Moonbeam and I were trying to extract Storyteller," he whispered.

"And you thought bombing Headquarters was the best way to do that?" Was I the only one who cared about Vivica's safety?

He furrowed his brow and shook his head. "Absolutely not. This wasn't us."

At least the Warriors hadn't decided to blow up the building with Vivica still inside. I wouldn't have been able to forgive them for that.

He glanced at the ceiling. "I'm not sure how much longer this building has before it collapses, but I don't want to leave Storyteller behind."

"Is Moonbeam in here?"

"No," Chad said. "She's waiting in the van at our rendezvous point."

I was glad Agatha wasn't in the building too. "I'll find Storyteller. Go back to Moonbeam."

His shoulders slumped. "I should help."

"Take care of your wife."

A woman with cuts on her face and arms ran by.

He didn't try to hide his relief. I couldn't blame him as I glanced around at the chaos. Police and firemen were starting to stream in. "Any idea on where Storyteller might be?"

"The SWEEP command center is on the nineteenth floor." He leaned closer. "The van is at Fifth and Jefferson."

"Got it. Now get out of here."

"Godspeed, my friend."

I saluted and took off up the stairs.

# CHAPTER 44

## *Vivica*

After trying to move the beam in front of the command center door, I'd gotten the building to creak and made dust rain from the ceiling, but that was the extent of my success. I needed a different path. When I'd pretended to trip on the loose tile, Jillian had mentioned that she never used the entrance near the offending tile and used one by her office instead, so that was where I needed to go.

I stepped over debris, listening for sounds of other survivors or for indications that the building was going to collapse. When I came to the stairwell door, I wrenched it open and hastened down a flight.

This floor still had walls intact, so I made my way down the hallway more quickly. However, the smell of smoke got stronger as I neared the command center, and I stopped, ripped a piece of my dress, and held the scrap over my nose and mouth.

As I reached for the door that I hoped would lead to Jillian's office, she careened out. Her white hair was frazzled, and she grabbed both of my arms. "Someone destroyed the server room." She pointed to the ceiling. "It's right above us." She paused and stared at me. "Did you do it?"

"Dressed like this?" I looked down at my attire. "Are you kidding me? I was caught in the blast."

"We need to get out. The building's unstable. I've tried to reach security, but I can't. They're probably trying to get his lordship out."

I wasn't going to be the one to break the news about Navid. "What about Hurricane Sigourney?"

Jillian shrugged. "It's on track to hit the Coastal Republic."

My mind whirred as I thought about the nanobots that would help to steer the hurricane. "Do the nanobots need a signal from the server?"

"No. They get their signal from the drone that's in the eye of the hurricane, collecting data, and I programmed the drone before the server got blown up." The building creaked, and Jillian looked over her shoulder. "I'm out of here." She disappeared into the stairwell.

I had to see if she was telling the truth. I might be able to reprogram the drone to send different signals to the nanobots. I hurried through Jillian's office and into the command center. The radar screen was black. The emergency light in the corner cast a yellow-green glow over the room, but the computers were working. There must be a back-up generator.

However, when I sat down at the computer station, I determined Jillian had been telling the truth about the server. I couldn't access any information.

Now what?

I still had to find a way to stop the hurricane. Scanning the room, I wracked my brain for an idea. There was only one possibility.

And it all depended on me getting out of this tower alive.

The building emitted a metallic groan, and I scurried through Jillian's office and ran into a man's broad chest.

"Sorry." I backed up and attempted to dart around him, but he caught my arm.

"My dear, it's—" Drake lowered his head and kissed me.

I wrapped my arms around him. I didn't know how he'd gotten here, but it didn't matter.

I pulled away, and he rested his hand on my cheek. "Are you okay?"

"Yes." My mind buzzed with a thousand questions, but the building moaned.

He took my hand. "Let's get out of here." We ran down the hallway and into the stairwell.

There were a few other stragglers, but everyone was so focused on evacuating, the only sounds were footsteps and opening and closing doors. We reached the ground floor and filed onto the street where hundreds of people milled about and looked up at the damaged tower.

"This way." Drake led me down an alley, and I stepped over a pile of broken glass. Something rustled in the recycle bins that we passed, and I pressed closer to Drake. "One more block," he said.

We rounded a corner and came face-to-face with Errol.

# CHAPTER 45

## *Vivica*

"Stop. Put your hands up, and get on your knees." Errol drew his gun. "Got Wilkins cornered in the alley."

Who was he communicating with?

Drake and I lowered ourselves to the ground, but as I raised my hands, I used my thumb to flick the volume on Navid's MD3 that I still clutched. I tapped the device, and the blast of a saxophone screeched through the alley. A cat scurried from behind the dumpster with a loud meow, and in the second Errol took his eyes off of us, Drake leaped forward, wrenched the gun from his grasp, and put him in a choke hold until he passed out.

We took off down the alley. Gunshots fired behind us. Asphalt tore the bottoms of my feet, but I ignored the burning.

Another gunshot blasted, and a bullet whizzed by my head. I widened my strides and pushed myself faster. My feet slapped the ground, jarring my teeth to the roots.

A van turned the corner and zoomed toward us.

"That's our ride," Drake said.

The van's door opened, and we dove inside just as the men behind us fired more shots. The door slid shut, and the driver backed down

231

the alley, turned, and floored the accelerator.

Behind us, there was a rumble, followed by faint screams. A vibration shuddered through our vehicle. When I lifted my head, a plume of smoke, illuminated by the city lights, wafted heavenward where Navid's tower had once loomed over the streets.

\*\*\*

While the van threaded through traffic, dodging emergency vehicles, I lay still and tried to catch my breath.

"You okay?" Drake asked.

I pointed at my bloody feet. "Sort of."

"Hey, Moonbeam. Got a first aid kit up there?"

I sat up. *Agatha?* "Moonbeam?"

The woman with chin-length blond hair turned and grinned. "At your service."

"Same here," the man with a Mohawk said.

"Sleuthhound?"

"That's right. Fit as a fiddle and ready to fight."

It was great to see Chad was well enough to be on a mission. I took another deep breath. "This reunion is wonderful. But we have to reroute a hurricane."

As I copied the contents of Navid's MD3 to Drake's courier, Drake worked on my feet. I tried to ignore the stinging and told them about the server being destroyed and what had happened to Navid. "Did the Warriors set off the bomb?"

"No way." Agatha said. "Our mission was to rescue you and get you to the SWEEP command center."

"Then who set off the bomb on the floor with the server?" I asked.

"Probably the same person who assassinated Navid." Drake closed the first aid kit.

"Navid's last words were 'Bahram wins.'" I drummed my fingers against my arm. "We'll worry about that later. All that matters now is that I find a way to reprogram the drone so it can send a different signal to the nanobots that are inside the hurricane."

"And how are you going to do that, my dear?"

"We need to fly into the hurricane's eye, so I can get close enough to reprogram the drone."

# CHAPTER 46

## *Vivica*

Drake stared at me. "You're joking, right?"

"No."

"That's crazy," he said. "Why can't we use our drone to shoot theirs down?"

"If we do that, it's possible the nanobots will continue to do what they've been programmed to do—which is steering the hurricane to shore and causing tornadoes. First, I have to try hacking in and reprogramming the drone, but I have to get close enough. If it doesn't work, then we'll have nothing to lose by shooting it down and hoping that'll stop the nanobots."

"There's got to be a better way," Drake said. "It's too dangerous..."

"I agree." Agatha pursed her lips.

I leaned forward. "Researchers fly into hurricanes all the time. Jillian told me about it."

"Okay, then. I don't know who Jillian is, but I'll see if I can make the flight happen." Drake took out his courier and began sending messages.

When the van arrived at an airstrip, a jet was waiting for us. We boarded, and Drake launched deep into conversation with Jethro about our next move, so I took a seat next to Agatha.

"Agatha?"

"Yeah?"

"Is Isaac okay?" I told her about the video of the rescue Navid had shown me. "I wanted to believe him, but I was so afraid to hope."

Agatha smiled. "Isaac's fine. Drake felt terrible about jabbing the poor little guy with a tranq dart, but—"

"Wait. *Drake* rescued Isaac?" I thought back to the man I'd seen on the video. He *had* been too tall to be Ben.

"He sure did. With Ben and Ally's help. They took good care of Isaac and got him back to Gabe and Alma. They're all in the Coastal Republic now."

"Right." Tears stung my eyes as the weight of that burden lifted. *Thank you, God.*

Agatha glanced at Drake, who was engrossed in conversation, and lowered her voice. "How was it seeing Ben?"

"Good. It was closure I needed." I stared out the window. "I'm happy for him, and I didn't want Ally to be cool, but she was."

"Yeah, she is. I met her when they stayed at the Mine."

I watched Drake, but he didn't notice. Agatha followed my gaze. "And Drake?"

"I love him," I said.

"I know." She leaned forward and rested her elbows on her knees. "But does he know that?"

\*\*\*

Halfway through the flight, Drake came over and sat next to me. Agatha stood. "I need to stretch my legs and check on my husband."

"I didn't mean to interrupt the girl talk," he said.

"You're fine," I said. "It's more important that you and I chat."

"Chat is probably an understatement."

"Pow wow?"

He cocked an eyebrow. "Summit might be more appropriate."

"No. I'd like to call it a symposium."

"Really, my dear? We can bat synonyms back and forth, or we can have an actual conversation." Drake swallowed. "And it needs to start with an apology from me."

I folded my hands in my lap.

"I never should've left the Warriors. I was being a coward, and because of that, you had to endure captivity. I'll never forgive myself for giving Navid the chance to hurt you—"

"He didn't touch me."

"Oh, thank God." Drake buried his face in his hands. "I prayed and prayed as soon as I heard you'd turned yourself in. I begged God to protect you."

"It worked." My throat tightened.

He looked up and tears welled in his eyes. "Will you forgive me?"

I'd never seen such sincerity and tenderness in his expression. "Yes."

"Thank you." He kissed the top of my head and put his arm around me. I rested my head on his shoulder while we sat in silence.

I leaned forward. "How do you figure the part with Navid was your fault?"

"I never would've let you turn yourself in." He pressed his lips together.

"You wouldn't have been able to stop me."

"No," he said. "We would've found a way to stop Navid. Together."

"Maybe so." I glanced out the window. "You weren't a coward for not fighting. You were right."

"How?"

"Sometimes we take a stand for justice and fight. Other times we let God battle for us—and it's the bravest thing we can do."

He rested his hand on top of mine.

"There's something else." My pulse quickened. "I should've told you I love you."

"If you meant it."

"I do love you." I grasped his hand.

His eyes danced as he leaned in, letting his lips hover just above mine. "Well, that's wonderful, because it turns out I love you too."

Unable to stand the teasing, I closed the gap and thought of nothing else but the feel of his lips on mine.

\*\*\*

When we landed at an airfield in the Coastal Republic, the sun was rising and several members of our new country's military greeted us at the border and confirmed our identities before sending us back to the Mine.

Drake gathered my father, Nathan, Jethro, and Liam into a conference room. When I entered, my father rushed over and hugged me. "Vivibear, I'm so glad you're okay."

"Me too. God protected me."

He took a step back. "I want to hear about it some time."

Jethro cleared his throat. "Let's get down to business." I sat beside Drake and waved at Nathan, who grinned.

"I've been in contact with the CR military. They got a plane, an experienced pilot, and a team you can use to get into the hurricane's eye." Jethro surveyed me. "These folks are a bunch of mavericks looking for a thrill, so it oughta be okay. You sure you can pull off reprogramming that drone?"

I smiled. "I'm a better hacker than liar."

Jethro stared at me with the same skeptical look he'd given me the day I met him.

Drake coughed but didn't manage to cover his laugh.

"Good. We ain't got much time, and we've already started evacuating people along the CR's coastline." He brushed his fingers over his courier, and a radar image projected on the wall. My stomach flopped when I saw the massive storm swirling in the Atlantic. "Latest data shows the thing's morphed into a Category 5."

I folded my hands and rested them on the table. "Then we'd better finish this meeting and go save our country."

***

Drake, my father, and I waited outside to board the plane that had just arrived. The wind had picked up, and dark clouds had started to gather.

"Vivibear, I'd feel better if you stayed on the ground. I can handle this."

"Dad—"

"What if this doesn't work?" my father asked Drake. "Is the CR government prepared to respond?"

Drake snorted. "What government? Right now, the military is running the country and keeping order. We need a constitutional convention ASAP. Plus, aren't we supposed to be about helping each other and not relying on a government to swoop in and save us?"

I wondered if a government-dependent mindset would be easy for people to overcome. No wonder Navid had been so confident a hurricane would be the end of our new country.

My father surveyed Drake with disdain. "Convince her to stay."

"I can't make her do that."

"Have you tried?"

"No." Drake's forehead creased.

"Dad. Drake." I held up a hand. "We don't have time for this. Let's go."

My father pursed his lips but turned and boarded the plane. Drake took my hand, and we followed. The plane's interior was far different than the jets I'd used to travel. A wall of computers stood outside the cockpit.

A man sitting in front of a radar stood. A fringe of hair lined the circumference of his scalp, and he had a pug nose. He extended his hand. "Howdy. Name's Sloan. I'm your flight director." He pointed toward the cockpit. "Carolina's your aircraft commander. Heath's the copilot."

Heath saluted. He looked about thirty and had muscular arms.

"Hey, Drake." Carolina waved. "Drake's friends." She resumed her pre-flight check. Her gray hair was short, and she appeared to be in her early seventies.

Sloan continued. "She's one of the best. Been flying for years. Heath's a pro too."

Drake smiled at me. "Carolina served in URNA's Air Force with my dad."

A short man with red hair boarded, and Sloan pointed at him.

"And this is Jon, your flight engineer."

"Good day for a ride," Jon said and sauntered to the back of the plane.

Sloan motioned toward some seats with shoulder harnesses in front of the equipment. "Y'all better get buckled in."

***

The first part of the flight over the Atlantic Ocean was peaceful. While I waited for the action, my father dozed, and Drake talked to Carolina.

I swiped through my courier to get updated on the latest news, and my heart sank when I saw the headline that Bahram Zahedi had been voted secretary general of the Council of World Peacekeepers.

He'd be far more brutal than his brother, since he most likely assassinated a family member to usurp power.

I skimmed another article that indicated the new secretary general would address the Peacekeepers about the Coastal Republic three days from now—after the storm.

Drake returned, sat next to me, and buckled his seatbelt. "Carolina says we're close to the eye wall, and we're going in at an altitude of 5,000 feet." He looked at my father. "Make sure you're all fastened in and your equipment's secured, because it's going to be rough. He handed me a barf bag and held up one of his own. "Just in case." He tossed a bag to my father.

I showed Drake the article about Navid's brother.

"No surprise there."

"Are you worried?" I asked as the plane descended.

Drake shrugged. "Probably should be, but we can't do anything about it."

I gazed out the window. Gray clouds enveloped us. Lightning flashed and thunder roared above the plane's engine. I gripped the edge of my seat as the plane plummeted like a roller coaster car.

My stomach hit my throat and bounced back in place, diminishing my scream into a pathetic whimper.

Drake grasped my hand. "You okay?"

"Maybe," I squeaked.

"Just turbulence." Sloan said, then spoke to Carolina through his headset. "Come right ten degrees."

"Falling out of the sky counts as turbulence?" The plane bucked and sheets of rain blocked my view from the window.

My father groaned and opened his eyes. "Tell me this is a nightmare."

The plane convulsed.

This time, I closed my eyes and focused on the task ahead. I'd need to be ready as soon as we were inside the eye because the fewer times we had to circle, the better. We had to be mindful of fuel.

The sun broke through the clouds, and the turbulence weakened. Blue sky blazed overhead, and white swells danced in the ocean below. A fortress of roiling gray clouds loomed in angry layers on my side of the plane.

I turned to my computer screen and pored over the radar that would help us locate the Azar 646 drone.

My father pointed. "Is that it?"

"Yep." I began searching for a signal to see if I could hack into the drone, but I couldn't. "We need to get closer."

Drake reported to Carolina, and as she circled, the plane descended to a lower altitude while Sloan called out adjustments to keep us in the eye.

"We're at 2,000 feet," Drake said.

I held my breath as our system locked on to the drone. "Yes!"

My father gave me a high five.

I unzipped my jacket and pulled my hair into a ponytail "Anyone else hot?"

"Yeah," Sloan said. "Temperature's higher inside the eye."

I concentrated on hacking into the drone.

"I don't like what I'm seeing." My father shook his head. "I'm not sure we're going to be able to reprogram it."

"Yes, we can."

My father groaned. "The Azar's security is impeccable." His mouth settled into a thin line. "Now might be a good time to get Inspector DART ready for the back-up plan."

Drake and I exchanged glances. Inspector DART was the nickname for the Warriors' drone—defense and reconnaissance tool.

My father wasn't known for his optimism, but we'd come too far to give up. I wasn't ready to use our drone to take out the Azar and risk letting the nanobots continue guiding the hurricane on its destructive course.

The constant circling was taking its toll, and I buried my head in my barf bag. But in spite of concentrating as hard as I could, I wasn't able to keep my last meal in my stomach.

My father took over.

I moaned as Drake rubbed my back. "Hang in there."

When Drake handed me a water bottle, I rinsed the acid from my mouth and tried to think.

A few seconds later, I glanced up at the radar. The Azar was coming right at us. "Dad?"

"I see it."

Our radar went dark.

# CHAPTER 47

## *Vivica*

Transfixed, I stared at the blank screen.

My father unbuckled his seatbelt, knelt down, and examined the computers. I started to undo my belt, but Drake pressed his hand against mine and shook his head. "Don't."

My father straightened. "Equipment's fine. Something else knocked out my radar."

"I'm on it." Jon hurried to the back of the plane.

A tense silence flooded the cabin until Jon returned. "Can't find anything else wrong." Confusion lingered in his expression.

"Dad, what if—?" My stomach rolled, and I covered my mouth.

My father pointed at Sloan. "Why is *your* radar still working?"

"You'd better be glad for that, if you want to make it through this mission in one piece," Sloan said.

"Answer my question."

"I'm not the engineer, so I have no idea." He shot my father a dirty look. "Shift five degrees left," he said to Carolina.

"The Azar could have a defense system that we activated when we hacked it," I managed to choke out. "What if it targeted our specialized radar?"

My father studied me. "Maybe." He turned toward Jon. "You think that's possible?"

"Could be, since we added your equipment especially for this flight and our plane's automated defense system isn't protecting it." Jon pulled on his earlobe. "Let's go look again to be sure, and then we'll release Inspector DART."

I closed my eyes. That option gave us no guarantee of success.

My father stood. "Drake, come with us."

Drake kissed my forehead and got up. I gave him a weak smile. After a few sips of water and some deep breaths, the nausea's choking grip began to fade.

My father and Drake returned, and from the grim look on Drake's face, I knew they'd released Inspector DART.

"You did it, didn't you?" A part of me hoped I'd misinterpreted Drake's expression.

"Yes," my father said.

Drake motioned for me to join him on the opposite side of the plane. "You can see them both from here." He handed me a pair of binoculars.

I staggered across the aisle, buckled myself in, and took the binoculars.

"Inspector DART is the orange one," Drake said.

The DART chased the Azar, and a few seconds later, our drone began firing. The enemy drone dodged the shots and zipped in a circle, zooming closer to the plane.

"The Azar is coming at us." I handed the binoculars to Drake.

"Yes, it is." He spun toward Sloan. "We need to adjust course."

Before Sloan could respond, the DART flew upward. The Azar released a spray of ammunition that slammed into the DART. Our drone exploded in front of our plane's wing.

I screamed.

Carolina banked to avoid the debris, and darkness shrouded us as a wall of clouds jutted in front of the plane. Sloan swore as we accidentally reentered the eye wall. The bucking started again, and I gripped my seat's armrests and tried to hold my body still—to no avail.

"God help us," Drake muttered as he tried to buckle his harness.

I wanted to think, but another wave of nausea pummeled me. The plane jerked violently, throwing my father, Drake, and Jon to the floor. As they stood, the plane plunged, and their heads cracked against the cabin's ceiling before they collapsed.

I hurled into my barf bag.

"Yeehaw!" Carolina yelled from the cockpit.

Sunshine flooded into the cabin. We were back in the eye, but none of the men were moving. Sloan started to step from his station, but I held up my hand. "I've got it."

With my heart thudding, I stood, held onto the edge of the seat, and moved toward Drake. I felt for a pulse and started breathing when I found it—steady.

I checked my father and Jon. Both were still alive. I dragged Drake to a seat and buckled him in and then did the same for my father and Jon.

The plane shuddered, and Carolina groaned. "Not good."

"What's wrong?" I shouted.

"We lost engine four," Heath said. "Probably got hit with ammo from their drone—or debris from ours."

I joined them in the cockpit.

"We need to start climbing, so we can get back through the eye wall at a safer altitude," Heath said.

"No!" I clutched my head. "I still have to stop their drone. I'm the only one left who can do it."

The crease in Carolina's forehead deepened. "I've got to keep everybody safe. Which means we need to get back to shore ASAP."

"There has to be something I can do."

We continued in heavy silence. Everything the Warriors had fought for was about to be destroyed.

"I've got an idea," Carolina said. "But you look pretty green around the gills. I'm not sure you can pull it off."

"Please," I said. "I have to do something."

"You willing to risk your life?" She stared me down, and something in her expression reminded me of the day Jethro had suggested I didn't have what it took to be an agent with the Warriors.

"What would you call this?"

She cleared her throat. "This plane's carrying a V-32 Lobo Solitario. I was transporting it when I got the call that y'all needed me. That little thing's got room enough for one."

I swallowed. "Does it have a computer?" I could try hacking into their drone one more time, and I might be successful using different equipment.

"Best available."

"What if I can't figure out how to fly it?"

"Ain't hard. Like driving a car." She snorted. "I suppose you haven't done much of that. Most kids your age don't know how." She shook her head. "Stupid driverless cars are ruining society."

"I know how to drive." I hadn't done it for a while, but I could do it. My bodyguard, Bobby, had taught me a long time ago when my mother was governor of the Great Lakes Region.

"The biggest risk is you don't have a flight director telling you where the eye's moving so you can adjust."

I nodded.

"But if you're willing to get in the Lobo, I'll dump you off. We'll start climbing to a higher altitude and be ready to shoot out of the eye as soon as you're done. Sound okay, Heath?"

"Yes ma'am." His confident tone didn't match the uncertainty in his eyes.

"Work fast, and when you're done, the Lobo'll doc itself back in my cargo hold."

"What if I'm not fast?"

"Then we're out of options," she said. "I can't leave you behind because the Lobo's not heavy enough to withstand the updrafts and downdrafts in the eye wall… Plus, you don't know what you're doing."

"Why couldn't I fly up out of the eye and over the storm?"

"The Lobo's not meant to fly that high."

I closed my eyes and pictured myself accidentally slamming into the eye wall and plummeting to my death. I recoiled.

"We'll head back to shore now, missy. Just say the word."

"I can do it." Too many people's lives depended on me, and the hurricane was getting closer and closer to the Coastal Republic. Other men and women had made sacrifices in our fight.

I had to be willing to do the same.

***

I passed Drake, my father, and Jon on the way to the cargo hold. All three men were still unconscious. I paused and gave Drake a kiss on the forehead.

Would he ever forgive me if something went wrong?

"Take care of him, God," I whispered. I feared he'd never forgive himself for not being able to protect me. But then, this plane might not even make it back to shore.

Clenching my fists, I marched toward the cargo hold door and descended into the cavity that held the tiny aircraft, just a tad bigger than a small car. I opened the Lobo's hatch and climbed inside.

When I turned on the power, a navigation screen illuminated, and the engine roared to life. Just as Carolina had told me, there was a place for me to sync my courier with the aircraft. I connected my device and waited for her command.

The plane began to lurch. I rested my head against the seat and closed my eyes.

*Please God, help me do this.*

Carolina's voice boomed through the speakers. "I'll eject you on three."

"Copy that." I thought that's what I was supposed to say.

"One. Two. Three." A door beneath me opened, and the Lobo dropped from the plane.

The aircraft plunged downward before steadying itself. Ignoring my churning stomach that had nothing left to expel, I grabbed the controller and steered toward the drone.

Sunshine poured into my tiny cockpit, and I set the Lobo to run on autopilot while I tried to hack the enemy drone again. Every so often, I looked up to make sure I wasn't about to slam into the eye wall.

This time, I was careful of the Azar's security measures, but it was too late—the drone had protected itself, and there was no way for me to reprogram the nanobots.

"No, no, no!" I wailed. "Please, God."

There had to be something I could do.

And then I knew.

When we'd tried shooting down their drone, we'd bet on the possibility that the nanobots were completely dependent on the drone, and without nanobots steering the hurricane, there was no guarantee the storm would continue on its path to the Coastal Republic.

But as long as the Azar remained active, the hurricane was sure to hit the country—the nanobots would guide the storm to a direct hit.

We were running out of time—and other options.

I had to use the Lobo to destroy the drone.

Tears pooled in my eyes as my last hope of a happy ending vanished. I thought of the wedding I'd never experience. The children I'd never have. The son I'd never see again.

I could sacrifice my life, and it wouldn't even make a difference.

But if I didn't *try*, then Isaac wouldn't have a chance of living in a free country. Everything the Warriors fought for would be gone if I was unwilling to give my life for the cause.

I touched the communication button. "Carolina? It's Vivica."

"Go ahead."

My throat ached, and I could hardly speak. "I can't hack the drone and reprogram the nanobots."

She muttered a curse. "Fly up toward us. When I open my plane's cargo hold, the Lobo'll slide itself right in and dock."

"No. There's only one way left to stop the drone."

Silence. "You don't have to do that, missy."

"Yes, I do. Tell Drake and my father I love them."

I disconnected my courier and took a deep breath. "God, I'm going to do my part. Please do what I can't."

Locating the drone on the radar, I lined up the Lobo and increased my speed. Just a few more seconds, and I'd be in Heaven.

Would I see Melvin?

Was there a chance my mother had repented in her final hours?

The Azar was in sight. I braced for impact. At the last second, the drone darted left and fired on my plane, but I adjusted.

An explosion rocked my aircraft. My head thumped against the hatch, and I screeched at the blinding pain.

Fire.

Falling.

Darkness.

# CHAPTER 48

### *Drake*

I opened my eyes. Something was wrong. I could sense it in my gut. No turbulence, only the smooth feel of an aircraft circling. Harrison and Jon slumped in their seats. Sloan hunched over his workstation calling out commands to Carolina. He didn't seem to notice me.

Where was Vivica?

I rubbed my sore head and tried to remember what had caused the knot.

The drone battle. Turbulence.

I unbuckled the seatbelt that I didn't remember fastening. "Vivica? Where are you, my dear?"

I checked the lavatory door. Unoccupied. Making my way to the cockpit, I tried to ignore the foreboding that was making me sweat.

"Carolina?"

The pilot turned. Tears streamed down her wrinkled cheeks. Heath glanced over his shoulder and gave a slight nod.

"Where's Vivica?"

"Oh, son. I'm so sorry. She's gone."

My heart slammed against the floor. "That doesn't make sense. It's not like she'd parachute out of here." I mopped my forehead with my sleeve.

"She took the Lobo I was transporting."

*No.*

She wouldn't. She didn't know how to fly one.

But flying the Lobo was easy. Vivica could figure it out, and that stubborn woman would do whatever it took to stop the hurricane.

"So Vivica flew closer, hacked the drone, reprogrammed the nanobots, and she's on her way back?" I wanted that to be the answer.

Needed it to be.

"Oh, son. I wish I could say yes." Carolina sniffed. "But that girl told me to tell you she loves you right before she crashed her plane into the drone to stop it."

\*\*\*

As soon as our plane landed, Harrison and I huddled together over a computer in the hangar and attempted to trace the Lobo using the GPS tracker.

I balled my fists and shoved them deep in my pockets, while I tapped my foot against the concrete. This couldn't be happening. She'd risked her life with no guarantee the sacrifice would work.

But she'd done it before. Only this time it was over.

It seemed like God was playing a cruel joke. Or he was giving me what I deserved for abandoning the Warriors and leaving Vivica to fend for herself.

Still, knowing Vivica, we might have ended up in this very place.

Yet as bleak as things looked, I wasn't quite ready to accept that I'd held her in my arms for the last time.

"Any luck?" I asked.

Harrison clenched his jaw and kept working.

I thought about the Lobo's specs and tried to remember if it was solid enough for someone to survive a fall into the ocean and the inevitable beating from a hurricane.

Maybe. If God gave us a miracle.

\*\*\*

Two hours later, Harrison turned from his computer, and he'd aged about ten years. "There's nothing more I can do. I can't get a GPS signal."

"We can't give up!" Fury blazed in my chest.

His shoulders sagged. "I need a minute." He trudged out of the hangar, stood in the rain, and covered his face with his hands.

I pulled my courier from my pocket and selected Jethro's number. When he answered, I explained what had happened. "I need the Coast Guard's help. Use your connections."

"Freeman, I'm sorry, but no one in his right mind is gonna head out now. Not with Sigourney heading at us."

I closed my eyes. The hurricane was still going to hit the Coastal Republic. "We can't just do nothing."

"Praying ain't doing nothing."

I didn't have a response because I hadn't found the words to pray.

"Look, there ain't nothing else we can do. The Coast Guard'll send out a team on a recovery mission once the storm has passed."

"I thought you said you were praying."

"I am. But I'm a realist. And unless the man upstairs gives us a miracle, we're gonna be going on a recovery mission."

I disconnected. No way I was giving up hope. Not yet.

*God, please fix this. Give Vivica and me another chance to be together.*

\*\*\*

The wind howled and rain pelted the hangar's metal roof while I beat a throw pillow and tried to get comfortable on the lumpy couch in the office. Reaching for my courier, I sat up, looked at the radar, and blinked. I had to be seeing things.

The hurricane's path had shifted.

Though the outer edge was still skimming the Coastal Republic's coastline, meteorologists at the National Weather Federation had issued warnings to the people in URNA's Atlantic Region to brace for a direct hit.

Even though Liam and I still weren't speaking, I called him.

"Can the Peacekeepers find another way to route the hurricane back at us?" I asked.

"Dude, what time is it?" He sighed. "But no. Not since Tower One of North American headquarters collapsed and took out the SWEEP command center. One of our agents told me they're scrambling to get another drone here from the command center in South America, but there isn't time."

"How soon can we get a team out to look for Vivica?"

"Probably as early as tomorrow, but Drake, you need to prepare yourself."

"We'll find her."

"You're in denial. I went through the same thing with Ophelia."

"No, I'm not. I've been reviewing the specs on the Lobo. The thing's rock solid. They used the same materials that manufacturers put on spacecraft, so they can withstand reentering the earth's atmosphere. The self-healing materials are buoyant too."

"Denial is normal," he said. "When I first heard about Ophelia, I didn't want to believe it. It was too awful to accept. But I had to."

"I don't have to accept anything. Vivica's still alive. I know it."

"God will give you strength to deal with losing her."

I massaged the bridge of my nose. Maybe I *was* in denial and should prepare myself—on the off chance that I was wrong. "I know. He already is."

But God was also giving me hope.

Liam cleared his throat. "Look, Drake. I'm sorry for blaming you. Please forgive me for being a jerk—and for almost killing you."

"You didn't even come close to killing me." I chuckled. "But, yeah. I forgive you."

"Thanks, man. I'm praying for you."

# CHAPTER 49

## *Vivica*

I floated, but suffocating dampness surrounded me. My eyes flew open, and I choked back a gasp. Ocean spread as far as I could see. The storm was over.

While I'd drifted in and out of consciousness, wave after wave had engulfed the aircraft, tossing it to and fro.

But somehow the Lobo had remained afloat, and now it bobbed in choppy water. The cockpit had grown unbearably warm. The hatch door was a spider web of cracks, and I had no idea how it was holding together. My head throbbed, and my body ached. I brushed my sweat-dampened hair off my forehead.

I couldn't survive a fall from the sky and a hurricane only to be lost at sea. Holding my breath, I pushed the aircraft's power button and prayed the navigation screen would blink to life, but it remained dark. My stomach rumbled. Had I been unconscious for hours? Days? My tongue stuck to the roof of my mouth. Had Hurricane Sigourney hit the Coastal Republic?

Shifting, I searched under the seat in hopes of finding supplies, but there was nothing. Resting my head against the seat, I closed my eyes.

*Please God, help someone find me.*

***

The thwack of a helicopter roused me from my stupor. Sitting up straighter, I pushed against the hatch, popping it open.

Fresh, salt-tinged air rushed into the confined space, and I breathed deeply. I shaded my eyes with one hand and waved with the other.

"Hey!" My voice came out in a faint croak. "Help!"

The helicopter drew nearer, and I continued to shout and wave. Someone lowered a cage-like apparatus from the helicopter, and I choked back a sob.

# CHAPTER 50

## *Drake*

I held Vivica close and put a water bottle to her mouth. "Drink. You're dehydrated." She needed an IV, but the Coast Guard had been so sure we'd be on a recovery mission that they hadn't spared a medical team, especially since a lot of members were aiding URNA's citizens in the Atlantic Region.

She took a few sips of water. Then her head lolled, and the headset she wore for us to communicate above the helicopter's noise bit into my shoulder.

"Did it work?" Her voice was hoarse.

"Crashing the Lobo into the Peacekeepers' drone?"

She lifted her head just enough to nod.

"Yes." I stroked her hair. "The hurricane shifted and slammed into the Atlantic Region. It was devastating."

"Those poor people," she whispered.

Thousands of Coastal Republic citizens had donated aid and supplies in spite of our unstable economy.

"Try to relax, my dear. There's no need to talk right now."

Her forehead creased, and her eyes flashed. I grinned. She was going to be okay.

257

"How long was I gone?"

"Two of the longest days of my life."

She smiled. "I had to survive to annoy you."

"I wouldn't have it any other way." I kissed the top of her head and said a prayer of thanks as we approached the shoreline.

# CHAPTER 51

## *Vivica*

I lounged in the sand in front of Drake's stepdad's beach house and watched the tide roll in. Two weeks after my rescue, I was finally feeling back to normal. Though my new country had avoided a disaster, questions lingered in my mind about my own future.

"God, what do you want me to do next?" I let a handful of sand sift through my fingers. I wanted to get my next step right.

But God didn't give me an immediate answer.

My father strolled down the beach. When he drew closer, he waved, strode over to where I sat, and joined me.

"You feeling okay, Vivibear?"

"Yeah. Praying about my future."

"You're serious about your faith, aren't you?"

I traced squiggly lines in the sand. "Why did you think I wasn't?"

"I didn't. Just an observation." He stared at the water. "I have some news about your mother's death."

"You were able to prove Navid killed her?"

"No, Navid didn't do it." My father picked up a shell and examined it. "Bahram Zahedi's people tampered with your mother's health data. But since they didn't cause the ruptured aneurysm, we don't have a case—not even if we were still a part of URNA."

"So there's no justice for her." It was the perfect crime.

"If you want to take on Bahram Zahedi, I'll help you find a way."

I drew my knees to my chest. "That's not something I'm willing to do without airtight proof."

"Unfortunately, I agree."

I'd have to let God fight that battle. I gazed at the waves crashing into the shore.

"I have an idea for your next move," my father said.

"What's that?" I was thankful for the change of subject.

"Even though several governments have officially acknowledged our new country, we're still concerned about defending against the Peacekeepers. They're putting together a department of defense and have asked me to develop a system that protects against weather weaponization. I'll be leading the project, and I'd love to have you on my team." He studied me. "What do you think?"

"It's a good idea—the defense system." I bit my lip.

"But…"

"I don't know if that's what God wants for me."

"Will you at least consider it? It's a great opportunity."

"I appreciate the offer," I said. "I'll pray about it."

***

The next week, Drake and I boarded a jet to fly back to the Mine. After we were in the air, he leaned over and took my courier out of my hands. I gave him a playful nudge with my elbow. "Give that back."

"Nope." He winked.

"I was—"

"I have a surprise for you."

My stomach fluttered. "What?"

"We're going to make a stop on the way back to the Mine. There's a little boy I thought you might like to see."

I squealed, leaned over, and kissed Drake on the cheek. "Do Alma and Gabe know we're coming?"

"They're excited to see you."

\*\*\*

Isaac grinned, put a blue block in his mouth, and wobbled over to where I sat on Gabe and Alma's living room floor. I held out my arms, and he giggled. His brown eyes had the same light that sparkled in Ben's.

Isaac plopped down on my lap. I smoothed his hair and handed him the stuffed frog that I'd brought—a belated birthday gift. He dropped the block and squeezed the frog.

"And he's completely okay?" I asked Alma.

She nodded. "We had a doctor check him out."

"I'm sorry." I didn't know what else to say.

"It's not your fault."

I fidgeted with one of Isaac's blocks. Alma might not feel that way if she knew how I'd stood up to Navid, but she never needed to know.

"Thank you for letting me see him again." I took Isaac off my lap and stood. He held out his arms, so I picked him up.

"You're welcome any time. Have you figured out where you're going to settle?"

"No, but I'll let you know." I kissed the top of Isaac's head and handed him back to his mother. My arms ached at the emptiness.

Alma studied me. "Thank you for your sacrifice."

My stomach flipped, and for a moment I thought she'd found out about how I'd refused to yield to Navid. But then I realized she meant giving up my child.

My words came out in a hoarse whisper. "It was the right choice."

***

When Drake and I returned to the Mine, we discovered several agents had already moved away to transition to careers that would help our new country's economy. However, the Warriors weren't disbanding, because we needed to make sure our developing government would protect our freedom. Plus, the Peacekeepers were still a threat, though our nuclear program was helping to keep retaliation in check. Bahram also had his hands full with the hurricane devastation.

I wanted to contribute to our nation's defense, but every time I prayed about joining my father's team, I sensed silence from God. There had to be something I was missing.

I stood with Commander next to the Mine elevator while Agatha and Chad dragged their suitcases inside. They were moving to the eastern portion of the Desert and Pacific Region that had successfully petitioned to leave URNA and join the Coastal Republic. They'd oversee the transition from one government to another.

She stopped and faced me. "Are you sure you don't want to come with us? You can get an apartment near our house and work on our project. That's what my brother is doing."

Chad leaned out of the elevator. He'd shaved his head to get rid of the Mohawk. "We'd even rent a room to you—temporarily."

I laughed. "I wouldn't want to invade the newlyweds' privacy." I stepped forward and gave Agatha a hug. "I'll be fine as soon as I figure out my life."

"You're always welcome," she said.

"Thanks. I'll try to visit as soon as I can."

She gave me another hug and patted Commander's head before getting in the elevator. They waved as the door closed, and I lingered, listening to the elevator's hum as they traveled to the surface.

Commander and I hiked back to my room. Perhaps I could buy

a house near Gabe and Alma. Then I could check on Isaac every so often. The thought put a spring in my step, but I wondered what I'd do with the rest of my time.

I could go to college with my inheritance. That decision would've pleased my mother, but I wasn't sure what I wanted to study. I could always work with technology, but after having my skills exploited, the thought of working behind a computer the rest of my life didn't thrill me, which was probably why my father's offer had so little appeal.

A cart stopped beside me. "Hey, Vivica."

I smiled. "Nathan."

"Just the woman I wanted to see." Commander pulled toward him. Nathan motioned for us to get in, so we did. "Where're you headed?"

"No idea." I bit my salty lip.

"Want to take a drive?"

"That'd be great."

We rode through the wide thoroughfare and passed several other carts as well as people walking.

"Why did you need to see me?" I asked.

"I'm joining your father's team."

"That's great." One more friend knew what he was doing with his future, while I floundered. I stroked Commander's head.

"Yeah, I'm pumped. We need to be able to defend ourselves against URNA—and the Peacekeepers." He nudged me. "Can I convince you to work with us?"

"I've been praying about it."

"That's good enough for me." Nathan grinned, but it faded when he met my eyes. He slowed the cart and pulled over. "What's wrong?"

"My life is confusing."

"How so?"

I shook my head. "I don't even know what I want any more—let alone what God wants."

"Have you and Freeman made up?" Nathan's eyes twinkled.

"Yes."

"Good. That's what I'd heard, but I wanted to make sure I wasn't believing a rumor."

"Just in case." I winked.

"Hey, you never know." He scratched Commander's back. "Seriously, though. I'm happy for you. I know how much you love him."

"That's what everybody keeps saying."

"Well, it was pretty obvious. And you've never been a great actress."

"You too?"

"Call it like I see it."

I rolled my eyes and gave him a gentle punch on the arm.

***

The next day, Drake insisted that we take a walk and have a picnic, and I didn't argue. My stomach fluttered because I wasn't sure what his purpose for the outing was. Of course, I had a few possibilities in mind, but I didn't know how I felt about any of them.

We strolled under a canopy of trees. Though the afternoon was warm, the air held a bit of chill that warned fall was approaching.

We stopped next to a pond that glimmered in the sunshine, spread a blanket, and relaxed. I pawed through the basket. "What did you put in here?" I removed a container of sandwiches and a bowl of fruit.

"There are even some cookies—with full sugar and fat. No more government bans."

"No way." I dropped the sandwich and fruit containers, found the jar with cookies, fished one out, and took a bite. I savored the sweetness and the gooey chocolate chips. "Oh my. Do you know how long it's been since I've had a cookie that tasted this good?"

"Probably forever."

"Right."

He smiled. "I thought this might be a perfect chance for us to talk about the future." He leaned closer and took my hand. "I want to get married, but I know how confused you are."

My shoulders drooped. "I'm sorry. I want to marry you, but—"

"I'll wait." He squeezed my hand. "It's okay. We've been through a lot and don't need to rush."

"Are you sure? I don't want you to think I don't love you."

"I know you do." He picked up the sandwich container. "I want our relationship to be right."

"Me too."

We ate, watched a family of ducks swim across the pond, and talked about light-hearted topics we'd never had time for before. Books, movies, music, silly childhood anecdotes. Then our conversation drifted back to more serious matters.

"Have you decided if you're going to accept your father's offer?" Drake asked.

"No. It doesn't feel right."

"Why?"

"I'm not sure," I said.

"Do you trust your father?"

"Yes. He's proven he's on our side." I flipped the edge of the blanket between my fingers. "But I don't believe it's what God wants me to do."

"Then you shouldn't."

"What if I'm wrong?"

"God will show you." Drake gazed at me.

"You have a thought."

He raised his eyebrows. "Now you read minds?"

"Not used to having someone figure you out, are you?" I grinned.

"I prefer to be enigmatic." He kissed me. "Except with you."

I rested my hand on his chest. "Tell me."

"Everyone has been so fixated on your abilities with technology that they've forgotten you're more than just a hacker."

"Thanks."

"I'm serious. You also have your mother's charisma."

It took me a second to realize where he was going with that statement. "Uh-uh." I pulled back. "You can't be suggesting what I think."

"That you could play a role in ensuring that our new government protects its citizens instead of trying to control them? How is that negative?"

I studied my hands. "I hate politics."

"You despised how your mother played political games in the old system."

"How will the new system be better? Politics is politics."

"We can make it better. Oliver can find a place for you."

"Drake, I'm eighteen years old. No one is going to listen to me." But even as I made the excuse, a peace that I hadn't felt in weeks began to settle over me.

"Start small and work on making a difference one day at a time." He sighed. "This is your decision. Just pray about it."

"I will."

He smiled. "It almost feels strange, having the freedom to dream about a future."

He was right. We'd been fighting for so long that it was hard to imagine life after the battle. "What are you dreaming about?"

"A life with a beautiful woman by my side. Children."

I smirked. "How many?"

"I'll let my wife decide since she'll be the one to endure childbearing."

"Sounds fair." I cleared my throat. "But what else do you want? We've talked about my future, but what about yours?"

"I want to keep working in intelligence. Holding off the Peacekeepers."

"Perfect." I squeezed his hand. "We have a lot to be thankful for, don't we?"

# EPILOGUE

## *Vivica*

Twenty-five years later in the Coastal Republic…

I poured some coffee in a travel mug and glanced at the clock on the kitchen wall. One of my life-long goals was finally going to be achieved today, and I couldn't be late for work.

My husband grabbed me around the waist and kissed me. For a moment, I was transported back to our first kiss in the presidential compound.

Drake grinned. "Have a wonderful day, my dear. You know I'm proud of you, right?"

"Yes." I loved how his touch could still make me dizzy. "I couldn't have done any of this without you."

"I know." He gave me a peck on the cheek and bolted out the door to his job at the National Investigative Services.

"Kids, hurry up!" I shouted. "You're going to be late!"

Twelve-year-old Ellery bounced down the stairs and smoothed her dress. "Is this outfit okay?" Her forehead creased like Drake's did when he was worried—and she was concerned about the debate after school. There was no need for her to be because she'd inherited her ability to argue from Drake, though he insisted it came from me.

I gave her a hug. "It's perfect, and you'll do great." Her tense expression relaxed into a smile.

Everett emerged from the study. At ten, he was already as tall as Ellery, which annoyed her. I smoothed his cowlick and marveled at how much he looked like my father.

He pulled away and took his lunch box from the counter. "Mom, do you have the money for my soccer uniform?"

"I put it in your account this morning."

"Thanks."

They left, and I locked our suburban colonial and got in the car that waited at the curb. The car drove me into our nation's capital, Emancipation City. Technology had improved to the point that I could multitask while the car eased through rush-hour traffic. I used the time to sip coffee and check security briefings each day, but today I had a call to make first.

"Call Agatha."

When Agatha answered, her face projected onto the car's windshield. She was folding laundry. She and Chad had moved to Emancipation City so he could work for the NIS with Drake.

"Today's the big day, isn't it?" She squealed and clasped her hands. "Chad came home late last night and told me URNA's representatives had an agreement."

"That's right. And to celebrate, Drake and I would like to have dinner with you and Chad. I have a break in my schedule next week."

"Yes. Absolutely." She put a towel on a stack. "No kids. A double date night. Sound good? Olivia can babysit. They'll have a blast."

Olivia was their sixteen-year-old daughter. "They'll probably terrorize her."

Agatha grinned. "Nah. Not your angels. Can't speak for her siblings, though." She and Chad had three more children—twin boys who were Ellery's age and drove her crazy and a nine-year-old girl who was Everett's buddy.

We chatted a while longer and then disconnected. The car took me past an elementary school where children swarmed around the building waiting for the day to begin. I hoped someday they understood how lucky they were to live carefree lives—and the sacrifices that had made it possible. I thought about the other people I cared about and how they were enjoying the freedom we'd earned.

Isaac, engaged to a gorgeous girl named Selina, worked in the Defense Department with my father. Ben, Ally, and their three children lived in another city where Ben flew for a commercial airline. Nathan had married Danielle from the Mine. Liam had remarried, and he and his wife had three children. Though we'd all hoped for a change in Faith, we'd learned that she'd died when the Council's Headquarters had collapsed.

God had blessed us and protected us, and for that I thanked him every day. I also vowed to serve him to the best of my ability.

The limestone building that held government offices stood tall. I exited the car and climbed the steps, greeting a few men and women who were also arriving for work. We kept our government as small and as efficient as possible, and I reminded myself daily that my fellow citizens had entrusted me to serve them.

I loved my office for its old-fashioned feel. An antique desk dominated the room. The aquamarine walls reminded me of the Caribbean Sea, and Drake said the color matched my eyes. A Bible—an authentic version—sat open on my desk.

As I was settling into my chair, my assistant Carlyle hurried in. "Good morning, Secretary Freeman." He flashed a smile and adjusted his bowtie.

"Good morning."

Carlyle had been my faithful assistant ever since I'd worked in local government after graduating from law school. With a flourish, he placed a crisp sheet of paper in front of me. "URNA's ambassador had this delivered a few minutes ago."

I smiled at their symbolic gesture of actually printing the document on paper. "Wonderful." It had taken years of work and negotiations to get to this day. Even though it had come, the Peacekeepers wouldn't be happy, and we'd have to stay vigilant.

Bahram Zahedi still loved population control and continued to fight for global domination in an international community that had seen an increase in the number of independent nations. Twenty-two years ago, we had faced a tense few months when Zahedi had threatened to bomb our capital. He'd backed down after negotiations and threats of nuclear retaliation.

I pushed the thought aside and decided to dwell on today's victory.

Tears welled in my eyes as I read the opening line to the document that I'd spent my time as Secretary of State negotiating with URNA's government.

*We the representatives of the United Regions of North America, declare that the following document is intended to preserve the God-given rights of life, liberty, and the pursuit of happiness for all citizens. As such, effective immediately, the Posterity Protection and Self-Determination Act is null and void. No woman shall be forced to terminate a pregnancy for any reason.*

I read the remainder of the document and thanked God that the Coastal Republic's government had been able to help URNA's see reason.

We would still have battles to fight, but I'd continue to use my office and influence to help the people of URNA—as well as my own country—because the freedom we had in the Coastal Republic was the happy ending I'd fought for.

And it was a legacy I was proud to leave our children.

# FROM THE AUTHOR

I hope you've enjoyed the conclusion to the Emancipation Warriors series. You'll find discussion questions on the following page.

If you missed books one and two, check out *The First Principle* and *The Liberation*. *The Agitator* is a companion novella that gives you a different glimpse into the Warriors' world.

For updates on my new releases, subscribe to my mailing list at www.marissashrock.com. I'd love to have you join and won't share your email address with anyone.

Finally, I'd be grateful if you'd leave a short review on the website where you purchased the book.

# THE PURSUIT DISCUSSION GUIDE

1. Throughout the story, many futuristic components involve technology. Which ones would you like to see happen? Why?

2. In this novel, some chapters are written in Drake's point of view. Did this change your perception of him? Why or why not?

3. Vivica must live with the uncertainty of her mother's eternal fate. How can this fictional example motivate us to share the gospel with those we love?

4. Agatha encourages Vivica to seek God's will as she chooses a mate or decides to remain single. Do you agree with Agatha's advice? Why or why not?

5. Drake is uncertain if the Warriors' mission is truly God's will. According to the Bible, what is the proper role of government?

6. Inspired by King Jehoshaphat (2 Chronicles 20), Vivica chooses to stand firm and let God fight for her—even though her son's life is in danger. What would you have done? Why?

7. Have you ever experienced a time where you had to let God fight for you? Describe the situation and how God worked.

8. Vivica faces uncertainty about her future. Describe a time when you experienced similar feelings.

9. Did Vivica's career choice at the end of the story surprise you? Why or why not?

# CREDITS

Cover Art & Design by Anita B. Carroll at Race-Point.com
Cover Photos

- iStock.com/Yuri_Arcurs
- The Beginning of the Tornado © Victor Zastol`skiy | Dreamstime.com
- Sunset Tornado © Solarseven | Dreamstime.com

Editing by A Little Red Ink
Formatting by Polgarus Studio
Marketing Copy by JR2 Marketing & Advertising